Let's Face the Music and Die

Let's Face the Music and Die

Sandra Scoppettone

LITTLE, BROWN AND COMPANY

Boston   New York   Toronto   London

First Edition

Library of Congress Cataloging-in-Publication Data
Scoppettone, Sandra.
    Let's face the music and die / Sandra Scoppettone. — 1st ed.
        p.   cm.
    ISBN 0-316-77664-5
    1. Laurano, Lauren (Fictitious character) — Fiction.   2. Private investigators
— New York (N.Y.) — Fiction   3. Greenwich Village (New York, N.Y.) —
Fiction.   4. Women detectives — New York (N.Y.) — Fiction.   5. Lesbians —
New York (N.Y.) — Fiction.   6. New York (N.Y.) — Fiction   I. Title.
    PS3569.C586L4   1996
    813'.54 — dc20   96-5858

10 9 8 7 6 5 4 3 2 1

MV-NY

Published simultaneously in Canada
by Little, Brown & Company (Canada) Limited

Printed in the United States of America

In memory of Harriet Laine,
a dear friend and an ardent reader,
who faced the music with courage and dignity.

November 12, 1941–November 28, 1995

Let's
Face the Music
and Die

One

The siren shrieks sorrow.

But this time I don't wonder what it means, whether it's a crime, whether someone died. This time I know because I sit and stare at the dead body. It's not a sight anyone should see and I'm here because I've been called by my friend Elissa, who has discovered her aunt and didn't know whom to call but me.

I'm the one who phoned the police and asked for my friend, Lieutenant Peter Cecchi. We are within his precinct, so I expect he'll be coming.

Elissa is crying. I have my arm around her as she sobs into my corduroy jacket. Comfort is hard to give. There's nothing to say, to do, when death comes to loved ones, especially in this brutal way.

Ruthie, Elissa's aunt, has been stabbed and slashed to death. Blood splashes are everywhere, making patterns on walls and floor that under other circumstances might be interesting, like an abstract painting. But these spatters signal the end of life and are not creative.

Rape may also be a factor; we can't know that yet.

The knock at the door is accompanied by the bell ringing. Police like to use all their options. I hug Elissa to me, then go to open up.

Cecchi has come and I'm grateful to see his craggy, handsome face.

"Lauren," he says, and shakes his head in a way I understand to mean *What are you doing here? Why are you involved?*

I answer his unspoken questions. "Elissa's a friend. It's her aunt."

He nods and enters with another detective, O'Hara, and two uniformed cops. I know all of them and we exchange greetings.

"Jesus," Cecchi mumbles when he looks at Ruthie's ruined body on the floor. He's seen worse, I know, but he's told me he never gets used to it. This is one of the things that make him a good cop.

O'Hara says to me, "You're gettin' to be a regular Jessica Fletcher, Laurano."

I give him my weakest smile. "A P.I. has to live, O'Hara." I don't enjoy the banter but know if I don't respond in kind, he'll keep it up.

I understand why he says this; it does seem that friends and relatives of friends are dying all around me. I still haven't totally recovered from the murder of my oldest friend, Megan, several years ago. And last summer there was the death of my lover's brother who had AIDS, an assisted suicide. That was different. The police closed their eyes to it but Kip and I could not, and that, plus the death itself, has visited damage on our relationship ever since.

An Assistant M.E., Barbara Butcher (no joke), arrives and Cecchi and I take Elissa into the bedroom. It's dark in here: the furniture heavy walnut, the drapes a thick maroon velvet. Cecchi, with gloved hand, switches on a light.

Elissa's naturally olive skin is pale, brown eyes red-rimmed and puffy from crying. Black curly hair surrounds her face like a cherubic frame. She wears a green hooded sweatshirt and old jeans, her feet in scuffed clogs.

Cecchi and Elissa haven't met before, though he's heard me speak about her, but I know he'll be compassionate, as he is with anyone in her position. Elissa sits on the bed and he and I continue to stand.

"I have to ask some questions," he says gently.

She nods.

"When did you find her?"

Elissa looks at me.

"You called me about nine," I prompt.

Elissa says, "I guess it was about ten minutes or so before that. I didn't know what to do. It was such a shock . . . I think maybe I just stood there staring for a while. Couldn't move."

"Sure," Cecchi says. "Understandable. So why did you come over here this morning?"

"I was worried about her. I called her all day yesterday and she didn't answer. I should've come then," she says more to herself than to Cecchi. "Maybe if I had . . ."

"No," he says. "I'm not an M.E. but I'd say she's been dead for more than twenty-four hours. She's already out of rigor mortis."

" 'Out of'?" Elissa asks.

"Yeah. Well, first you go into it, then out. People think you stay that way, but you don't. So that would account for more than a twenty-four-hour period. I'd guess it happened night before last. See what I'm saying?"

"Yes. Still, it wasn't like her to be out all day. I should've known something was wrong."

"It wouldn't have mattered, Elissa," I say.

She nods, trying to believe me.

"I went to the movies last night. I should have come here instead." She looks up at us both, a rueful smile rumples her lips. *"Shallow Grave."*

"Huh?" Cecchi asks.

Sometimes he's not exactly au courant. "It's the name of a movie," I explain.

"Oh. Oh, sure."

I know he's never heard of it but Elissa doesn't. "Don't you think that's ironic?"

"Definitely," Cecchi says. "Anyway, let's get back to today. When you couldn't reach her, you decided to come over . . . is that it?"

"Yes. I have a key."

"Was it locked?"

"Yes. But it locks automatically when you leave. The police lock wasn't in place, that's what scared me."

"What did you touch?"

She thinks for a moment. "The doorknob, of course. Both

sides of the door. Then . . . well, I saw her right away and . . . God, I don't really remember."

"That's okay."

"The phone," I add.

"Yes, right," Elissa says.

"You didn't touch the body?"

Pain swamps her face. "God, no."

"I know this is going to sound stupid to you, Elissa, but I have to ask. Your aunt have any enemies?"

"Aunt Ruthie? I can't imagine. Can you, Lauren?"

"No. Not those kinds of enemies, Cecchi."

"Didn't think so. Elissa, you have any idea who might have done this?"

"How would I have any idea?"

"I have to ask," he says and touches her shoulder in an avuncular way. "Do you think you could come down to the station and make a statement?"

"I'll go with you," I offer.

Elissa nods.

"That's good. You should get out of here now anyway."

"Let's have some coffee first," I say to her, put out my hand, help her up from the bed although she's perfectly capable of rising by herself.

"Yes, coffee. I need to go to the bathroom," she says. "Is that okay?"

"Better not do it here before forensic checks out everything," Cecchi explains.

"Right."

"C'mon," I say to her. "We'll go to the Peacock." I know she likes it there.

We file out of the bedroom, Elissa leading. Cecchi taps my shoulder.

"Just offhand," he whispers to me, "I'd say this is the work of the Granny Killer."

It's been in the papers for months — someone preying on older women who live alone, robbing and murdering them — but Ruthie being done by the Granny Killer hasn't crossed my mind.

"Doesn't he pick on older victims?"

"Usually. But anyone over sixty would fit the profile. Don't say anything." He indicates Elissa with a jut of his chin.

We go through the living room, where all the machinery of the investigation has begun. The place is filled with personnel and I steer Elissa out of the apartment, wishing she didn't have to see any of this. But the truth is, she's seen the worst. A person hacked to death, an aunt who, the last time Elissa saw her, was vital and funny, as I knew Ruthie to be. People scurrying around doing their jobs is the least of the horror.

Outside, the street is blocked off by blue-and-whites; a cop stands on the front steps. People are gathered as though waiting for a show to start, and of course the media have arrived.

Terry French of Channel 4 shoves a microphone in my face. "Laurano, what's happening here?"

I know a lot of reporters from working on a high-profile case a few years ago that involved Cybill Shepherd. That brought them all running like scampering mice. Terry French is not a favorite.

"You think I'm going to tell you, Terry?"

"You involved?" she asks. Her hair is unnaturally black, like patent leather.

"Excuse us," I say. And try to push past her.

She says in a cold, controlled voice, "We hear it's another of the Granny Killer's work. Any truth to that?"

I look at Elissa, whose mouth drops open. Then back at French. How did she hear this so fast? How do they ever hear?

"You know, Terry," I say, "I never noticed it before but you're getting gray hair."

She looks at me quizzically.

"Sort of grannyish," I explain, unable to control my great big mouth.

Two

═══════════════

I've noticed that lately we don't seem to have spring. It's always been a favorite season of mine and now it's practically nonexistent. Both Elissa and I wear outer clothing that would normally be a bit too heavy for this time of year. Still, the sky is clear, the ozone behaves — so that's something.

New York, at least Manhattan, is crawling with coffee bars, a trend brought to us from Seattle. These places are often small with counters and stools. They serve various blends like Eastern Mingo Mongo Margo Macadamia Roasted Blue at six hundred dollars a cup. Elissa and I are not interested in this scene and go to our old standby, the Peacock, on Greenwich Avenue.

We sit at a window table. Verdi plays in the background.

" 'Requiem,' " Elissa says. "Perfect." She starts to cry, lip trembling first, chin puckering. "I can't believe it," she mumbles into her napkin. I cover her hand with mine and remain silent because there's nothing to say. I've become very good at this, unfortunately. Dealing with death on a regular basis has almost made me an expert.

It takes Elissa a few minutes to recover. The waitress approaches. I've never seen this one before. She looks twelve and a half but must be in her twenties. And she chews gum, something one would never expect to see a waitress do here. Her hair is long and black, a dark-haired Alice in Wonderland.

"Getcha?" she asks.

I have to assume that this is her way of asking for our order. "Two cappuccinos," I say.

"All?"

"Yes." Is she too tired to form a complete sentence? What could someone so young have to be tired about?

She snaps her gum and slogs toward the back. I notice that she wears a short brown skirt exposing a great deal of thigh. It's not that I wish to show off my thighs or wear skirts, but I know that I'll never display them again, except in a bathing suit and then only to a select few. Age has become an obsession with me and it drives Kip nuts. I refocus my attention on Elissa.

"She was a big pain sometimes, but oh, God, this is . . . I don't know. It's so weird that both Ruthie and Harold died in these horrible ways."

"It is," I agree. Harold, Ruth's husband, had died five years earlier by falling overboard a cruise ship. His body was never recovered.

"Did I hear that reporter say something about the Granny Killer?"

"Yes. But she . . ."

"She wasn't even a grandmother."

We look at each other and start to laugh. Inappropriate as it is, this isn't an unusual response to death, even murder. It releases tension.

When we stop laughing Elissa says, "Why did that reporter say that, do you think?"

I shrug. "Sensationalism. You know how they are."

"You mean like *Hard Copy* types?"

"Yeah. They'll say anything, write anything. Ethics are a thing of the past," I say, realizing I sound like Kip. I wonder if we're merging and worry that we have.

The child waitress, still snapping gum, returns with our caps. "You. You," she says as she sets a cup in front of each of us, then meanders away.

"Maybe she doesn't speak English," Elissa suggests.

I hadn't thought of that; instead made a judgment. And I thought I'd changed! "Possible," I say, only able to give an inch because in my marrow I know it isn't the case. I know this is what has happened to a whole generation . . . they've lost not only the art of conversation but the art of speaking full sentences. Do we blame this on Wayne or Garth?

"When did you see Ruthie last?" I ask Elissa.

She looks at me, her large eyes like bits of a glazed chocolate doughnut. "Middle of last week. We had supper. . . I mean dinner. . . guess I'll never get over being from the Bronx. Anyway, dinner at five-thirty. You know Ruthie, she can never wait to eat."

Elissa speaks of her aunt in the present tense because she hasn't absorbed the truth yet. It takes some people months.

"We ate at Woody's. Ruthie likes the quesadillas there."

"Me too," I say, wishing I had one right now. One of my favorite meals there is the chorizo quesadilla and mud cake.

"You know, she always has to order whatever is the most fattening thing on . . ." Her eyes fill up quickly and I know this is because she realizes that she's speaking of her as though she were still alive.

"Oh, God. Listen to me."

"It's natural. Drink your cap, it'll get cold."

She looks down at her cup. "I guess I don't want it."

I've never seen Elissa reject any kind of coffee. "Want to go to the station and get that over with?"

"Yeah. And then I want to go home."

"Should you call Deanna?" This is her partner.

"You know, I didn't even think. She's probably in session now." We have many things in common, among them that we both have mates who are therapists.

"After the station I'll walk you home and you can call her then. I'll stay with you until she gets there. You know her schedule?"

"She works until seven tonight."

It's twelve forty-five now. There's a lot I have to do but I don't want to leave Elissa alone. I pay the check and we go out onto Greenwich Avenue.

A man wearing a shabby coat and knickers with holes in them steps in front of us. "Could I have forty-five cents, please?" He holds out a hand that hasn't seen soap in centuries.

"Why forty-five cents?" I ask.

He sizes me up, tilts his head to one side, strokes his ragged beard. "I wanna buy a BMW," he says.

"I don't like your values," I say, but give him a quarter.

Elissa and I cross Greenwich and start down Tenth Street toward the Charles Street police station.

"Have you noticed how they can't answer straight anymore?" she asks.

I have. Every beggar has a quip now, as though they're competing to be the best stand-up. I tell Elissa this and then we're silent. I reflect on why we're going to the station and assume she's doing the same.

It's almost impossible to believe Ruthie's been murdered . . . or even to acknowledge she's dead. She's been such a part of Elissa's life for so long. Elissa's parents died fairly young, and Ruthie and her late husband were surrogates. After Harold died five years ago Ruthie moved to California, then to Florida, and finally back here, where, as she often said, "I'm like Dolly, back where I belong." And it was true. Ruthie was a quintessential New Yorker.

Although Elissa has always supported herself, Ruthie and Harold, and then Ruthie alone, supplemented her income because they had a great deal of money and no children of their own. Suddenly, I feel a chill run through me as I remember what we've all always known, sometimes joked about. When Ruthie dies Elissa will be very rich!

I, of course, know that Elissa didn't kill her aunt. But that's because I know her. The law will be looking for MOM — means, opportunity, and motive — and there's no doubt about Elissa having a motive if she wanted one. Money.

"Elissa, you do have an alibi, don't you? What were you doing Saturday night?"

She looks at me, startled. "Why?"

"Do you?"

"Lauren? You can't think I —"

"No, I don't. But it's not me you have to worry about. Let's look at it this way . . . exactly how much do you stand to inherit?"

"Oh, I see," she says meekly.

"How much?"

"Well, I'm not sure."

"Ballpark."

Our eyes meet and I see fear in hers.

"Ballpark?"

"Yes."

"A few million."

"Ohmigod." I suppose I always knew this but to hear it now, after what's happened, causes a frisson of fear to race across my shoulder blades and down my spine.

"What kind of an alibi do I have to have?" Elissa asks.

"A very good one."

We stop in front of an unassuming building, the police station.

"A very good one," Elissa repeats, as though by her saying this out loud it'll be true.

"You don't, do you?" I ask. "Have a good one."

"Is 'being at home alone reading' a good one?" she asks, knowing the answer.

I look at her, somber-faced.

"That's what I thought," she says, then shrugs. "Well, it's the only one I have. Deanna was away at a conference for the weekend and I took the opportunity to have time in the apartment alone."

I understand this need. I've had little of it myself and love it when Kip goes away for a few days.

"Guess what?" I say.

"I'm in deep doo-doo," she states.

"Right."

Three

By the time I arrive at the house Kip and I share on Perry Street, it's after eight but I know she's still in session, so I go into my small home office and turn on the computer. The one I have here is a PC which I had built for me. It has a 1.2 gig hard drive and it's black.

You have no idea how hard it is to find a black computer. The manufacturers insist on producing these putty-colored machines. I was able to get this from a place on Canal Street and Sixth Avenue called Micro Computers. I happened to see the store one morning on one of my fast-walks. The computer I was using at the time was only a 386 and it was ugly. Okay, so I didn't *need* a new PC — but what's that got to do with the price of Pentiums? Kip says I'm a consumer, and I guess that's true. Anyway, I love this machine. I even have a black mouse.

While it boots up, I go through my snail mail. There are lots of bills and sometimes I don't know how I'm going to pay them. Like now. At the moment I don't have a case and my savings are running low.

I open on Norton Commander, type in *win:* to get to Windows, where I have configured my desktop to show a picture of the Mona Lisa. The sound that goes with it (for the moment) is a clip of Margaret Hamilton, as the Wicked Witch, saying "I'll get you, my pretty, and your little dog too!" and then laughing hysterically. I used to have Robin Williams saying "Good morning, Vietnam" but I got bored with it.

The reason I have all this good stuff is more consumerism. Kip and I had a big fight about it at the time because she said I couldn't afford a Sound Blaster CD-ROM drive kit, I said it was my money, she said I didn't contribute enough to household expenses to warrant buying it, and I won because basically I do what I want. Anyway, I bought it and spent about two months installing it myself. But does Kip appreciate that I do this to save money? No, all she cares about is the time I spend on the installation. I think it went something like this:

KIP: You haven't been out of your office for weeks.
ME: I'm trying to get it to work right.
KIP: Why is it that whenever you buy a new computer thing, it never works?
ME: What does that mean?
KIP: Gee, I wonder which word it is that you don't understand?
ME: You're implying that *I* don't know how to make these things work. It happens to everyone.
KIP: That's exactly why I don't want to get into it, computer/Internet stuff. Whatever new thing you or anyone else gets, it takes days and years to . . . to, what do you call it?
ME: Install.
KIP: Right, install. I don't know how you stand it. You waste half your life with this stuff.
ME: It's my life.
KIP: And welcome to it.

It was not a pretty scene. But I've never regretted buying the kit. I can get lost for hours in *Cinemania,* a CD that's all about movies: pictures, sound bites, movie clips — the works.

After Margaret Hamilton stops screaming I click on the icon for NWDC (New World Data Corp.), which is my Internet provider. Bulletin Boards are a thing of the past for me. Now I'm only interested in surfing the Net. Darren Klein runs NWDC and charges fifteen bucks a month, which is more than reasonable. When I asked him why he was so cheap, he said he didn't believe that providers had to charge more than that. A wonderful guy! He is, actually. He returns my calls and gives me any and all the help I need. I click on Netscape, my Web browser, and a dialog box comes up. I type in my password, click CONNECT, and listen while my modem dials.

Eventually, I'm connected to NWDC. I launch my news reader, called Free Agent. A colorful picture of a guy wearing a trilby, sitting on a bench, reading a newspaper, appears. When he vanishes another screen comes up, this one with three partitions: groups, headers, and the messages. In two more clicks I begin to download the Usenet newsgroups I read, like: alt.conspiracy.jfk; soc.motss (a gay and lesbian group); alt.showbiz.gossip; rec.arts.mystery; and about seven others.

While it does its thing I write some checks, hating every moment of it. Eventually, Free Agent finishes retrieving everything and I close it. Then I click on my E-mail icon (a dog with a letter in its mouth). The program's called Popmail. Don't ask.

In the upper left corner it says FETCH, which is what I click to get my mail. I have three messages. There's no way to know who they're from until they're . . . yes . . . fetched.

The list tells me there's a letter from Mallory Kates (a producer/writer in Los Angeles I met on-line), another from Rosey (a male computer person) in Scottsdale, and one from Alexandra Thomas in New York. She is a woman I met a year or so ago when I was hired by Danitra Kandrew, the designer, to look into who was cooking her books. Alexandra is her assistant. I'm surprised to hear from her because I barely know her, and even more surprised that she would know how to reach me. I go immediately to her letter. The date is at the top.

From: Alexandra Thomas (athomas@panix.com)
To: Lauren Laurano (laurenl@NWDC.com)
Subject: Hello
Dear Lauren Laurano,
    You probably do not remember me but I am Danitra Kandrew's assistant. We met when Danitra had a problem here and hired

you. We talked a little bit about E-mail and at that time I did not have it or know much about it. Now I do and I thought I would drop you a line just for fun. Hope you do not mind. I got your address from a post you sent in the JFK conf. Yes, I am a hopeless buff on this subject too. I am a novice at this modem thing, so any help or suggestions you want to give will be welcomed. Well, that is it for now. Back to work, and who knows if you will even get this.
Alex

I try to remember what she looks like. Suddenly, her face flashes on my mindscreen. How could I have forgotten? She's beautiful.

"In a trance?" Kip asks.

I whirl around. "Oh, hi."

"If I didn't know better, I'd say you're blushing."

"Then it's good you know better." I *am* blushing. I can feel it. But why? I haven't got a clue.

Kip looks great as always. She's taller than I, but who isn't? Alex Thomas?

Tonight Kip wears a powder-blue silk blouse and charcoal slacks with matching shoes. Each day I notice that Kip gets more gray in her hair. I find it becoming but she hates it. Her soft brown eyes look into mine but I can't read them. Since her brother's death she's become more and more remote, and I don't know how to reach her. I often feel lonely even when we're in the same room.

"Are we having dinner together?" she asks.

"Yes. If you'd like to." How formal we've become.

"Fine. Feel like pizza?"

"Sure."

"I got a movie earlier today," Kip adds.

We must've watched five million tapes since Tom died. It's all Kip ever wants to do. Fortunately, I love movies. "What'd you get?"

"*Serial Mom,*" she says.

"Really?" I'm disappointed. Kathleen Turner isn't a fave.

"I hear it's very funny."

"Okay."

She leaves my office without saying anything further, but more important, she hasn't asked about my day. How long has it been since she's asked or cared? I notice it in particular today because of Ruthie's murder. Kip knew her too. So why didn't I just tell her? Why do I have to wait to be asked? It's this new and horrible mode we're in: a lack of intimacy, something I never thought we had a problem with.

Ruthie will be buried next week, even though she's Jewish, because of the nature of her death. When we were at the police station and Elissa was being questioned, I could see the look pass between the detectives when she had to admit she was sole heir. Thank God she has Deanna, because I have a feeling this isn't going to be easy for her.

I glance back at my monitor, and my screen saver is whirling around making pretty patterns. I tap a key and there's the letter from Alexandra Thomas. *Alex.* I don't know why, but I create a folder called Alex in which to save her message. I'm still on-line, so I write a quick reply.

From: laurenl@NWDC.com
To: athomas@panix.com
Subject: I Remember You
Dear Alex Thomas,
   I do remember you very clearly. Yes, this is a lot of fun. If there are particular things you want to know about being on-line, feel free to ask. This is just a quick note so you'll know I received yours.
Best,
Lauren

I click on SEND and watch while it shows me the progress. When it's gone I log off NWDC and get ready to read the other mail off-line. I feel strangely giddy.

The movie's a drag and we don't bother to watch the whole thing. When we shut it off Kip turns to me.

"I didn't know how to tell you but I'm leaving on Wednesday to do a series of lectures at U of M."

I find this news staggering. Wednesday is two days away. "For how long?"

"A month."

My mouth drops open.

"Close your mouth," she says, smiling. "You look like a moron."

"Are you being funny?"

"About your moronic look?"

I don't answer.

"Look, Lauren, we haven't been getting along and you know it."

"So? What's that got to do with you going away for a month and not telling me before this?"

"Everything. I think it'll be good for us to be separated for a while. And I didn't tell you, because I knew you'd make a fuss."

"A *fuss?* Oh, thanks."

"Well, look how you're acting now."

I feel furious. As controlled as I can possibly be, I say, "If I'm acting any way in particular, it's because you've just dropped a bomb and you know it, Kip. What about your goddamn patients?"

"I've taken care of that."

I laugh ironically. "What that means is you told them but not me, right?"

"Right," she says, with an appropriate expression of contrition.

"Call me crazy, but that just doesn't seem fair. Telling them and not me."

"I was afraid."

I'm shocked. "Of *me?*"

"Oh, I don't know." She puts her head in her hands.

I touch her shoulder and she shrinks away, catches herself, then looks at me helplessly.

I charge ahead, angry at her involuntary reaction to my touch. "Since Tom died you've been, I don't know . . . impossible."

"Thanks."

"But it's true. You've changed."

She sings mockingly, "You've changed, that sparkle in your eye is gone."

"Okay, never mind."

"Oh, Lauren, where's your sense of humor?"

"I sent it to Chicago for the week," I snap.

"Frankly, I think this separation will be good for us."

"So you said. Maybe you're right . . . a separation might help."

Now she looks stricken. Funny how that happens when ideas flip-flop.

She says, "I'm not suggesting anything permanent, you know. I mean, I still love you."

"I still love you," I say but feel empty, dead.

We look at each other, hoping for answers, knowing there are none right now, both of us afraid of unexpected possibilities. And then the phone rings.

"Saved by the bell, as always," she says.

I answer. It's Deanna.

"Lauren, thank God you're there."

"What's wrong?"

"Elissa's been arrested."

Four

It is after eleven by the time we get back to Elissa and Deanna's apartment. I'd called my lawyer, Irene Sullivan, but Elissa wasn't charged, because all they had was her lack of an alibi, which wasn't enough to hold her.

Deanna has short white hair, which she's had since the age of twenty-eight, worn full around a face that is attractively sculpted in large, broad strokes. Her eyes are brown and have the look many therapists eventually get: a deep and immutable sadness, as though there's no way they can fix the horror they hear. Kip has this expression also.

Elissa holds Deanna's hand as they sit close to each other on their white couch. They've been together six years and are devoted.

I think of Kip and me at six years and remember that it was a bad patch, but we got through it. If you don't walk away, you can manage these troubled times. I have to face that we're in one of those now and wonder, will we weather it again?

Elissa says, "I had my problems with Ruthie but how can they think I killed her?"

"It's the inheritance," I say.

"They don't even know about that."

"Actually, they probably do. Not how much exactly, but that you're a beneficiary."

Deanna shakes her head in disbelief. "Two million and change."

"How d'you know?" I ask.

Elissa says, "Robert Rosenwald, Ruthie's lawyer, told me today."

I'm surprised. "You asked?"

"No. He called me to express his sympathy and then he mentioned it. I thought it was sort of odd. But he sounded like a little kid, like he couldn't wait to tell me something I didn't know."

"And did you know?"

"Not the amount, as I told you." She seems irritated.

"I have to ask you these things. Anyway, I don't think the sum is going to make any difference. The motive stays the same."

Elissa looks at me quizzically.

"I mean to the cops. Not to me."

"Phew. You had me worried there for a moment, pal."

I reassure her. But what *I* know about Elissa won't cut it with the police. "They're going to focus on your lack of an alibi, try to get you on that, try to place you outside your apartment."

"That's why I want to hire you."

"Hire me? Are you crazy? I can't take your money."

"Lauren, I'm rich now."

"Not yet." What I don't say is that she never will be if she's charged, tried, and convicted.

"Well, I will be. Besides, Kip will have a fit if you aren't paid."

This is certainly true. Our money issue is more severe than ever. "I wouldn't feel right having you pay me."

"Get over it," Elissa says. "You want the job or do I have to let my fingers do the walking?"

A dilemma. It's true that Elissa would hire someone else if she didn't know me; it's also true that I could use the money. "Okay."

Deanna asks, "What do you charge?" She's always pragmatic, which is good, because Elissa never is.

I toy with the idea of giving a lower rate than usual but know if this were discovered, it wouldn't sit well with anyone. So I quote my standard fee. But I can't help a caveat: "You may not need a P.I."

"Lauren, I know you love Cecchi and I admit, he's a super guy and a great cop, but they're not all like him. I need you to find out who really did this. If the cops are putting all their energy into proving *I* did it, they aren't going to look for anyone else. Hey, I watch *NYPD Blue*. I know how it goes."

"So," Deanna chimes in, "we want to take precautions and we want the best. You." She has a wonderful way of making you feel special, because she's not afraid to tell you what she thinks.

"Okay," I say. "I'm yours."

"Glad that's settled," Elissa says. "You'd think we were asking you to go hiking or camping."

Everyone knows the great outdoors is my worst nightmare.

"Where do we start?" Elissa asks.

"Does anyone else stand to gain by Ruthie's death?"

They look at each other.

"Besides Deanna," I say.

"You mean from the inheritance? Rosenwald didn't say, but I suppose she left something to my brother. Probably not much, considering his problems."

Andy, Elissa's brother, lives in London and is a heroin addict.

"Anyone else?"

"I don't know. It didn't sound like it. Maybe you should ask Rosenwald."

I know it's doubtful that he'll tell me. "I think you'd better ask."

"Okay. First thing tomorrow."

"What about this Granny Killer?" asks Deanna. "Doesn't Ruthie's murder fit?"

"I'm not entirely sure. I'll have to get the skinny from Cecchi." I like to say *skinny*. It makes me feel like I'm in the forties even though it's still used by certain cops and gossip columnists. "You have to give me a list of Ruthie's friends."

"You're kidding. You're *not* kidding. Do you actually think one of her friends would do . . . would . . ." She trails off, unable to put the deed into words.

"Elissa," I say gently, "you can't question everything I do. Okay?"

"Sorry. I didn't mean it that way. I'll make up a list."

"Anybody you can think of, even if she knew them only slightly."

"Right." She goes to a desk and gets a pencil and paper and begins the list while Deanna and I wait, for once at a loss for words.

Around one in the morning, when I get back to Perry Street, I bump into Rick, who is on his way out carrying two suitcases. Rick and William rent an apartment from us . . . from Kip . . . and have been together for about ten years. Rick's a screenwriter and goes back and forth to L.A. but it still seems odd for him to be leaving at this hour.

"Hollywood calling?" I ask him.

"You could say that," he answers enigmatically.

I hate it when he gets like this. "Well, it is or it isn't," I say, snappish.

"Ask William. I'm late for the plane."

"Is he up?"

"Yes."

I watch him as he lurches, under the weight of his luggage, toward the street and hails a cab. After he gets in he doesn't turn to wave and I wonder what the hell is going on.

I should go to bed but I have to know what's happening to my friends, and if there's anything I can do, so I ring William from outside.

"Yes?" There's an angry but urgent sound in his voice.

"It's me," I say.

"Oh." He's definitely disappointed.

"Can I come up?"

"Sure."

He buzzes me in even though I have my key. I go upstairs to their apartment, where I find him slumped in a club chair, his long jean-clad legs sprawled like discarded tree limbs.

William is exceedingly handsome with brown hair that he now wears in a crew cut. He also has a mustache and short beard. Since he's begun working out at a gym he's become muscular but hasn't overdone it. His demeanor tips me to the certainty that he's depressed.

"I just ran into Rick," I say.

"He's gone."

"To L.A., you mean?"

"Yes. But not for a visit."

"Meaning?"

"He's gone for good."

"What?" I'm shocked.

"We're finished."

"William . . . what happened?"

"It's been coming, Lauren. You must have known that."

I guess I haven't wanted to know. Maybe about a lot of things.

"I can see that you *didn't* know. Well, we've never been right since Rick found out about my coke habit."

I feel panic. "But you're clean now, aren't you?"

He arches a perfect eyebrow. "Are you asking?"

"No. Not really. I'm sorry I made it a question." And I am.

His clear blue eyes show he's not completely sure I'm telling the truth. It makes me want to protest more but I know it will only confirm his suspicions.

"He doesn't think I'm using now," he explains. "It's all a matter of trust. He's never gotten over that I lied to him, says he'll never trust me again . . . oh, hell, it's finished, that's all."

"That's all?" I ask, appalled. "I mean, this is how it ends? Just like that?"

I know I'm thinking of my own relationship. When friends split up it's always threatening. Especially when you've known the people only as a couple.

"It's not catching," he says sarcastically.

He guesses what I've been thinking. I bring it back to him, where it belongs. "Are you very upset?"

"You could call it devastated . . . but I wouldn't. I suppose I should be. Strange that I'm not."

"What are you then?"

"As in animal, vegetable, or mineral?"

"Stop it." He does this when he doesn't want to deal with things.

"Let's see. If I'm not devastated, then I must be something else. Should we name all the things I could be?"

"Why are you acting like this?"

"Oh, I don't know," he says, sighing as though he's sick of himself. "I guess I don't know what I feel or how I should act. Feelings aren't my strong suit, in case you've forgotten."

"I haven't." Even though he's been clean and going to NA meetings for several years, getting to his feelings is still a problem for him, as it is for any addict.

"This may sound curious," he says, "but I think there's a big part of me that's relieved. Rick's been like a watchdog ever since I got out of rehab."

I can't help wondering if this relief has something to do with his starting cocaine again.

"Not that I intend to have a slip or anything," he says, reading my mind once again. He pulls in his legs and stands up to his full height of six five. "Want anything? I'm going to have some juice."

I say no and follow him to the kitchen. "You seem too calm," I say.

"What's *too* calm?" He pours juice into a crystal glass.

"Is there someone else?" I ask, not knowing why.

He turns, looks at me solemnly. "Not on my part."

"On Rick's?"

"Funny you should ask."

I wait but he doesn't say more. We return to the living room, where we sit on the couch together.

At last he says, "I can't prove anything but my guess is that there *is* someone. And that he's in California."

"Oh, William," I say.

"What?"

"You must be so hurt."

"Why? Just because my lover of ten years turns out to be a cheat, a liar, and wants to blame our break-up on me? Why should that hurt me?"

I touch his arm. "I'm sorry."

"Thank you." His voice is shivery. He turns away from me and I can't help wondering if he's crying. It's not something he does often or easily. Face still averted, he says, "The reason I think he's seeing someone is that he doesn't want anything from here. If that's not a sure sign of guilt, I don't know what is. He left an answering service number too. I bet he's moving in with someone."

"But who? I mean, things don't happen all of a sudden like this."

When he turns back to face me I note that his long lashes glisten. I want to take him in my arms but know he wouldn't like that, would prefer I ignore the evidence of his sorrow. "Who says it's all of a sudden? He's been in Hollywood about eight or ten times since my drug disaster."

"And you think he's been seeing someone all this time?"

"I have no idea how long it's been going on."

"Surely, you'd know."

"Don't call me 'Shirley,' " he says. This is our standard line, but it's not funny right now.

"Stop," I say.

"Can't help it."

"Yes you can. Did you suspect?" Why do I need to know these details? I suppose it's normal.

"I did and I didn't. I asked him but he denied it. I wanted to believe him, so I did. But in retrospect I see all the signs." He shakes his head. "What a simpleton I've been."

"No you haven't. As you said, you didn't want to know. Who would?"

"Maybe somebody with a little more spine. Have you been faithful to Kip all these years?"

I don't know why this startles and upsets me, but it does. "Yes."

"I thought so. What about her?"

"I assume she has."

He smiles dispiritedly. "You really *know*, don't you?"

Do I? "I think I know."

"WASP," he says cryptically.

"WASP?"

"We don't cheat. Unless we're on drugs, of course. Even then, I didn't. But Kip never would. It's not her style."

I know he's right. And I hope I know the same about me.

Five

When I come down to breakfast Kip's sitting at the kitchen table and my heart doesn't leap up when I see her . . . it almost thunks in despair. I'm not used to feeling this way and I don't like it.

She gives me a wan smile and I know she's not thrilled about seeing me either. "Hi."

I greet her in kind and sit opposite. On the table there's an open copy of *Time* magazine. Is she going to begin a rant about the state of the union, so to speak?

"Don't worry, I'm not about to go on a diatribe," Kip says. Another mind reader. There's something to be said for knowing someone so well.

Nick and Nora, our Persian cats, sit curled up together at the far end of the table. They're full-grown now. I try to remember what they were like as kittens but can't. When I look at them, my heart tap-dancing with love, it's hard to believe there was a time when I didn't want them.

I pour myself a cup of coffee and fill a bowl with Apple Jacks, my new favorite cereal. "Rick's left William," I blurt.

"What's that supposed to mean?"

"What word don't you understand?"

"Nice," she states.

We've both used this expression hundreds of times, but this morning it doesn't fly. "It means that Rick has left William and moved to California."

"Are you serious?"

"Would I make it up, Kip?"

"But . . . just like that?" She snaps her fingers. "No warning, nothing?"

I shrug. "Who's to say what warnings there are, what people choose to notice or not notice."

"Are you talking about us?"

I'm startled. "I didn't think I was."

"But maybe you are?"

Am I? I dive into denial. "Of course not. Couples always feel threatened when their friends break up."

She nods because she knows this is true. "Is he all right? William?"

"Naturally, he's upset, but he says he's relieved in a way. Rick never forgave him for his coke addiction."

"Is there someone else?"

"For Rick? William thinks so."

"Well, this is a helluva thing," she says.

"When are you leaving?"

She laughs. "Why, got a date?"

I shove my chair from the table and stand up. It's this new edge Kip has that I don't like. She might have said the same words another time and they would've made me laugh, but now there's a blade of ice that accompanies her humor. "Will you stop it!" I yell. Both cats scamper away in fear.

"Hit a nerve, did I?"

I feel furious. "What nerve?"

"You tell me," she says.

"Well, what was that supposed to mean, 'got a date?' "

"It seemed to fit. You said Rick had left William for someone else and then you asked when I was leaving." She shrugs.

"Heavy evidence," I say.

"Look, Lauren . . ."

"Don't say 'look.' "

"You're impossible." She stands up and takes her cup to the sink.

"*I'm* impossible? This separation is right on schedule." I

leave the kitchen and go into my office. By now Nick is on my desk, sitting next to my computer. I turn it on.

"It's you and me, kid," I say to him, and he makes his funny squeaky sound.

As I'm about to log on to NWDC, Kip knocks once on my open door. I cancel my dial.

She stares at me. "You know, you may think I've changed but you have too. Ever since you got into this damn computer stuff you've been absent, missing. You were going to do it just now, weren't you?"

"Do what?" I stall.

"Disappear into the so-called information highway."

"It's relaxing."

"It's a nightmare," she says.

I pretend innocence of what she means. "How would you know? You've never tried it, never had any interest, never let me show it to you."

"Lauren, your use of it is a nightmare. You've been gone for years."

"That's ridiculous."

"Is it?"

"Are you accusing me of not being there for you when Tom was dying?"

"No. You were wonderful then. I'm talking about before and since."

"And you think you've been present?"

She stares at me as though she has no idea what I'm talking about. Perhaps she doesn't.

Then she says, "I've felt so alone," and begins to cry.

I get up, take her in my arms. I'm a sucker for tears. She feels thin and I realize it's been some time since I've held her this way. We *have* drifted . . . where have I been? Maybe she's right.

"Oh, Kip, I'm so sorry," I whisper.

"For what?"

"I don't know . . . for everything, I guess. Do you think we're in trouble?"

"Yes, I think we are and I don't know what to do about it."

"Maybe separating *isn't* the best thing."

"Maybe not, but it's too late now."

We hold each other for a long time. This is the place where we would normally go to bed and make love but it's clear that's not going to happen, neither of us wants that. I'm not certain why, but I know it's true. I can't remember a time I've felt so sad with Kip, excluding deaths. Is this a kind of death or dying? I hope it isn't. We have so much together . . . or did. How can this be happening to us? I almost ask her but know she has no answers.

I suppose we'll have to see what happens. We can't know the ending now. This is the hardest thing for me to bear but I don't have a choice.

"I have a patient," she says. "I can't look like this." She means her tears.

I nod. She wriggles out of my embrace and I let her go without a struggle and hope this isn't a metaphor for our relationship.

"We'll talk later," she says over her shoulder.

"Right." When she's gone I shut down my computer without logging on for mail and go upstairs to dress for the day ahead.

As I head down Perry toward my office, I pass the storefront where it seems that AA meetings are held around the clock, and wish as always that my mother would seek the help of this program, but know it's unlikely.

At Fourth Street I take a left. This is a fairly quiet street during the day, with only a few stores, brownstones, and a number of restaurants. As you get closer to Seventh Avenue, the noise level rises.

My office is to the right of what was once Tiffany's, a Greek coffee shop which tarted itself up, added a bar, raised prices, then went under. At the moment the space is empty.

I enter my building, take the stairs to the second floor, and walk down a short hall. LAUREN LAURANO PRIVATE INVESTIGATOR is painted on the glass of my office door. I still get a kick when I see it. I stick my key in the lock and am gratified that it turns. I always expect it to be open and to have been burgled.

The place is small, one room, but it's big enough for my purposes. It houses a desk, two chairs, a coat rack, and a filing cabinet. I hate frills.

After I hang up my jacket, take my usual peek down at Seventh Avenue, I sit at my desk and drape my purse strap over my chair. Inside there's a .38 Smith & Wesson. In my desk drawer is a .44 Magnum and strapped on my ankle, a .25. You can't be too careful these days. The desk itself is devoid of anything personal and has only the essential tools of my trade: phone and a recently purchased AST color notebook, with a PCMCIA Megahertz modem. I bought it from CompUSA and don't have to pay for six months. Kip was not amused. From my jeans pocket I take the piece of paper which has the list of Ruthie's friends Elissa drew up for me. There are six names on it.

    Joe Blades
    Harriet Weiss
    Miriam Verber
    Lisa Stein
    Ben Newman
    Maggie Vitagliano

All their phone numbers and addresses are listed. I dial Mr. Blades first. He's an NA — no machine. The same goes for Weiss. I wonder why these people don't have machines and at the same time admire them for their refusal to enter the late twentieth century. A woman answers Miriam Verber's phone and turns out to be Miriam herself. She sounds on the frail side but when she hears who I am and why I want to speak with her, her voice takes on a resonance that suggests she gains strength. We make an appointment for an hour from now.

Newman's phone has been disconnected. Stein is another brave old soul in an new world, but Vitagliano has a machine and I leave a message.

Having completed this round of calls, I turn on my notebook, go into Windows, and log on to NWDC.

After *fetching* my mail I click off the system and return to Popmail. I feel nervous and anxious and when the list of my E-mail comes up, I realize why. There's a letter from Alexandra Thomas.

From: athomas@panix.com
To: laurenl@NWDC.com
Subject: Getting To Know You
Dear Lauren,

Thanks for responding to my letter. I honestly did not know if you would remember me or have time to answer. I am glad you did. I was wondering if you liked to correspond with strangers . . . for all intents and purposes I guess that is what we are, although I feel I know you, do not ask me why or how. Anyway, I think it might be fun. I know we live in the same city and if we wanted to, we could talk on the phone or meet but, as you know, this is a whole new way to get to know someone. What do you think? I will start by telling you something about myself, if you are interested, then you can do the same. It does not have to be an everyday thing.

Meanwhile, here is a piece of hot news: hemlines are going to be knee-length next season! Now how could you live without knowing that? Hope to hear from you.

Yours,
Alex

I read it twice. I smile at the formality of her writing . . . no contractions . . . and I also wonder what's going on here. Why does this stranger want to become not a stranger? I tell myself it's nothing. It's innocent and it might be fun. I immediately write back.

From: laurenl@NWDC.com
To: athomas@panix.com
Subject: I Don't Know Enough About You (I've decided to follow her song theme for the subject)
Dear Alex,

Got your letter. Sure, why not? You'd be surprised at how much time I have. I do have a case now but lots of being on a case is

waiting around for things to happen. Let's get the facts up front: height, weight, eye color, hair color . . . all that stuff. Maybe this is because of my training. It's not that I don't remember what you look like; it's just that I want to be 100% sure. If I recall, your eyes are blue, right? BTW how old are you? Hey, babe, I don't fool around. :) Oh, yes, thanks for the news on the hemline status . . . you're right, couldn't live without it.
Lauren

Miriam Verber lives on the Lower East Side. I've been walking fast, as though there's something I want to get away from. Not much has changed in this part of town. Orchard Street is still the mecca for cheap shopping, although the prices have risen in the last decade like everything else. Hester Street will always be Hester Street . . . just like in the movie, except the people wear more current clothing.

Clothing. This makes me think of Alex Thomas and the letter I sent her. Why did I call her *babe?* Well, I call lots of people *babe*, don't I? Yes, but usually not strangers. And why did I ask her what she looked like? Is this pertinent to an E-mail correspondence? God, will she think I'm flirting? I'd give anything to get the letter back, but there's no way. I push it from my mind like detritus.

Verber lives on Suffolk between Delancy and Stanton, closer to Stanton, nearer to Avenue B, which is on the fringe of a big drug-selling area, and I wonder how safe it is here.

The street is narrow, with tenements lining each side. I look for Verber's building and when I find it there's no surprise . . . it looks the same as the others: dingy and defeated like a ten-cent-a-dance girl grown gray, grotesque.

As I reach out to ring Verber's bell, a boy bumps into me. He has one long curl in front of each ear, wears a yarmulke, a black suit, and looks frightened. After politely excusing himself he darts off. These children who are raised to be Orthodox Jews . . . is it what they want? Do they have any choice? What becomes of them?

After waiting about four thousand hours for a response I

suspect that perhaps the bells on this building no longer work. It's only then I realize that the inner door isn't locked.

Inside, my nose twitches to the wonderful smell of frying onions laced with a hint of garlic. The hallway is dark, paint peeling, but it's clean. Someone takes care of the building, though only in a cursory way.

There's no elevator here, so I walk up the three flights and find Verber's apartment at the end of another dark hall. Whoever cleans is not good about replacing lightbulbs. A mezuzah on the door frame is barely recognizable, as it's been painted over many times. From within comes the unmistakable murmur of a tuned-in television set. I look for a bell but see none, so I knock a few times. And wait. And wait. This time I knock louder and suddenly the TV sound is gone.

"Who?" comes a voice from the other side of the door.

I identify myself and remind her we have an appointment.

"Who?" I'm asked again, as though she hasn't heard word one or doesn't recall our phone conversation. I repeat the whole business.

"Who?"

I can't believe this. "Do you know Ruth Cohen?" I ask.

"Who?"

"Ruth Cohen."

"What about her?"

"I'd like to talk with you about her, as I told you on the phone."

"Phone?"

"Yes, we spoke about an hour ago."

"Who are you?"

I want to scream. I don't. Instead, I patiently explain once more.

"A private eye like on the television?" she asks.

"Yes."

"How do I know you're telling me the truth?"

"I'm going to put my card under your door."

"Don't bother. It could be anybody's card."

She's right, of course. "Well, how can I prove to you I'm who I say I am?"

"Get in a line-up, maybe?" She giggles like a schoolgirl.

Funny, though it doesn't quite make sense if you think it through. And it's hard to know how to respond. "Mrs. Verber, I commend you for being so cautious but I really am who I say I am and I would like to talk with you. I guess you could call a cop friend of mine and . . ."

"I'll believe, I'll believe."

There's the sound of bolts and locks being undone and then she opens up, chain still on. She peeks at me. Looks me up and down. "Ech, you're just a little bit of a thing . . . I could take you myself if I had to."

Mrs. Verber definitely watches a lot of television. She undoes the chain, steps back, and lets me in. She's a woman in her seventies, on the tall side (at least to me), and is wearing a plaid blouse covered by a blue cardigan with a lighter blue skirt, which has a hemline well below her knees. That I'm even noticing a hemline is bizarre. I think of Alex Thomas and smile inwardly. Maybe this correspondence will put me in touch with the fashion world. Just what I've always wanted.

"You want a glass of tea, something?"

"No, thanks."

Mrs. Verber has hazel eyes and lines on her face like little razor cuts. She indicates that we should sit at the kitchen table, which has a once-white Formica top, metal around its edges.

"As I said, I'm investigating the murder of Ruth Cohen."

She puts a gnarled hand to her forehead. "I can't believe it. Why would anyone want to kill her?"

"I thought perhaps you could help me with that."

"Me?"

"Why not? How did you know her?"

"I knew her." This is said with finality.

Why doesn't Verber want me to know how she knew Ruthie?

"Yes, I understand that. But *how* do you know her?"

"We went to school together."

Verber looks so much older than Ruthie that this is hard to believe. "What grades?" I ask gingerly.

"Grades? What do you mean, *grades?*"

I don't ask her which word she doesn't understand. "Grammar school or . . ."

She gestures with her hand as though swatting away a mosquito. "No, no, adult education."

"Oh, right. So you met taking a course."

She nods, looks down, wipes away imaginary crumbs from the tabletop. It's as though she's embarrassed about this. "It's great that you want to continue your education," I say, hoping I don't sound patronizing.

"Continue, shminue. Never went past the fourth grade."

"Then it's even more impressive."

"*You* I don't need to impress," she says.

Whoops.

"In fact, girlie, I don't need to impress anybody. That's the upside of being an old lady. Who cares what people think?"

But she does care, because she doesn't want to tell me what course they took. "Right. Who cares? So what class did you take?" She knows I have her now.

Slowly, she raises her head, gives me an eyeball challenge, but I don't back down.

"Belly dancing one-oh-one," she snaps.

My mouth drops open uncontrollably.

"Hold your water, I was only in my late sixties then."

"I was surprised that Ruthie would take a class like that," I recover. Nicely too, I think. Besides, I *am* amazed.

"So her you're surprised at but me, no?"

I can't win and don't try. "And you became friends at school and stayed friends."

"Ten years."

"Did you see her often?"

She shrugs. "Who can say what's often?"

"Did you know her other friends?"

"Some."

"Did she have any enemies, anyone who'd want her dead?"

"Ruthie Cohen, enemies? If you knew her . . ."

"I did."

She shrugs. "Then you know."

"No. I'm a friend of her niece. I didn't know about her life in the way you might."

"Have you looked for a man?" she asks, leaning close to me as though she's got valuable info.

"A man? What man?"

"You know how they always say, *cherchez la femme?* So what's the opposite? *Cherchez la* what?"

"I don't speak French. Was Ruthie seeing a man?"

"Maybe yes, maybe no."

Exasperation is sneaking up on me. "Mrs. Verber, this isn't a game. If you know something, you should tell me."

"A game? You think I think a murder of my good friend is a game?" She is deeply offended.

"I'm sorry, but do you know if she was or not?" I ask gently.

"You know Ruthie, you maybe knew her husband, Harold, too?"

"Yes."

"Devoted they were. Devoted. And he was only fifty-five when he died. Did you know he was younger than Ruthie?"

"I did, yes."

"Good, because she'd kill me if she knew I told." She claps a hand over her mouth, realizing what she's said.

I smile sympathetically. "Another man?" I prompt.

"As I say, they were a devoted couple, but a person gets lonely."

"Of course. So she *was* seeing someone?"

"Seeing, shmeeing. I'm not sure what that means. Did they sometimes go to a show in the afternoon? Yes. A walk in the park? Yes. Is that seeing?"

"I think so. What's the man's name?"

Mrs. Verber rises stiffly, walks to the stove, turns on a kettle. "I don't want to get anybody in trouble," she says, her back to me.

"I just want to talk with him."

"What could a man like Ben Newman know about a thing like this?"

I mentally thank her. "What's Mr. Newman like?"

She faces me with sparkling eyes. "A doll."

"Can you give me his address?"

"Sure. Washington Square Park. The fourth bench from the MacDougal Street entrance."

"Are you saying he lives there?" I recall that Newman's phone is disconnected.

"We don't ask the man. He deserves respect, dignity. You're a detective, you find out if he lives there."

"Thanks," I say. "I will."

Six

Washington Square Park has changed considerably over the years. The landscape has remained pretty much the same, but the atmosphere and the people who frequent it are different from fifteen or twenty years ago. I can remember a time when no one offered me drugs as I walked through the park. Really. Sometimes it's hard to believe that a lot of people didn't do drugs back then.

The day has warmed up and I unzip my jacket. High in the sky is a bright round sun like a smiley face without the features. Before we know it that same round ball will be devastatingly hot and everyone will complain, especially Kip, who hates the heat and the cold and can't stop talking about it. I wonder what Alex thinks of the various seasons.

I walk along the bottom edge of the park to MacDougal and enter from there. This is where the chess players congregate. The tables are always filled and people surround the players, giving unwanted advice.

I join a group from where I can keep an eye on the fourth bench from the end, which is, at present, unoccupied. If Ben Newman lives there, he's out.

Something pokes my side. It's the elbow of the small man standing next to me. He wears a blue beret rakishly angled over his left ear, a matching turtleneck sweater, and faded jeans. Glasses ride the bridge of his prominent nose, a brush-cut mustache below.

"The man don't know how to play he wouldn't know a knight from a rook from a bishop," he says to me.

My uncle taught me chess when I was young, so I know he's referring to chess pieces. I also know that what this man has said about the player can't be true. I smile noncommittally.

"You think I'm wrong?" he asks in an aggressive way.

"Of course not," I say.

"Because I'm speaking truth. I'm the uncle of the one and only Bobby Fischer."

Oh, boy.

"You don't believe me. I can see it in your eyes. You think I'm a nut."

I'm tempted to agree but I can't be sure where this route will lead, so I opt for safety.

"I don't think that at all," I say.

"Sure you do. Why would I be Bobby Fischer's uncle, huh?"

"Why not?"

He stares at me, his sleek blue eyes narrow, and the expression says that he's never thought of it this way.

"Yeah, why not?" He smiles.

I see a man sit down on the fourth bench from the end. "Excuse me," I say to the beret.

"Sure. Have a nice day."

"You too."

I walk to the bench and sit. Not too close. I observe. The man is in his late sixties, early seventies, wearing a pin-striped suit, conservative tie, a shirt that's seen whiter days. A fringe of gray hair circles his skull like a ruff. He opens the *Times* and expertly folds it — clearly a man who's read the paper on the subway or train for years.

"Excuse me, sir?"

"Yes."

"Are you Ben Newman?"

He looks shocked, as expected. "Yes, I am. Who are you?"

I tell him my name and what I do.

He smiles. "A private detective?"

The usual response. I try to ignore it. "Mr. Newman, I'd like to talk with you about Ruth Cohen."

His face darkens. "Ruthie," he whispers, like the hiss of a snuffed wick. "She's dead."

"I know. That's why I want to talk. When's the last time you saw her?"

He puts his paper on his knees. "The police have already asked me questions."

I nod. "This is a separate investigation. You don't have to answer me but it would help . . . help find the killer. I'm sure you'd like that to happen."

"Yes, sure, naturally. But the police . . . they're looking into it."

"They have a lot of cases. I have only this one."

"You don't mind me asking, how'd you get to be a private eye, a girl like you?"

I grit my teeth. "I could tell you the whole story but it'd take a long time."

He laughs, showing tiny teeth. "Time I got, Miss Laurano."

Time I don't got, I want to say. "It isn't relevant, Mr. Newman."

"To who?"

I sigh. "To you, this case, to anything."

He looks hurt. "Just interested."

"I appreciate that. So let's just say it was a one-thing-led-to-another deal, okay? It's not an interesting tale anyway." The truth is, it is a good story, but in the interest of time, I've told a lie. "So, Mr. Newman, will you cooperate with me?"

He shrugs. "Why not? What do you want to know?"

I ask again when it was that he last saw Ruthie.

"I guess it was the night before she . . . she passed."

I've always thought this euphemism absurd, but I let it go. "What did you do?"

"When?"

"The last night you saw each other."

"Oh. Yeah. We went line dancing. There's a place we go every Friday night."

It's much easier to picture Ruthie line than belly dancing. Easier too than picturing Mr. Newman. "Where?"

"Here in the Village. It's in a church on Christopher Street."

I think I know the one he means. "Between Bleecker and Seventh?"

"That's the one."

"You and Ruthie went every week for how long?"

He stares at the sky as though the answer will be spelled out by the clouds. "I can't remember. Maybe two, three months."

"Did you make friends there?"

"Sure. Everybody was friendly. All of us *altacockas,* we stick together. Not that Ruthie was an *altacocka.* That was part of the trouble."

"Trouble?"

"Well, you know, me being an older man. I always knew I was too old for her but well . . . I kept hoping. I'm seventy-six."

I'm surprised. "You look great."

He shines. "Thanks. Still, I was twelve years her senior."

"Did she care?"

"She said she didn't; I always thought she did."

"Mr. Newman, at the line-dancing place, was there anybody especially friendly, you know, more than the others?"

"Well, there's this other couple we sometimes would have coffee with after."

I take out my pad and pen. "Names?"

"I don't want to get nobody in trouble."

"I just want to talk to them, the way I'm talking to you."

"Thing is, I only know their first names."

"And you don't know where they live, right?"

"Right."

Why is it this is almost always the situation on any case I get? "How about the people who run the line-dancing thing?"

"Nobody runs it. Not really. We rent the space, contribute what we can every week. Ruthie contributed for us both."

"So this couple, think they'll be there next time?"

"Why not?"

"Then tell me their names."

"Clarice and Stuart."

"And when's the next meeting?"

"It's not a meeting."

"Dancing, then."

"Well, they have it twice a week but me and Ruthie only go once. I think Clarice and Stuart go twice, so that'd be tonight. It rhymes with Harris."

"What does?"

"Clarice. That's what she always says. People want to call her Clareese but that's not how she says it."

"I heard you say Clarice."

"I was just thinking if you saw it written or if you wrote it correct in that notebook."

I spell it back to him and he acknowledges that I've gotten it right.

"What time does it start?"

"Six-thirty."

"Tell me something about them, Clarice and Stuart. Are they married?"

He laughs, high and tinny, strange for a man. "If they were married, they wouldn't be line dancing. Nobody goes if they're married. You only do these things when you're single. Too bad, too. The married ones stay home, don't do nothing, don't go nowhere, just sit and petrify in their old grudges. I know. I did it with my wife." A look of bitterness flicks across his face.

"So stupid," he goes on. "They die, then we go out, start to have fun. Not Ruthie though. I mean, she did go out and have fun but she really cared about her dead husband, Harold. That's another reason, aside from the age thing, why I couldn't get her to marry me."

"You proposed to her?"

He nods. "On one knee, you can believe it." He laughs at the picture of himself. "Right here it was. We was sitting on this bench and I got down on the ground on one knee. I tell you, it wasn't no piece of cake neither. I got bad knees."

"What did Ruthie say?"

"In a word, no."

"Why did you want to marry her?"

"Why? Why does anybody want to marry anybody?"

Sometimes I wonder. "Tell me why *you* wanted to marry *her* in particular."

"She was a good lady. I liked her a lot . . . maybe I even loved her. Was it passion? No. Passion is for kids."

"Kids?"

"Well, kids to me is anybody under fifty. You get my age, you don't have passion . . . you don't need it. Passion means pain."

A philosopher. Still, I wonder if he's right. "Did you know that Ruth Cohen was very rich?"

"I cannot tell a lie. I did."

"Did that have anything to do with wanting to marry her?"

"I cannot tell a lie. It did."

"Thanks for your candor."

"You're very welcome. But what I said before is also true. She was a swell dame. Classy. I hope you get the sonofabitching bastard who killed her."

"Me too. You can't think of anybody who'd want her dead, can you?"

"Nope. Certainly not me, Miss Laurano. Hope springs eternal."

"Meaning?"

"I intended to try and get her to hitch up with me, and I think I would of worn her down eventually. She was lonely just like we all are. Funny thing is, there's always one in a couple who ends up alone . . . usually it's the woman but we men lose our brides too. There ain't no happy endings, you know. Can't be."

I stand up, put out my hand to shake his. He takes it.

"I'll be here, you need me again."

"Thanks."

As I walk through the park I think about what Newman said: *No happy endings.* It's true, of course. Whether you leave or are left or whether one person dies and the other lives on. I think of a couple, Ginny and Terry, who'd been together almost forty years when they were killed in a car crash. It shook up all of us but perhaps that was a happy ending after all.

Then I think of William and Rick again. I would've put money on their staying together. I'm doing everything I can to not think of my own situation. And just what is *my situation?* Tenuous, at best.

This is ridiculous. Absence makes the heart grow fonder

and all that. I sit down on a bench near the MacDougal and Waverly Place entrance, take out my cellular phone, and punch in the number of Joe Blades, one of Ruthie's friends I haven't been able to reach yet. But I can't get that phrase, *there ain't no happy endings,* out of my mind and it makes me feel depressed. Instinctively, I know it ain't because of the grammar.

Seven

Ruthie's friend Joe Blades finally picked up his phone and even though I'm going to see him in less than forty minutes, I run up to my office, turn on the computer, and dial in to NWDC to see if I have mail. This is crazy. I've already done this today. What's it all about? As if I don't know.

I have mail and they're both from Alex. I experience a shock wave of excitement. Uh-oh. After I sign off the system I go back to my reader, click open the first message.

From: athomas@panix.com
To: laurenl@NWDC.com
Subject: Sentimental Journey
Dear Lauren,

I guess this is the letter where I tell you something about myself, right? I am having a harder time with this than I thought I would.

L> If I recall, your eyes are blue, right?

My eyes are brown. I am blonde. You should never ask a woman about her weight. Yes, I am stalling. I am sure you did not mean that you wanted to know where I went to kindergarten, etc. So here is a brief journey (see subject) through my life. I was born in California but I grew up in Scarsdale. I went to Skidmore. My mother has been married six times. She lives in Washington, D.C., because her present husband is in the Clinton administration. I have a lot of siblings but they are all halves

or steps and most of them — no, all of them — are gorgeous. For instance, Karel, my eldest stepbrother, looks like Robert Redford when he was younger and it is all uphill from there. I went to thirteen different high schools. So that is enough for now. It is your turn. Same information, please.
Yours,
Alex

The second one is very short.

Dear Lauren,
    If I could get back the previous letter, I would. I feel stupid. What do you care about where I lived or my family? I am sorry it was not more interesting.
Yours,
Alex

I feel bad that she's embarrassed about her letter to me, because they are exactly the kinds of things I wanted to know. I glance at my watch. I don't have time for anything profound or long.

Dear Alex,
    Please don't be embarrassed. I loved your letter and was glad to learn these things about you. I have an appointment now but will write more later.
Best,
Lauren

On my way to meet Joe Blades I make a stop at Three Lives Bookstore, which is run by our best-female-friends couple, Jenny and Jill. Suddenly, I wonder about them. They've been together longer than Kip and I have; in fact, they introduced us. I've always assumed they're happy but now I worry that perhaps they're not, perhaps it's all an illusion and nobody's happy. This is crazy.

The store is on the corner of Waverly Place and Tenth Street. This is one of the last independently owned bookstores in town. Not to mention the best. Jenny built it with some help and it resembles an English bookshop.

Both the Js, as we call them, are here today. Jill is in her midforties. She has dark red hair and greenish eyes and is taller than Jenny and me — but who isn't? Alex? *Stop that, Lauren.* Jill's attractive and adores Jenny. I think of Jill as smart, warm, and compassionate. We often read and like the same books. Her major fault is that she talks too fast: her mind sprints beyond how quickly she can impart information.

Jenny, who's forty-two, is fascinated by everything, always wants to know what's going on with her friends and in the world. Still, she plays it rather close to the vest when it comes to herself, offering as little information as she can get away with. She's got curly brown hair, not a touch of gray yet; wears glasses; and is very cute and cuddly-looking, although she's not open to that from anyone but Jill.

"So, what's happening?" Jenny asks.

Before I get a chance to answer, a customer pushes me out of the way and leans against the counter.

"Do you have it?" the woman asks breathlessly. She's dressed entirely in black, which isn't odd for New York, but she's not a kid and her lips and nails are painted black as well. And then there's the hat.

"Have what?" Jenny asks, in a less than adorable way, although I can tell she's trying.

"The new Anne Rice, of course," says the customer condescendingly. The hat is black too, and huge.

Jenny says, "Ah, which Anne Rice do you mean?"

"The newest one," the woman snaps, now totally disgusted.

"Jill," Jenny calls, "this woman wants the latest Anne Rice."

"Okay."

"She'll bring it over," Jenny says to the black-clad customer.

Jill goes behind the counter with the book and places it in front of the woman, who screams when she sees it, scaring us all.

"Are you insane?" the woman shrieks. "This is *Taltos*. I don't want this. I have this. This is *Taltos, Taltos, Taltos, Taltos . . .*"

"Okay, okay," Jenny says. "It's *Taltos*. I can see that."

Jill says, "You said you wanted the latest Rice. Well, this is it."

"Are you going bizarre?" the woman shouts.

I think of leaving but can't pull myself away. Jenny and I make eye contact and we both start laughing.

"This isn't funny," says the woman. "This is a travesty." She turns to face the open space of the store, holds up the thick book. "This is *Taltos, Taltos, Taltos*. This isn't new. I got this last fall. I read it in one night, as I do all Ms. Rice's work. They're trying to pass this off as the latest book, when we all know this is *Taltos*."

"Don't say *Taltos* again," admonishes Jenny.

"Excuse me," Jill says to the madwoman. "You may have read this and it may not be new to you, but it is the latest Anne Rice book."

I don't understand how Jill can manage to sound so sane.

The woman's eyes bug out like snails' shells. "Liar, liar, pants on fire. The latest book is *Memnoch. Memnoch. Memnoch.*"

"Don't say *Memnoch* again," Jenny says, "or I'll have to hurt you."

"Shush, Jen." Jill says this because she's afraid for Jenny, knowing the woman is a nut and unsure of what she might do.

"You must give me *Memnoch*." The woman falls to her knees, her big-brimmed hat flops over her face so that she resembles a pile of black rags.

"Get up," Jill says calmly but with heft.

It sounds as though the woman is weeping.

"Madam, get up, please. Now."

She raises her head, startled. "What did you say?"

"I said I want you to get up now."

There's something about the way Jill says this, because the woman does.

"And now," Jill continues, "I want you to leave my store."

"Not without —"

"No!" Jenny yells. "Don't say it."

Jill takes the woman by the arm. "Listen very carefully. *Memnoch the Devil* is not due out until this summer. When *we* get it, you may buy it. In fact, I'll put a copy aside for you."

"But I must have it now."

"You can't. It's not published yet." Jill has her almost to the door.

"Why should I believe you?"

Jill says sanely, "Because I don't lie."

"I'll get it at another store if this is how you feel."

"Fine. Why don't you go to Barnes and Noble. I'm sure they'd love you to have a coffee there as well as buying a nonexistent book."

The woman throws back her shoulders, wriggles from Jill's grip. "You-people-are-barbarians. You-people-know-nothing. I-will-never-shop-here-again."

"That's fine," Jill says and opens the door for her.

"I will go to a civilized place from this moment on."

Jenny says to me, "Oh, please, she's not going to break out in song, is she?"

Jill ushers her through the exit, then closes the door behind her.

"Well done," I say to Jill.

She takes a deep bow. "Just another normal day in the shop."

Jenny adds, "And just another pretty face."

I glance at my watch and see that if I don't leave now, I'll be late. "Got to go."

"But we didn't even talk," Jenny says. "I didn't find out what's happening."

"Nothing's happening. Just stopped by to say hi. Thanks for the show."

"You're very welcome," Jill says. "Anytime."

Blades is waiting for me at the designated spot. A seedy kind of bar on West Fourth Street. His choice. I hardly ever pick bars, because they almost never offer anything of the chocolate persuasion.

I recognize him right away from his description of himself. He wears a flannel shirt and jeans, is very tall, probably six seven or more, and he's thin, as though he were made of a garden hose.

I'm surprised because he's not a peer of Ruthie's, but instead a man in his late thirties, early forties. He stands at the bar, his large thin fingers gripping a half-drunk glass of beer, the empty brown bottle next to it.

As I'm the only woman here, he smiles, guessing who I am.

We shake hands and he offers to order me a drink. I ask for a Diet Coke. I like the taste even though I'm not on a diet, God forbid. While Blades buys another beer for himself, he looks at me dubiously, as though my not ordering something alcoholic makes me suspect.

"Let's sit down," he says.

I follow him into the recesses of the bar and we slide into a well-worn booth with green benches and a scarred wooden table.

"You're young to be a friend of Ruth Cohen's," I say.

"Oh, yeah? Why's that?"

Good question. "Her other friends are much older."

"I could say you're short to be a P.I."

"You could, but you won't, right?"

"Right." He smiles and two pronounced dimples appear in his cheeks. "I think you'll find that Ruthie had all sorts of friends."

"I've met two and they were both around her age. I guess I made a bad assumption."

"You did, indeed." He pours the last of his beer into his glass. "It's hard to believe she's dead. Ruth was a very vital person."

"Yes, she was. How did you happen to know her?"

"Actually, we met at the movies. It was an afternoon flick at the Waverly and she sat one seat away from me. We began talking before the film started. I liked her. Afterward we went for coffee. Then we became friends, saw each other about once a week, usually to go to the movies."

"What'd you see?"

"When?"

"That first day, when you met her."

"*Schindler's List.* You see it?"

"Yes. So you haven't been friends for that long."

"Define *that long*," he says.

I find Blades annoying. "More than two years, under three."

"That's about right. But that doesn't mean I'll miss her any less than someone else who knew her longer. Quality is what counts."

"And you and Ruth had a quality relationship."

"I think so. She would've said so too."

"Did she talk to you about personal matters?"

"Like what?"

I take a long swallow of my Coke and peer at him over the rim of my glass. This is meant to disconcert him, but I don't think it works. "Like her personal life," I say.

"Yeah, I guess. Her life was her friends and her niece."

"What'd she tell you about her niece?"

"Just that she's her favorite, even though she's a dyke, and she was going to leave her all her money."

"Did she actually say that?"

"That she was going to leave her money to her?"

"Yes. And the other thing . . . 'even though she's a dyke'?"

"She said the thing about the money but maybe she didn't call her a dyke."

"What *did* she call her?"

"Let's see." He furrows his brow to show he's trying to remember. "A ladylover, I think. Yeah, that was it. Ladylover."

This does sound like something Ruthie would say. "What was her attitude about that?"

"That she was a dyke?"

I control myself. It's one thing for me to use the word, another for him, but I can't get into this now, so I just nod to show that this is what I'm asking about.

"Well, she didn't understand it . . . I mean, she knew what it meant but she didn't get it. Said she thought it must have something to do with the niece's upbringing, crazy mother and father, I guess. But she didn't condemn her for it or anything, if that's what you mean."

"That's what I mean."

"She said she thought Alizza—"

"Elissa," I correct.

"Right. She thought Elissa was happy with her girlfriend, so that was the only important thing."

"Did you think she'd leave you money?" I ask abruptly.

He pulls back as if I'd slapped him. "Me?"

"Yes."

"Why would she leave me money?"

"You were friends."

"Yeah, but not like that. I mean, like you said, under three years."

"And you said you had a quality friendship."

"Yeah, but that doesn't mean she'd leave me money." He finishes his beer. "You don't think I did her, do you?"

The words *did her* give me pause. They're not the words of the average person. "What do you do, Mr. Blades?"

"Do?"

"For a living."

"Oh. I'm almost an anachronism. I set type, work nights."

"And you were working when Ruthie was murdered?"

"I don't know exactly when that was."

Neither do I, yet.

"But whenever it was," he goes on before I can say anything further, "I didn't kill her. Why the hell would I?"

"I don't know. Can you think of anyone who would want to?"

"Besides the niece?"

I know why he says this. "Yes."

"Far as I know, the lady didn't have any enemies. Heard it might be the Granny Killer, though."

"Where'd you hear that?"

"I didn't actually *hear* it. I read it in the paper."

"That could be, but Elissa's a prime suspect."

"Yeah. Tough."

Why is it I don't believe he really thinks it's tough? Why is it I don't believe a damn thing he's said? I slide out of the booth and stand up. "Well, thanks a lot, Mr. Blades."

"Joe."

"Joe." I give him my card. "In case you think of anything that might help."

"Sure."

We shake hands and I leave. I have to face the fact that even if ordinary people don't use the term *do her,* they do go to the movies and they do pick up lingo. Joe Blades is obviously a moviegoer and likes being kind of a tough-guy type. Still, there's something about him I don't like, believe, trust.

When I hit Sixth Avenue the vendors are out in full force. Nothing stops them. They sell videos in front of Blockbuster, CDs in front of Sam Goody's, books in front of Dalton's, and nobody gives a damn. Mayor Giuliani made a difference for a while, but it didn't last. Like everything else, change is ephemeral.

I think I'll go to my office. I owe a letter.

Eight

From: laurenl@NWDC.com
To: athomas@panix.com
Subject: All The Things I Am
Dear Alex,

I hope my earlier note assuaged your fears. I have a little time now, so I'll try to fill you in on me. I'm five one, have brown hair and eyes, and am forty-five. I noticed you didn't tell me your age. I'll take a guess . . . thirtysomething.

How I became a P.I. is a long story but I'll give you the microversion. When I was seventeen I was parked in a make-out spot in New Jersey (sorry, but that's where I'm from) and two men killed my boyfriend, raped me, and left me for dead. In the hospital I was recruited by the FBI (not kidding) and after college I went to work for them. In a freak accident I killed my partner and even though the Bureau didn't want me to leave, I did. So what to do? It took me a while to decide but with the help of friends, I chose this line of work. I've never been sorry even though I often see the seamy side of life. Et vous? How you got into your line of work, that is.

My parents have been married for forty-six years. I can't imagine having a mother who's been married so often. It must've been hard on you. Also, I'm an only child, so I have no experience with siblings. But don't let that make you think I had a perfect, happy, normal childhood. My mother is an alcoholic who's still in denial about it. I guess she's been one all my life but it's gotten progressively worse as these addictions do. So she was never really there, something I'm trying to come to terms with now. But that's a heavy subject and for another time.

What's your relationship with your mother like? Are you friends with the steps and halves and others? Guess that's it for now. I look forward to hearing from you . . . and please, say anything you like.

Best,

Lauren

After I read this about seventeen times, with some trepidation I send it, log off, and leave my office to meet Cecchi for lunch.

Ruby Packard, the smiling waitress of the year, almost collides with me when I enter the Waverly Place Luncheonette. I stumble; she doesn't.

"Watch where you're going," she barks. Her sprayed Ann Miller hair doesn't ripple.

"Sorry, Ruby," I say.

She makes a grouch sound and slides away on her sturdy legs, her thick square body like a tank.

This is a well-known cop hangout. It's one room with a counter and stools, booths, and freestanding tables. When Cecchi and I are not having cappuccino in a café this is where we meet because he can have the kind of lunch he likes: egg salad on toasted white, cole slaw on the side.

Cecchi calls to me from his usual booth.

I sit opposite him. "Anything new?" I ask, referring to Ruthie's case.

"*Nada.* This guy is slick, Lauren."

"You sure it's the Granny Killer?"

"Got all the earmarks . . . but we might know something more when the M.E.'s report comes in. All I have now is the prelim. What bothers me is her age. She's definitely the youngest of all the victims."

"She certainly could be a grandmother at sixty-four."

"Sure. But our mutt usually goes for the over-seventy-five group."

"You think he actually knows how old they are?"

Cecchi shrugs. "I thought so, but now I don't know."

"What if it isn't a Granny killing?"

"Then it's a whole new ball game. You got anything?"

"Nope."

Ruby hovers. "So?" she asks. This is her pleasant way of asking me what I want. And what I *want* and what I order are two different things.

"Dieting, huh?" Ruby asks.

I'm surprised she bothers, as she usually speaks only to Cecchi, even if I ask her a question. "Cholesterol problems," I explain.

For reasons I can't fathom, this sends her into a paroxysm of laughter which continues all the way to the kitchen.

"Delightful," I say to Cecchi. "Lovely woman."

"Ahhh, she's okay." Cecchi always defends Ruby because he knows how much she adores him. Not that he has any romantic interest in her. Cecchi's been married forever to a fabulous woman named Annette. By design, they have no children. Kip and I have spent some great evenings with the two of them. Occasionally, it's like having a workshop about our respective relationships — something I'd normally hate, but it works with them. Maybe Kip and I should . . . it feels like a kick in my gut when I remember that she's leaving tomorrow.

Cecchi says, "Did you know Ruth and her husband well?"

"Fairly well."

"She take it hard when he died?"

"Yes. It was so strange how it happened too."

He lifts a black eyebrow. "Oh?"

"Funny, I thought I told you about it at the time."

"If you did, I don't remember."

"They were on vacation . . . on a cruise. They went to bed in their cabin at a reasonable hour and the next morning nobody could find Harold. They weren't worried — except Ruthie, who worried about everything — until late in the afternoon, once they'd searched the entire ship and hadn't found him. They concluded that he'd gotten up in the night, taken a walk on deck, and somehow fallen overboard."

"Was he drunk?"

I laugh at the idea of Harold being drunk. "No. He never drank. They led pretty quiet lives, except they traveled a lot."

"Suicide?"

"He had no reason. It was ruled an accidental death. They'd always had a lot of money — he was a broker — but Ruth inherited a pile."

"And now Elissa is going to inherit it," he says matter-of-factly.

"That's right."

"Hey, you don't have to be so defensive."

I'm never aware of my tone, so his statement takes me aback. "Was I?"

He nods. "So they ever recover Harold's body?"

"No."

"I suppose taking late-night walks on deck was a habit with him?"

"Yes, smartass, it was."

"Just asking."

"What'd you think, Ruthie pushed him over?"

"Stranger things have happened. Elissa wasn't on the cruise with them by any chance, was she?"

"I can't believe you're thinking what you're thinking," I snap at him.

"Just asking," he says again.

Ruby is back and throws my food on the table in front of me. I'm surprised the dishes don't break.

"You want anything else?" she asks Cecchi sweetly.

He declines and Ruby goes away.

I stare at my boring salad, completely indifferent. Why would I want to eat this?

"And that was how long ago?" he asks.

"Harold's death? About five years ago."

"You know what I hate? Deaths where they don't ever find the body."

"Cecchi, they were in the middle of the Atlantic Ocean."

"Yeah, yeah."

"Oh, please . . . what do you think, he swam to shore a trillion miles away?"

" 'Course not. Terrible thing to die like that. Forget it."

"Forget what, Cecchi?"

"It was a stupid idea."

This man rarely has stupid ideas. "Let's hear it anyway."

"Nah."

"Do I have to beg?"

"It's just that I never understand how people fall overboard from big cruise ships. You?"

The truth is, I don't. But I know it's possible. At least, I think it's possible. "So what are you saying?" I fork some lettuce into my uninterested mouth.

"I don't know. I just don't get it, that's all. Obviously, they couldn't prove suicide and foul play was ruled out, so that means that a, what, a sixty-year-old man —"

"Fifty-five . . . Harold was fifty-five when it happened."

"So a fifty-five-year-old man jumped up on the railing, or whatever the hell it's called, and fell over, right?"

It does sound preposterous.

"The thing is, Lauren, these cruise ships are built so even old drunks can't fall overboard."

"When the insurance people investigated they found a few places where it could've happened." The truth is, it always has seemed strange to me but I focused more on Ruthie and Elissa's loss than on anything else. "I have to admit, though, I can't quite see Harold *jumping* up on the railing."

"Can you see him climbing up?"

"Why not? Fifty-five isn't that old."

"No, that's not what I meant."

"Then what?"

"I meant, *Why?* Why would he climb up on the railing?"

"What does this have to do with anything?" I've never tasted anything flatter than this salad.

"Nothing. I thought it was interesting."

"What's interesting is that both Harold and Ruthie should die unnatural deaths."

"Yeah, I find that interesting too."

"But does it mean anything?" Fleetingly, I consider ordering something else . . . something with butter and mayonnaise.

"Don't know," he says.

"But you think it does?"

"Don't you?" As he takes a big bite, egg salad squirts from his sandwich onto his plate.

It looks soooo good. "I think it's what you said, *interesting*, which means, I guess, it might mean something."

"Lot of qualifiers there," he says, smiling and looking especially rakish and handsome.

"Is that a good egg salad?"

"Want a bite?"

I shake my head. I know once I start, I'll be in trouble.

"I can see you're crazy about your salad."

"You know what it tastes like? Straw."

"Which you've eaten your share of?"

"It's what I imagine straw would taste like," I say bitterly.

"So just how high is this cholesterol thing?"

"I don't know. Too high."

"So shut up and eat your straw. Wouldn't want anything to happen to you."

Again he smiles, our eyes meet and wordlessly express our mutual fondness and respect. I don't know what I'd do without Cecchi. Not just as a cop connection, but as a friend.

Ruby is back with coffee and a check. "You're not eating," she says to me.

"Not hungry."

"Bet you would be if it was greasy and filled with calories, right?"

Does everyone have my number? I can't let her have the last word. "No, I'm just not hungry."

"A first," Ruby says, and exits laughing.

She has the last word. "I hate her," I say softly to Cecchi.

He laughs because he knows I don't really mean it. "Drink

your coffee. So back to Harold. You're not convinced it was an accident?"

"I've always wondered but I could never figure out what could've happened, since there was no way Ruthie could be involved in it."

"Yeah. I bog down there too."

We finish our coffee and after we pay, we go outside and stand on the corner of Waverly Place and Sixth Avenue. Two drag queens in full regalia pass us.

Cecchi stares after them. "I've seen better," he says to me.

"Where?"

"In jail. Glad they don't bust them anymore. I always hated that. People are stupid."

"It was ever thus," I say.

He nods in agreement. "Where you off to now?" he asks.

"I have an interview with another friend of Ruthie's."

"Which one?"

"Maggie Vitagliano."

"Talked to her last night."

"And?"

He shrugs. "You'll see."

"What's that mean?"

He smiles enigmatically for an answer and I know he's not about to tell me more.

"Yeah, well, I don't expect anything but you never know," I say.

"You learn something interesting, you tell me, right?"

"Have I ever not?"

He pats my cheek, as if to say I've always been square with him.

"So I'll talk with you later. Give Kip a kiss for me," he says.

"Sure will." I turn quickly so he doesn't get a good look at me. I haven't told him about her going away yet. Next time.

Nine

Usually, the only time I come to SoHo is early in the morning when I do my fast-walk. It's amazing what's happened here. Not only has it become a hot spot for galleries, shops, restaurants, and high-priced real estate, but tourists teem almost any time of the day or night and especially on weekends. SoHo (which means south of Houston) is arguably one of the richest neighborhoods in the city.

When I'm here to do my exercise I see basically two types of people: those who are going to work and the homeless. The homeless lie in doorways under blankets if they're lucky, but sometimes in the middle of the sidewalk. The suits (both sexes) who step around them have that intense look of those who hate what they do but have no choice if they want to continue to live in SoHo.

Maggie Vitagliano resides here. It's after two in the afternoon, and the livin' ain't easy, because although it's a weekday, the tourists don't seem to care. They maneuver, jockey, jostle, bump, and annoy, completely oblivious to anyone or anything but their needs. Most of all, they forget that people actually live here and they treat the streets like litter pans.

Vitagliano, to my surprise, lives in a very chic loft building on Prince Street. I realize that I've done some stereotyping. Because of the Italian name I assumed she was one of the old residents of SoHo who have lived here since before gentrification. Wrong. At least, I think so. I'm unable to picture one of those women living at this address. I can't believe I've done in my head what I scream about all the time . . . people portraying Italians as mobsters or lower-class immigrants who wear black dresses or, if they're men, undershirts at the table. I think Martin Scorsese has finally gotten to me.

I ring the bell and in moments a mellifluous voice asks who I am.

I tell her, and after instructing me to go to the back of the building and get in the elevator, she rings me in. I do as she says and don't bother pushing the third-floor button in the elevator, because I know that it's she who has to bring me up. When the door opens I step directly into the apart-ment/loft. I'm not positive which of the two things almost knocks me over: the place or Vitagliano. They're both gorgeous.

The loft is huge; Vitagliano isn't.

"How do you do," she says, extending a beautifully mani-cured hand.

I take it and she winces, then tries to cover with a false smile. I know I didn't squeeze too hard and she doesn't look like a woman who's ever washed a dish, let alone anything that might require manual labor. So it must be something else. I'll keep my eyes open to see what's wrong with that hand.

Maggie Vitagliano is, quite simply, a looker. She's at least five ten and wears a simple white T-shirt, tucked into white jeans, no belt. White Adidas sneakers and socks complete the outfit. No one's asking, but I'd have to give her figure a ten.

Her black hair, parted on the left, falls into two neat curves around her face like shiny shields. The eyes are large and brown, the lashes long, lightly mascaraed. Her nose is the per-fect Italian one with a hint of a rise on the otherwise straight bridge. She has pink lavish lips like velvet ribbons.

I stare as I try to remember if Alex is as good-looking as this woman. What is wrong with me?

"Thanks for seeing me," I say.

"You're entirely welcome." With a practiced nod of her head, she indicates that I should follow her. I take in the loft, which is all wood and brick, columns and beams. Walls define rooms but we're in an immense open space: eight enormous windows across the front.

In the living room area we sit on white leather couches that surround a black marble table on which there are two Dresden cups and saucers, a pot covered with a tea cozy, and a plate of yellow, blue, and pink petit fours (something I haven't seen in years).

"Shall I be mother?" she asks.

I feel like I'm in a BBC program. "Fine."

She removes the flowered cozy and pours us each a cup from the matching teapot. "Sugar?"

Why not? I tell her yes and also accept lemon. She picks up the cup with her right hand, then immediately switches it to the left. I see then that in the U between thumb and first finger she has what looks like an open blister — red, raw, obviously painful, and clearly what had evoked her earlier pain when we shook hands.

"Now," she says, leans back into the couch, her cup in her left hand, "what can I do for you?"

There's something off-putting about the way she says this, as if I'm here to solicit for a charity rather than to discuss her murdered friend.

"As I told you on the phone, I'd like to discuss Ruth Cohen."

"Yes, of course, dear."

"How long did you know her?"

"Let me think . . . oh, I'd say about twenty years."

By my calculations this would put her in her early twenties then. "How did you meet?"

"Through Harold."

"How did you know him?"

"I worked in his brokerage firm. That was, of course, before I married. Hugo didn't want me to work."

"Hugo Vitagliano?" It seems an unlikely name.

She giggles like a schoolgirl. "Oh, no. Hugo was my first husband, darling. My third was Orlando Vitagliano."

I wish she'd stop calling me *dear* and *darling*. "Are you Italian?"

"Yes. And you are, also?"

"Yes. So you met Harold twenty years ago and stayed friends with him all that time?"

"What part of Italy are your people from, dear?"

I know this is a snob question. I recognize it from my own family: grandfather, father, and his siblings.

"Rome and Naples," I say.

"Mmmmm," she utters approvingly.

I hate this. I know she wants me to ask her the same question but I don't. "I was inquiring if you'd stayed friends with Harold for the twenty years since you first met."

"No, not exactly. Not at all, actually. When I worked at the brokerage company we weren't friends at all. Then I remet him about seven years ago, dear. Remet both of them. Orlando is also a broker and we ran into them at a cocktail party. If the truth be known, Harold hardly remembered me." She takes a delicate sip of tea.

"Is that when you started a friendship with the Cohens?"

"Well, we did see them socially, but we weren't close friends or anything."

"So when did you become close with Ruth?"

"My friendship with Ruth developed after Harold died. I still can't believe the circumstances of his death."

"What do you mean by that?"

"You know, dear, how he died? It seems so fantastic, falling off a ship."

"What are you suggesting?"

"Oh, I don't know. They ruled it death by misadventure, so I guess I should simply accept that. But it's always bothered me."

"Did it bother Ruth?"

"Yes. We talked about it often."

"What was her theory?"

"Well, naturally, she ruled out suicide. I do too. Harold simply wasn't the type. Of course, one never knows who the type is, isn't that so, dear? I mean, you must come across odd suicides in your line of work."

Line of work is said as though I were a reporter for the *National Enquirer.* "Yes, I have. So what was Ruth's theory?"

"We both suspected foul play."

Not having heard a person actually say the words *foul play* in real life, I find them jarring. "What do you mean?"

"Pushed or thrown or something."

"And the motive?"

"Well, a crazed person, of course. There wouldn't have been a motive, because he didn't know anyone onboard before they took the cruise. It would be hard to develop a true hatred of Harold in such a short time."

"What about over a long time?"

"Sorry?"

"Where are you from?" She sounds more English every moment.

"From? You mean where was I born, grew up, that sort of thing?"

"Yes."

"I was born in Florence but grew up in Australia. Then I went to England before I came here when I was twenty-two."

"I wondered about your accent."

"Oh. Do I still have one, dear?"

She knows she does, so I smile enigmatically. "Let's get back to Harold. Do you think he had any enemies?"

"No. He was a very nice man. And she's a . . . *was* a lovely woman. It's all too peculiar. I mean, that he should die the way he did and that Ruth should be murdered. How often does something like that happen if there's no foul play, I wonder."

"So you befriended Ruth after Harold died?"

"I wouldn't put it that way, dear. We were already friends. We just became closer, that's all. She needed me. Shock, darling. That's what she was in, shock."

"So what did you do together?"

"Do?" She offers me the plate of petit fours; I decline and she takes a pink one.

"I mean, how did you spend your time?"

"Oh. Well, we'd dine. Occasionally, we'd go to the cinema. That sort of thing."

"Did she ever tell you anything that might lead you to believe that she was afraid of someone? Did she mention threatening phone calls or letters?"

"Never, dear. I mean, nothing about phone calls or letters. But her niece concerned her."

"What about her concerned Ruth?"

"You're married, darling, aren't you?"

I see that she's eyed my wedding ring. "Yes."

"Well, Elissa isn't."

"And that concerned Ruth?"

"Her lifestyle, dear," she says in a hushed tone, as though uttering something unspeakable.

"You mean that Elissa's a lesbian."

She grimaces, shuts her eyes. "Oh, that awful word."

It continues to amaze me that people, both straight and gay, have trouble with the word *lesbian*. Even *dyke* is more acceptable. "Why is it an awful word, Ms. Vitagliano?"

Her eyes grow wide with astonishment at my question. She says, "It's so ugly."

It is? Funny, but I don't think so. Certainly the jokes made, like "les be on our way," aren't nice but that's a whole other story. I decide not to pursue this.

"So Ruth was concerned about Elissa's relationship?"

"They don't have any money, you know. I mean, not to speak of. And Ruth kept them supplied when they needed it. It galled Harold."

"It did?" This isn't how I remember things. I'd understood that Harold had no blood relatives and was happy to help Elissa when she needed help. I also wonder, if Vitagliano wasn't a close friend of Harold's, how she knew his feelings about money and Elissa.

"He thought the niece was a sponge or a *schnorrer*, as Ruth would've called her."

Ruthie thought nothing of the kind, and although *schnorrer* is a word she most certainly would've used, it wasn't one she'd attach to Elissa.

"So what are you saying, exactly?"

"You know that the niece inherits everything?"

"I do."

"Millions, darling."

I wait.

"Well, figure it out, dear. If you knew you were going to inherit that kind of money and your benefactor was in great health, what would you do?"

I find this an incredible question. "What would *you* do?"

She looks at me, shocked. "We're not talking about me, are we?"

"But you asked what *I'd* do."

"Yes, exactly."

"I wouldn't do anything. And you?"

She's ruffled and puts her teacup down. "Well, like you, nothing. But we're talking about this homosexual."

Another acceptable term. "What does her sexual orientation have to do with it?"

"She's not about to marry and have a man take care of her, is she, dear?"

What century is this woman living in? "What do you do for a living?" I look around the loft, indicating that I know its worth.

"Haven't you ever heard of alimony?"

"I see."

"You needn't frame it like I'm evil or something. Orlando can afford it."

I make a mental note to see what she's getting from Vitagliano. I hand her my card. "I guess that's about it. If you think of anything else, anything that might be of help, please call."

"By the way, who're you working for?"

"I'm not at liberty to tell you that," I say mechanically.

She walks me to the elevator. "Do you think the police have any leads?"

"I don't know."

"Elissa did it. There's no doubt in my mind."

"How well do you know her?"

"Well enough."

I'm not sure what this means, but anyone who really knows

Elissa would be sure of her innocence. Unless they had a vested interest in her being guilty. When the elevator arrives, I shake her hand, giving it a more forceful squeeze than I normally would.

The last thing I see before the door slides shut is Maggie Vitagliano, her smile attempting to cover a rictus of pain that I've inflicted. I may feel guilty, but I'm not sorry.

Ten

Back in my office I record my impressions of Maggie Vitagliano. There's something off about this woman. I can't imagine her as a close friend of Ruthie Cohen's. What could they have had in common? Or am I being a snob? Although Ruthie had money and was educated, she was still a girl from the Bronx and Vitagliano doesn't fit. I pick up the phone and punch in Elissa's number.

We exchange greetings, ask about each other's state of mind, as we always do, and then I get to it.

"Oh, her," Elissa says. "You want to know the truth, I never understood it. She's such a phony. I don't know what Ruthie saw in her."

I smile. The eye of the beholder. "What about what she saw in Ruthie?" I ask gently.

"Mmmm. I often wondered about that too. It was sort of like the odd couple or something. Not that they spent that much time together... but more than you might think."

"Like what?"

"Maybe once a week."

"Did Ruthie ever talk to you about her?"

"Sure. She said she was, and I quote, 'a very wonderful person for a *shiksa*' unquote. You know Ruthie, she tried not to be prejudiced but she always had to mention if a person was a goy or a black or whatever. I think it was that generation of Jews."

"Not just Jews. My mother does the same thing and thinks

of herself as a liberal. Anyway, why did Ruthie think she was so wonderful?"

"Because after Harold died Maggie was there for her. Well, everybody was, all her friends, but Maggie was . . . I don't know. . . solicitous or something. Ruthie didn't see it that way. Frankly, I think Ruthie liked her because the woman never bugged her about her weight and brought her candy every time she came over."

"How about Harold? Did he ever mention Maggie to you? Single her out in any way. . . . as a special friend of theirs . . . or say that he liked or didn't like her?"

"Harold never met anything that breathed he didn't like. You remember how he was, don't you?"

I do. "I know this is going to sound silly, but can you think of any reason Vitagliano would benefit from Ruthie's death?"

"She's in the will."

"What?"

"Yeah. I finally saw a copy. But don't get excited. Ruthie left her some jewelry. I think she once told me Maggie admired a gold bracelet."

"So that's it then. She wouldn't benefit in any other way?"

"Not that I can think of."

"Can you tell me anything else about Vitagliano?"

"Like what?"

"Do you know her last husband . . . or any of her husbands?"

"I met Orlando Vitagliano once. At Harold's funeral, in fact. But I can't tell you anything about him; I wasn't paying attention."

"Of course not."

"But I do know that Maggie split with him a few months later. I think I remember something about him leaving the country, going back to Italy to live."

"So he was an Italian citizen?"

"I guess. Now that I think about it, I recall he spoke with a heavy accent."

"She told me her first husband was named Hugo, didn't mention the last name. Nor did she tell me who the second one was. You know?"

"No, but I'll ask —" Elissa sucks in her breath and I realize from experience that she was about to say she would ask Ruthie.

"Eliss? You okay?"

"Yes."

"It's a natural thing to do."

"I can't get it into my head that she's dead."

"Time. A cliché, but true."

"I guess you'd know."

"Unfortunately, that's so. I'll get somebody to run a check on her. She's been in New York for over twenty years, so my guess is she married here all three times."

"Probably."

"One more thing. How did Ruthie and Harold book that fateful cruise?"

"They always used the same travel agency I use. Shaffer Tours."

I write this down. "Do you remember the date of the cruise they were on when Harold died?"

She gives it to me and I add it to my notes. Then I try to reassure her with the line they say in almost every movie: *everything will be all right.* Which is usually untrue. We make a date for dinner and hang up.

I turn to my computer and click on NWDC. Suddenly, it occurs to me that with Kip gone I can stay up all night wandering the Web if I want. Hurrah! Almost immediately, I plunge back to earth as I contemplate the other side of being alone. Then I sweep that under my mental rug. Perhaps I'm no better than my mother when it comes to denial.

After I log on, launch my E-mail program, Popmail does its thing and I get new mail. One from my friend Mallory in California and one from Alex.

Without taking time to log off, I move the cursor down to her line and hit my ENTER key. The letter opens like a new bloom.

From: athomas@panix.com
To: laurenl@NWDC.com

Subject: Lazy Afternoon
Dear Lauren,

I am so glad you did not think my letter was dumb. I guess I am not sure what the rules are or if there are any. Yes, I know I started this but suddenly I feel <u>typetied.</u> Anyway, thanks for dropping me the note to alleviate my discomfort.

As for the second letter. It is so interesting that your mother is an alcoholic. Mine is too. Well, she is not drinking at the moment but I would not want to bet my life she is not taking pills. Probably her alcoholism accounts for all the marriages. Yes, I am friends with a lot of my sibs. Oddly enough I like most of them.

What a terrible story (I should not call it a story) you have about how you got into being a P.I. When you say your partner, do you mean partner at the FBI, partner in life, or both? Whatever he/she was, I cannot imagine how you survived such a thing. I am really sorry you had to go through that.

Business is very slow here and it feels like a summer day. Too bad it is not, we might go for a drive. Oh, well.

Your guess about my age is correct . . . thirtysomething. :) I was a fashion photographer for a while but it really is not my thing. I find I like being on this end of things better. Just call me a control freak. Or call me Ishmael, if you like.

What is the case you are working on or is it wrong for me to ask? If it is not wrong, I would love to hear about it. Well, not if it is a divorce case . . . I hate divorces. Are you married? Enough babbling from me. Hope to hear from you soon. BTW, do you like Barbara Streisand?
Yours,
Alex

I read it twice. I smile at *typetied* and the spelling of Streisand's first name. Obviously, Alex is a fan but doesn't know the famous spelling of the name of the very famous Barbra. Will I tell her or not? I am perplexed by the marriage question. Is Alex straight or does she mean am I married to another woman? Why did I assume she was a lesbian?

What does she mean, we could go for a drive? *Okay, Lauren, what word don't you understand?* It appears to be an innocent enough suggestion, yet I don't think it is. And *yours*. That seems an intimate way to sign a letter. This is ridiculous. What am I thinking about? I close the letter and sign off NWDC. Then I open the letter again and as I start to reread, the phone rings.

It's my mother.

"Are we ever going to see you again?"

Oh, boy. "And how are you this fine day?" I retort.

"Never mind being smart-alecky. What's going on?"

I'm alarmed by the question but don't know why. "What's that mean?"

"It means, we haven't seen you for a month and you haven't called in two weeks."

"I've been busy."

There's a long silence. "Too busy to pick up a phone?"

I knew she would say that, wish I'd had money on it. "I'm on a case."

"Oh, Lauren, you're always on a case, what's that got to do with anything? I don't know how Kip puts up with you."

I almost tell her that she doesn't but I catch myself before crossing the barbwire boundary between us. There's no need for my mother to know anything about my life other than what I wish her to know. And I don't wish her to know this.

She says, "So when are you coming to visit?"

This is the last thing I want to do. "When the case is over."

"Then there'll be another case. We'll come in. How about Saturday?"

I panic. "NO. No, Saturday isn't good."

"Friday night?"

"No. Look, let me consult Kip and I'll call you. Is Daddy all right?"

"Yes, daddy's girl, Daddy's fine."

I'd like to strangle her. "And you?" I ask grudgingly.

"I'm just ducky. Now don't forget to call."

"I won't."

"Love to Kip."

We hang up. Why couldn't I tell her that Kip is going away

for a few weeks? When I do, it'll seem odd and she'll make a big deal out of it. Is it a big deal? I don't want to answer this question or any questions about Alex, so I power down my computer and turn my attention back to the case.

I phone Cecchi and ask him if his secretary, George, can do a computer check on Vitagliano's various husbands and some names, including her maiden one. He agrees and after I find the address for Shaffer Tours I set off for their offices, hopeful, and reasonably certain, that I won't run into Kathie Lee Gifford.

I get out of the subway at the Forty-ninth Street exit and climb up the stairs to beautiful midtown Manhattan.

With weather this nice, the streets are more crowded than usual. I thread my way through the people to Forty-sixth Street between Seventh and Eighth Avenues, where Shaffer Tours is a tenant in a new green-glass structure.

Inside there is the ubiquitous keeper of the building standing behind a tall thin desk that looks like a lectern. The poor guy wears a blue uniform with gold-fringed epaulets and brass buttons. On top of everything else, it's too big for him. He has a face like a Spanish onion.

"I'm looking for Shaffer Tours," I say.

"Shaffer Tours?"

I nod.

"Shaffer Tours, ya say."

"Right."

"Could you spell that out, young lady?" He flips through a book but doesn't actually look at it.

"You mean, you don't know whether they're in this building or not?"

"I'm filling in. Me buddy is down with the flu, ya see."

This explains the ill-fitting uniform. "And you don't know the building," I state.

"That's the ticket."

The ticket from hell, I suspect. "Could you please look up Shaffer Tours in that book?"

"I kin try, is all."

"Good. Thanks."

"But ya haf to spell it out."

"S-h —"

"Hang on. S, ya say?"

I can't believe this is happening. I tell him yes, S.

"S as in Sam?"

I concur.

He wets a nicotine-stained forefinger and slowly turns each page.

"S, ya say. I found the esses." He looks up at me, the battered blue eyes shining as if from too much booze. "Here . . . here they are, girl. Them esses."

"Wonderful."

"Next letter, please."

"H."

"H as in Harry?"

"Right." Call me crazy, but I have the feeling we're going to go right through the name, letter by letter, the next being something like A is for alibi. Where have I heard that before?

Finally, after the letter-by-letter gambit, he finds and tells me Shaffer Tours is on twenty-four . . . Room 2410, to be precise. And now I must sign the book. This kind of security is becoming de rigueur in office buildings. Terrorists have succeeded in making the average person's life a little more difficult . . . exactly what we need to add to our easy-to-maneuver, happy-go-lucky New York lives.

I sign and go to the elevator bank, where I wait fifty years. And then another fifty years before the captain decides that the thing is full enough and allows the elevator to shut its door and rise.

As this one is an express, it doesn't stop until twelve. I endure the rest of the ride, while it checks in at every floor, until at long last we reach twenty-four, where I disembark.

I wish I didn't believe the personal touch, rather than phone contact, is the way to go in these investigations. But it is what I believe and I'm sure I'm right.

The halls here are carpeted in gray. I wonder what it would

be like to see a paisley sometime. Room 2410 is indeed Shaffer Tours. Naturally, I have to press a buzzer.

"Yes?" A tinny voice over the intercom.

"May I come in?"

"Of course not. What do you think we have this system for?"

"If I can't come in, how can we do business?" I ask logically.

"We can't until you state your name and what you want."

"My name is Lauren Laurano and I'm . . ." I think better of telling the truth. "And I'm eager to book a tour."

"Which one?"

I panic but give the name of the tour the Cohens had taken and hope that five years later Shaffer Tours still has it. They must, because she buzzes me in.

The receptionist, who couldn't be more than seven or eight years old and who enthusiastically chews gum, asks my name again and what I want. I repeat what I've said because I know I'll have to see a salesperson, or whatever they call themselves. She tells me to take a seat and that someone will be right with me.

Yeah, sure.

I won't even say how long it takes. Ms. Recep. tells me that I can be seen now by Mr. Tachus, my tour pathfinder. I knew it. But I'd never have guessed *pathfinder.*

Mr. Tachus rises at my approach and sticks out a meaty hand. He has a beige-colored toupee above shaggy brows and lifeless eyes. The suit he wears is conservative and the tie, dull. I take a seat next to his desk.

"So, Ms. Laurano," he begins, "what path can we chart for you today?"

It takes everything I have not to laugh in his face. "I'm interested in the Caribbean tour."

"Ah, yes, a lovely tour. When were you thinking of going?"

"I wasn't."

He looks at me quizzically.

I give him my card. "I'm investigating a crime that may go back some years."

"Well, what in the world would it have to do with us?"

"A man on this particular tour went overboard in the middle of the Atlantic."

"He killed himself?"

"Very unlikely."

"Surely, this has been solved by now." A fine sweat, like rice kernels, appears on his forehead.

"Declared 'accidental death,' not solved. The body was never recovered."

"So what do you want from me?" he asks defensively.

"I'd like the passenger log of that cruise."

"You've got to be kidding."

"I'm not."

Tachus gives a patronizing little laugh. "Surely, you must know even if I could, I can't."

"Sir?"

"We're not allowed to give out that kind of information."

"In a possible homicide case I think you can."

"Homicide? Like the TV show?"

"Yes, exactly." Why is it when they can relate it to television they understand? Why do I ask? I know why. This is what everything has come down to.

"Even so, I'm not sure we'd still have that information available."

I glance at his computer. "How long has this office been computerized?"

"I don't know. I've only been working here three years and it was this way then."

"Think you can find out?"

He mulls this over as though I've asked him to explain the theory of evolution. "Yes, I guess."

"Good."

He puts both hands on the edge of his desk and shoves. The chair rolls backward across the floor to another desk, where a chic-looking woman is working. They confer and then he shoves off from her desk and returns to his own.

"Six years," he says.

"Terrific. Then you must have the list on there somewhere."

He sighs. "You really have the authority to get this?"

Of course I have no authority but I take a shot at it. "I showed you my card, Mr. Tachus."

"True."

It worked!

"So let's see what we got here."

He begins the computer process by going into a database.

"What do you use?"

"FoxPro."

"Good program."

"Yeah. Can you imagine if I had to do this by hand? Go through a lot of paper records."

"Awful."

We both know, but don't say, that he'd have found a way out of doing it. The search takes about four minutes and he's got the passenger list of Harold's last cruise.

"Now what?"

I smile winningly. "A printout, please."

This takes about thirty seconds. He gives it to me, we shake hands, and I'm out of there. In the hall I quickly scan the list. Oddly there's only one Italian female name. Margaret Narizzano. I'm willing to bet she's aka Maggie Vitagliano.

Eleven

From a phone booth I call Cecchi. He's out but his secretary is in and he can give me the info I need.

George says, "She doesn't have any arrests or priors. Not even a parking ticket. But from a marriage license database I got the full name of the first husband: Hugo Geiger. The second one was Jan Wilde. And her maiden name was Narizzano."

Bingo!

"Want any other information?" George asks.

"Not right now, thanks. When will Cecchi be back?"

"Who can say?"

I could tell George the significance of what he's uncovered, so he can tell Cecchi when he returns, but I prefer to do it myself. "You've been very helpful. Thanks."

"Whatever blows your hair," he says.

"What?"

"Forget it."

I thank him and disconnect.

The revelation that Maggie Vitagliano was booked on the cruise ship that Harold and Ruthie were on, under her maiden name, is stunning. I have no idea what it means or how she could've been on the ship without their seeing her. And why did she use that name? More important, why didn't she tell me about it? Did Vitagliano kill Harold? If so, why?

I hail a cab to go back downtown. I give the cabbie my office address, lean back to think some more about what all this means. If Vitagliano had something to do with Harold's death, she may've had something to do with Ruthie's. And now that I've interviewed her, she might be alarmed and ready to bolt or worse. I feel extremely vulnerable.

I'd forgotten to ask Elissa if she knew why Vitagliano might have a blister on her hand. I take out my cellular phone. I hate having one, despise people who walk along the street talking on them, but have to have one for my work. When I bought mine I vowed never to make a social call from it and I haven't. I punch in Elissa's number. When she answers I ask my question.

"What does that have to do with anything?" she says.

"She doesn't seem like the type of woman to do much physical labor and I thought it might be significant."

"Why didn't you ask her?"

"I didn't want to put her on guard in any way."

"Well, I have no way of knowing what she does. I didn't think she did anything."

"Exactly." Suddenly, it comes to me why I've been so focused on this. I recall that my mother used to get a blister in that same spot every year from digging in her garden. "Garden."

" 'Garden'? What's that mean?"

"Does Vitagliano have a garden?"

"In SoHo?"

"Roof, maybe."

"I don't know. Does she live on the top floor?"

"No."

"That doesn't rule it out but it's less likely."

"You ever hear her talk about a summer place?"

"No."

I thank her and hang up. I don't know why I think this blister thing's important. Gut instinct. And that's usually right. How it might connect is another question.

When I come out of this rumination I realize the cab's not moving. I look out the window and see that we're on Ninth Avenue in some kind of gridlock.

"Why did you take Ninth?" I ask.

"What is it, miss?"

"Ninth Avenue. Why did you take it?"

"Take it, miss?"

Here we go. "We're stuck now."

"Stuck, miss?"

Hopeless. I lean back and try to relax. Who am I kidding? Have I ever relaxed in a traffic jam? Do I relax at all? might be more to the point. We move an inch.

"I think you should try to get over to Broadway," I say.

"Get over, miss?"

"I'll get out here."

He turns and gives me what must be meant by *the evil eye.* "You what, miss?"

I open my purse and put my hand on my gun. He looks crazy. Rasputin comes to mind. "Turn the meter off. I'm getting out here."

"Meter off, miss?"

"Yes. Turn it off. I'm getting out," I say, raising my voice slightly, as though he's deaf instead of impossible.

He flips the flag on the meter, turns, and gives me the stare again. "You are ugly, miss."

"I beg your pardon?" I can't believe I've heard what I think I've heard.

"Ugly. You are ugly."

I *have* heard correctly. Ugly, huh? Let's see how ugly he thinks I am when I don't give him a tip. I hand him the exact amount and open the door. He looks at the money in his hand and screams after me as I disembark.

"You the ugliest woman I ever see. Ugly, ugly, ug—"

I slam the door and, with mild trepidation, turn my back on him to get to the sidewalk. When I glance his way I can see that he's still shouting, fist raised in anger. A bit of an overreaction, I think. The light changes and I cross Ninth and head toward Broadway, where I'll get the subway.

"UG-LY!" comes the shout to the left of me. I don't turn. I know, of course, who it is. All I want is to get back to my office.

And then home to say good-bye to Kip. But I don't want to think about that now.

When I leave my office the weather has changed again and I feel cold. I've been unable to reach Cecchi, even by beeper, but I've left a message on his machine for him to call me. Now it's time to face Kip. Why am I thinking of it this way? What does it mean, *face* Kip?

The walk from my office to home is about five minutes but I manage to stretch it to ten. She's still in session when I arrive, so I go into the kitchen, pop open a Diet Coke, sit at the table, and wait. There's a feeling in the air of impending doom that I suspect has to do with Kip. And then she comes into the kitchen, an expression of dismay and horror on her face.

"What is it?" I ask, alarmed.

"Cecchi," she says. "He's been shot and is on the critical list."

I jump up. "Oh, God. Where is he?"

"St. Vincent's."

I run down the hall, grab my jacket. Kip grabs hers. "I'm coming with you."

Silently, we hurry to the hospital, which is practically around the corner. Inside, the odor of hospital life rushes into my nose like the syrupy smell of sorrow. The last time either of us was in a hospital was to see Tom, and I know without asking that Kip is thinking this too. In the elevator we're silent, as are the other passengers, grim looks on every face.

We get off at four and hurry down the hall, our shoulders banging into each other from time to time, something that might once have been comforting but now is nothing, or maybe annoying.

I see Annette sitting in the waiting room. She's a pretty, petite woman, small-boned and delicate. Recently she's begun to color her gray hair and it looks great.

We hug. "How is he? What happened?"

"He's hanging in there," she says. "I don't have the details but I think it was an inadvertent drug thing. What I mean is, he and O'Hara were on a case about something else and went to interview a person who thought they were there to bust him . . . oh, hell, I don't know, Lauren."

"What about O'Hara?"

Annette's face changes as though a shade has been drawn down over the window of her eyes. "He's dead," she whispers.

I suck in my breath. "No. Oh, my God. O'Hara was only thirty-five or something," I say foolishly, as though if he'd been older, it would be all right for him to be dead. But we all know what I mean.

"What do the doctors say about Cecchi?"

"He's got a chance . . . a good chance."

A *chance.* I can't believe it's down to a chance. "Oh, Annette, I'm so sorry. God. I was trying to reach him and . . ." I trail off because what does any of that matter now? The only thing that's important is that Cecchi live.

The three of us sit down to wait.

It's near midnight when the doctor approaches us. We rise in unison. She goes to Annette and my heart plummets to my knees.

"He's going to make it, Mrs. Cecchi."

Annette bursts into tears. The doctor pats her, in the way that doctors do, and looks to us for help. I take Annette in my arms, then find myself crying too.

Dr. Bates talks while we cry. "He's a lucky man. If he weren't in such good shape, I don't know if he would've made it. It'll be a long, tough recovery but I think eventually he'll walk again."

This stops us midcry.

"You *think* he'll walk? What's that mean?" Annette asks.

"Mrs. Cecchi, his spinal cord was chipped and in these cases it's always iffy."

"You mean there's a real possibility he won't walk?"

"I'm afraid so."

"But his job, his —"

"Even if he does walk, Mrs. Cecchi, I'm afraid his career as an active policeman is over."

I can't believe I'm hearing this.

"But that's all he knows," Annette says.

"He won't meet the qualifications. At least, not to be on the street. He'll be able to handle a desk job, of course. Anyway, the important thing is that he's out of immediate danger. He's asleep, but would you like to go in?"

She nods. We ask her if she wants us to wait but she tells us to go home, we'll talk in the morning.

Even though it's after midnight when we hit the street it's still fairly well populated. *The city never sleeps,* I think. Kip and I don't speak on the short walk home and I realize this isn't because of the circumstances or the hour. The silence between us has been going on for a long time. It used to be that we always had something to say to each other, especially after an event of this proportion. But in the last year, coming home from dinner with friends or a party or almost anything, we didn't talk anymore. I'm not sure I can attribute it all to Tom's death. Something has happened between us, something not good.

When we get to the house we go immediately into the kitchen. All we've had to eat is half a hospital turkey sandwich each. I open the refrigerator and peer inside. Even if a big chocolate cake were staring back at me, I don't think I could eat it. I shut the door.

"I guess I'm not hungry," I say.

Kip puts her hand on my shoulder. "I'm so sorry about Cecchi."

I nod. "He'll never take a desk job."

"No. I don't think he will either."

"What'll he do?"

"Isn't that the least of it now?" she asks.

"Yes, I suppose. But I don't think he should know that he can't be on the street before he regains his power to walk. I have to tell Annette that. I know him: if he thinks he can't be a cop anymore, he might not care about walking."

"Don't you think Annette knows that?"

"Yes, of course. You're right."

We stand there looking at each other, neither of us with a

clue what to say to the other. Finally, Kip says, "I think I'll try to get some sleep."

"I'll be up in a minute," I say.

She gives me a patronizing smile as though she knows, without a doubt, that I won't be. Maybe she does.

"When are you leaving?" I ask.

"I have to make a ten A.M. plane at La Guardia. We should say our good-byes now. In case I'm asleep when you come up."

How do you say good-bye in a situation like this? Funny how helpless you feel when you haven't done something before. "I guess I don't know how to say good-bye," I tell her honestly.

"It's strange, isn't it?"

"Very."

She takes a halting step or two toward me, and I toward her, and then we're holding each other.

"I'm so sorry," she whispers.

"Me too," I say, even though I'm not exactly sure what we're talking about.

"I can't believe this is happening to us," she says.

I don't ask her what she means because I don't want to know. Anyway, I think I *do* know. We're a mess.

"I'll call you," she says. "And I want you to call me. I've left my numbers on your desk. Will you be all right?"

"All right?"

"Well, taking care of yourself?"

"Kip, I've been taking care of both of us for years."

"Yes . . . I guess you have. If you need any money I —"

"I'll be fine."

"I'll pay the mortgage from there," she says.

It's then that I realize she hasn't any intention of paying for anything else, like electric and phone, etc. And why should she? A slap of fear hits me. How *will* I manage? I'll find a way. I'll take on more jobs. Something. Anyway, it's only for a month.

"Maybe when I get back we'll feel differently."

"I hope so," I say, wondering if I really mean it.

"I'm going up now." She kisses me lightly. "Don't stay up too late."

I say nothing.

I watch her as she leaves the kitchen and listen to her footsteps along the hall and up the stairs. The bedroom door opens and shuts. I stand in the middle of the room, alone.

Is this what it'll be like?

No.

Worse.

Twelve

When I awake, Kip is gone. I look over to her side of the bed and realize that this is the way it will be every morning for the next month. Sadness snares me. She's been gone before — conferences and family visits — but that was different. It was never more than four or five days at a time and it gave me a liberated feeling.

I remember the time she was gone when I bought my first modem and became totally crazed and obsessed. I was delighted she wasn't around. And the other times too. When things are good with your lover it's fun to have time to yourself. But things are not good.

I'm tired because I stayed up late running around the Internet and then I got in a conversation through IRC (International Relay Chat) with a guy from Ohio whose mother had named him Lobos because she didn't want her kids to have ordinary names. I'd picked his conference because the topic was mothers. Soon after I got on, it switched to the weather, so he and I went into a private conference and continued. Mostly he told me about his mother and himself and, like so many people in real life, didn't ask much about me. Near the end when I volunteered that I was a P.I. he became fascinated but I was too tired to go on.

Abruptly, I remember Cecchi. Not that I've forgotten but it simply wasn't in my consciousness for these first waking moments. I feel as if I've been hit with a club.

I lean over and dial Annette. I get the machine and leave a message telling her that I'll be at the hospital soon. I don't know if she's home or there or if she'll get the message.

There is mewing outside my door, so I get up, quickly slide into my slippers, throw on my bathrobe, and meet the Ns in the hall.

"Okay, I hear you. What do you want for breakfast?" I ask as we all three go down to the kitchen.

Only Nick replies. I think he says *fish*, so that's the tin I open. Both he and Nora seem happy with the selection. And then she's not, and gives me a look as though I've betrayed her.

I flick on the coffee switch, go back upstairs, and throw on sweatclothes for my walk. When I get back I'll answer Alex's E-mail before I go to the hospital.

I bring Annette a cup of coffee along with a sticky bun, of which she's inordinately fond. She looks like hell. But why wouldn't she? Cecchi is the same as when I'd left the night before. When she finishes the coffee and cake she goes into his room for a while.

I've printed out my response to Alex and brought it with me. I take it from my bag. We are definitely into song titles for our subject entry. And they seem to be from the past. When I was writing this hundreds sprang to mind and they were all suggestive of something more than an innocent correspondence. But then I couldn't help myself and went with it.

From: laurenl@NWDC.com
To: athomas@panix.com
Subject: Just In Time
Dear Ishmael,

I'm sorry you have an alcoholic/pill-addicted mother. It's bad enough having a mother be one of those things, let alone both.

My partner in the FBI was also my lover. That's how we met. We'd been together two years when it happened. No one at the Bureau knew, of course. We were totally closeted. Afterward they did know.

OK, toots, thirtywhat? Thirtysomething just ain't good enough.

So how about you? Are you involved with someone? If so, who? How long and how's it going?

About my case. You may've read about it in the paper. A woman named Ruth Cohen was murdered in her apartment. A relative of hers has hired me. That's really all I can ethically tell you.

You may've also read that a cop was killed and another critically wounded last night. Well, the wounded cop is one of my best friends and I have to go now and see how he's doing.

Best,

Captain Ahab

Now she'll know if she didn't before. Telling her that the relationship was closeted is tantamount to saying I'm a lesbian. Why am I afraid to say this to this woman? What do I care what she thinks? Maybe I shouldn't call her *toots*. And why didn't I say that I'm involved now? What will she make of the subject entry? What did I mean? Just in time for what? A little place inside me knows the answer to all these questions but I'm not willing to look there. What will I say the song reference means if she asks?

The hell with it, it's too late now. That's how I sent it.

Annette comes into the waiting room; I fold up the letter and put it in my pocket, feeling guilty.

"He's awake," she says, smiling.

"That's wonderful."

"Would you like to go in? I know he'd be happy to see you even if he can't talk. He hears me, understands."

"I would."

She leads me to his room but doesn't come in. Cecchi is in an oxygen tent and lots of tubes and stuff are attached to him. I stand where he can see me and I smile.

"Hi there, big guy," I say. I may be imagining it but a tic around his lips looks like a smile.

"Thank God you're going to be all right." It's a white lie. "I sure could use you now but I guess I'm going to have to solve this case without you. Probably won't be able to. Maybe when you're a little better I can use you as a consultant."

HE NODS!

I'm sure of it.

"Don't want to tire you, Cecchi. I'll come back later."

He closes his eyes.

I leave the room. Annette is waiting outside the door.

"Well?"

"You're right. He understands, no doubt about it. I'll be back later. Anything I can do for you?"

"Thanks, Lauren, nothing."

I kiss her on the cheek.

"Sweetheart," she says. "Is everything all right between you and Kip?"

I can't believe she's noticed with everything she's been dealing with. But that's Annette for you.

"Fine," I lie. "She has a lecture gig she's committed to, so she'll be away for a month."

"You can talk to me anytime, you know that, don't you?"

"Yes, I do. Thanks. But everything's fine."

"Good."

I tell her I'll see her later and leave. When I get out on the street I stand there. I don't think I've ever felt quite so alone. I find myself walking down Sixth Avenue at a fast clip and the next thing I know I'm at Waverly Place, inside the coffee shop. I look all around, then spot her as she comes out of the kitchen balancing four plates on her arm. I never thought I'd be happy to lay my peepers on Ruby Packard, but I am. I wait until she's served her customers and then I call her.

She looks at me in her surliest way but comes over.

"What's up? And where's Cecchi?"

"That's why I'm here. He's okay now, but he was shot."

"Oh, no," she says, and slaps a hand over her heart.

"He's okay. He's going to make it," I reassure her. "I thought you'd want to know."

"Yeah. What happened?"

I tell her what I know, which still isn't that much.

"Hey, Ruby?" a customer calls.

"Blow it," she shouts back. "Go on, Laurano."

I'm shocked. I didn't know she knew my name. "I don't know anything else."

"So he's gonna be fine, huh?"

I know I can't tell her the truth. It seems all I'm doing is lying today. "The doctor said he definitely would make it."

"Thank Christ," she says. "He at St. Vinnie's?"

"Yeah. Intensive care right now."

"Think he'd like flowers?"

"From you? You bet."

Something streaks across her face and I guess it's a smile.

"Well," I say, "I thought you'd want to know."

"I would. I do." She nervously pats at her helmet of hair. "You want some coffee, somethin'?"

"No, I have to get to work."

"Yeah, sure."

"See you," I say and turn to go.

"Laurano."

"Yeah?"

"Thanks, kid." She rushes away and I watch as she yells at customers and screams at her boss. I laugh to myself.

Smiler's on Seventh Avenue is gone and it's now called Andy's, so I can go in there again. I'd experienced some homophobic stuff there and boycotted them. I like to think this is why they folded but I know it isn't.

The place is set up similarly to Smiler's, which means like almost any deli. And by the level of the argument that's going on it seems as though nothing has changed but the name of the place and the date.

CUSTOMER: You call that a sangwich?

CLERK: No, I call it a sandwich.

CUSTOMER: That's what I said, dumbbell, a sangwich.

CLERK: Yeah, I know. You said a *sangwich*, I said a *sand-wich*.

CUSTOMER: What're you, some type comedian or what?

CLERK: You want the turkey sandwich or not?

CUSTOMER: Why you think I asked you, "You call it a sangwich," in the first place?

CLERK: Beats me, mister. So you want it?

CUSTOMER: That all the turkey yer gonna put on that sangwich?

CLERK: It's a done deal.

CUSTOMER: Then I ask again, "You call that a sangwich?"

CLERK (puts the sandwich to the side): Next.

CUSTOMER: What, next? I want my sangwich.

OTHER CUSTOMERS: Grumble, grumble, grumble.

CLERK: Oh, now you want it?

CUSTOMER: I always wanted it, what the fuck's wrong with you?

CLERK: Look, pops . . .

CUSTOMER: Don' call me *pops*.

CLERK: Okay, dude. Now . . .

CUSTOMER: No *dude* neither.

CLERK: Sir, get the hell outta this store.

CUSTOMER: What? What you say? You throwin' me out? For what? 'Cause I want a decent sangwich?

CLERK: 'Cause I don't like your pukey face. Get out. Next customer.

CUSTOMER (turns to all of us on line): You hear that? You hear what he calls me? *Pukey face*. And he don' wanna give me my sangwich. What kind place is this?

EVERYONE: A deli.

CUSTOMER: Bunch of bums. All I wan' is a decent turkey sangwich.

EVERYONE: *Sand*wich.

Now the poor guy looks frightened, as though the rest of us might attack him, and he makes a hasty jog to the door and out.

I feel sorry for him, but I'm glad it's over and nothing violent happened. I hate it when I have to take out my gun and wave it around. Yes, I do.

Next to my booted-up notebook are my coffee and a chocolate doughnut, one bite gone. I stare at my notes about this case. So what do I know so far?

1. Ruthie was murdered in a manner that looked like work of the Granny Killer.

2. Elissa is the main beneficiary.
3. Harold, Ruthie's husband, died mysteriously at sea five years ago (body never found).
4. On the cruise during which Harold disappeared Maggie Vitagliano was a passenger booked under her maiden name, Narizzano. Why?
5. Vitagliano didn't mention this to me. On the surface I can't see what Vitagliano could possibly gain from either Harold's or Ruthie's death. But that's on the surface. I know I'm missing something here.
6. I still have to interview Stein and Weiss.

My phone rings. I answer. It's Deanna.
"Lauren, come over quick. Hurry, please."
"What is it?"
"Someone just tried to kill Elissa."

Thirteen

Eyes closed, Elissa lies on the Aubusson rug in their living room.

"Oh, God!" I shout.

"No, she's all right," Deanna says.

"My back," Elissa groans, and opens her brown eyes. "It's the stress."

"What happened?"

They both begin to speak at once. "Wait, wait," I say, feeling like Judge Ito.

"Elissa, you tell," says Deanna. "It's your life they tried to take."

"Who's *they?*" I ask.

"Well, him/her/it, I don't know," Deanna offers.

"So it was only one person?"

"One," says Elissa weakly.

"Tell."

"I was coming into the building and the lights were out. This made me suspicious but it happens from time to time, not often because Paul Keiler takes care of all that for us in this co-op."

"He's such a nice man, Lauren. Thanks for getting him for us."

"Deanna," Elissa objects.

"Sorry."

"So anyway, the lights are out. I go to the elevator, push the button, and bang."

"Bang, what?"

"Bang, a gunshot."

"What do you mean?" I'm horrified.

"A bullet. It misses me by a hair. . . I'm telling you, a hair."

"And then?" I prompt.

"The elevator door opens, I jump in, push CLOSE, another bang. God knows where it went. The door closes, I come upstairs. Here I am. Here I lie."

Deanna says, "I wish you could've seen her when she came in. White. A ghost. I've never seen her look like that."

"And you thought I was crazy," Elissa accuses. "She tells me to calm down. This is a therapist. I should calm down."

"I thought it was you being anxious."

"It *was* me being anxious. But I had a damn good reason."

"That's what I mean. I didn't know you had a reason."

"Even so, it doesn't help anything to be told to calm down."

"Elissa," I say, "did you see anybody?"

"See? How could I see? Pitch. That's what it was until the elevator opened. Pitch-black."

"So when it opened it shed some light. You didn't see anything then?"

"Are you crazy, Lauren? You think I was looking around? I wanted to get out of there and that's it."

"So how do you know it was only one person?"

"A feeling."

"*A feeling?*"

"That's right. A feeling. Take it or leave it."

I take it because Elissa has some interesting and extraordinary powers, like clairvoyance. Give her a package and she can tell you what's inside. Sometimes it seems there's no connection, like the time I gave her a present and she said she smelled fish. It was a book: Pete Dexter's *Paris Trout*. I've tried to get her to go to Atlantic City with me but she won't use her powers that way. In fact, she almost never uses them, because she says they make her ill. I trust her feelings, so I accept that there was one person.

I say, "When I came in now the lights were on downstairs."

"I called Paul," Deanna says. "He took a look, called me back, and said someone had unscrewed the bulbs."

"Did you call the police?" I ask.

"The police? No, why?"

"Elissa, someone took a shot at you . . . when people get shot at they usually call the police."

"But they think I killed my aunt. I don't want to talk to them."

"It doesn't matter what they think. Anyway, the fact that you were shot at might change their minds."

"Will they believe me?" she asks.

"I didn't check, but there're probably bullet holes, maybe some spent shells."

"You have a point."

"Thanks. So why do you think anyone would try to kill you?"

"I have no idea."

"Elissa, besides Deanna, who benefits if you die?" I ask.

"Don't."

"Don't what?"

"Don't say *die*. You know how I hate that word. Or any aspect of it. Die, dead, death. Phooey."

"Who benefits?"

"I haven't made a will yet."

"You haven't made a will? But you're a millionaire."

"Not yet, I'm not. Probate and stuff. Oh, God, I have to get up." She rolls over and gets on her hands and knees, then slowly straightens and grasps the edge of the couch as she pulls herself to a standing position. "I feel like a truck ran over me."

"Sit," Deanna says.

"I can't. I need to walk. You know that's the only thing that helps my back. Ohmigod."

"What?" Deanna and I chorus.

"How can I walk?"

"What do you mean?"

"I can never leave this house again."

This is a distinct possibility until the killer is caught. "Actually, I wish you wouldn't for a bit."

"Housebound," Elissa says, glumly.

"Only for the time being. So, you've seen Ruthie's will now. Did she leave anything to your brother, or does he inherit if you die?"

"She left him five thou and he doesn't get anything else — no matter who lives, who dies."

"Is there anybody in it besides you? Aside from small bequests like the jewelry to Maggie Vitagliano."

"Well, yes. You see, it was really Harold who set things up."

My detective's heart does the reggae. "Meaning?"

"He had a cousin he wasn't particularly close to, but he said if anything happened to me before Ruthie died, he'd like to see his money go to him. He was family, after all."

"And Ruthie put that in her will?"

"Yes. But it didn't happen. I mean, I didn't die before Ruthie." She stops walking back and forth, stares at me as it dawns. "Ohmigod. If I died now, before I have a chance to make my own will, before I inherit, this cousin would get it, wouldn't he?"

"Yes. What's his name?"

"Martin Goldstein."

"You know him?"

"No. Never met him. I didn't even know he existed until Ruthie mentioned him to me. In fact, she'd never met him."

"You mean *before* Harold died," I say with certainty.

"No. Never."

"How come?"

"Harold told her to stay away from Goldstein."

"Wait a minute. He wants to leave all his money to this guy if you and Ruthie die but he doesn't want his wife to meet him? That doesn't make much sense."

"Go know," Elissa says.

"And Ruthie didn't question this?"

"Ruthie never questioned anything Harold did or said."

"Did Harold say *why* she should stay away from him?"

"Said he wasn't a very nice person but he was family. Crazy, but that was Harold."

"It was? I never particularly thought of him like that. I mean, he seemed like a very steady guy, very upright, downright."

"Yeah, that's true. Still, he had his quirks, like anybody."

"Where can I find this Goldstein character?" I ask.

"Haven't the vaguest."

"You're kidding."

"On my life. I have no idea where the man is. Maybe Ruthie's lawyer knows."

"Give me Rosenwald's address."

Wall Street is a strange place. There is actually a street named Wall, but one thinks of it more as an area. The streets are narrow here, twisting and turning, and it's sometimes difficult to find an address if you don't know where you're going. Since this is another place I walk in the mornings when I'm feeling like a long walk, I know it fairly well.

Rosenwald's office is on Ann Street in an old but classy building, gargoyles glaring from corners of the upper floors.

There's no security guard or doorman in the small lobby and only one elevator. On the wall is a directory and I easily find Rosenwald's name. I push the button for the elevator and listen as it creaks its way down from the seventh floor. It's impossible to measure how many years it takes to reach me.

When it opens I'm surprised to see that it's automatic, no attendant. I hit the button for five. And it sits. And sits. I push again, then hit CLOSE. Nothing. Obviously, this conveyance is on its own schedule and I must exercise patience, of which I have so much.

When I step off the elevator on five I turn right. It's the second door. Rosenwald's office holds no surprises. The walls are dark wood with velvet draperies over the windows. Brown leather chairs grace the waiting room and the secretary sits behind a mahogany desk.

"No, I don't have an appointment," I say to her before she can ask.

"The very fact that you're saying that makes me know that you know that you have to have one, so you might as well make one for another time."

Janice Blau, as her nameplate reads, is a woman in her late fifties, with hair the color of canned peaches, has carefully applied makeup, and wears a conservative green wool dress.

I take out my P.I. license and show it to her.

"You think that's going to get you in, you got another thing coming, Phillipa Marlow."

Phillipa Marlow? What planet's this one from? "Look, I have to see Mr. Rosenwald about the Cohen will. It's a murder case."

"Who cares? He's a busy man. All lawyers are busy or didn't you know that?"

I eye the door with Rosenwald's name on it.

"I see where you're looking. I know what you're thinking of doing and all I have to say is, don't try it. I run the New York Marathon."

This is one tough cookie. I weigh my chances of beating Ms. Marathon to the door. She's already closer but she's sitting down, while I have the advantage of standing. What can I lose? In a burst of speed I go.

She's up, she's running, she's there before me, her body plastered against his door, arms and legs spread-eagle like she's protecting the Holy Grail.

"Ha!" she barks.

Now what?

"Back," she orders.

"You win," I say dejectedly, turn around, and start to walk away. When I hear her step I make my move and this time I'm successful. I feel her grab my leg, slide down it, and clasp my ankle as I drag her into the office with me.

"What the hell?" says a young man behind a huge desk.

"I'm sorry, I'm sorry," she yells from the Oriental rug where she lies, my ankle still in her grip. "Oh, Mr. Rosenwald, I tried everything."

He rises and looks over his desk. "What are you doing, Janice?"

"She doesn't have an appointment."

"Let go and get up," he commands civilly.

"But . . . she's an intruder."

"Janice. Please."

She releases my leg. It seems like everybody is lying on the floor today.

Janice rises, grunting. "Should I call security, Mr. Rosenwald?"

He holds up a hand to silence her, asks me who I am. I answer and explain why I'm there.

"It's all right, Janice. I'll take care of this."

"You will?" She's clearly bewildered and maybe a tad annoyed.

"You can go," he says.

Now I feel sorry for Ms. Blau. The woman was willing to lay down her life for this putz and he dismisses her.

"I think you should commend her, Mr. Rosenwald."

"Excuse me?"

"Well, don't you think she's gone beyond the call of duty for you?"

"Say, do you want to see me or not?"

"Sorry. She's your secretary." But I still feel I'm right.

Ms. Blau leaves, her head hanging, spirit squashed. I already don't like Mr. Robert Rosenwald, Esquire. I see at once that he's a type. Maybe thirty, he wears a narrow-pinstripe suit, rep tie, white shirt with French cuffs, gold links. His chestnut hair is combed back, no part, and he has the lean, bored face of a whippet.

"Sit down." He motions to a maroon leather chair on the other side of his desk.

"Mr. Rosenwald, as I said, I'm here about the Cohen will."

"What about it?"

"I understand that should Ms. Rosner die before she's able to inherit, or make her own will, everything will go to a Martin Goldstein."

"Yes, that's correct."

"Do you know Mr. Goldstein?"

"I haven't had the pleasure."

"But you have an address for him."

"Actually, I don't."

"Then how would he get the money?"

"When Mr. Cohen originally made the will he said that Mr.

Goldstein would be in touch with me should it come to that, but he doubted very much that it would."

"Meaning he assumed his wife would die before Elissa."

"Right."

"Then why did he bother to . . ."

"Miss Luanno, I —"

"Laurano."

"People do a lot of strange things with wills. Surely you've heard about cats inheriting and things like that?"

"This is a little different."

"I'm not sure how."

"According to Elissa, Harold didn't even want his wife to *meet* Mr. Goldstein, because he said he wasn't a very nice man. I guess I can't understand why he'd leave him a fortune of that size . . . or anything, for that matter."

"Family. Don't you have special feelings about family, no matter who they are, what they're like?"

I think. It would be like my leaving my money to my cousin's wife whom I despise.

"No. I mean I have feelings, but I wouldn't leave money to someone I didn't like."

"So be it. That's you. This will is not unusual. Trust me."

I never trust people who ask me to trust them.

"So, let me get this right. Should Ms. Rosner die before the will is probated, Mr. Goldstein is the benefactor?"

"That's right, Miss Leraner."

"Laurano. And you'd be expected to wait until he came forward?"

"Exactly."

"What if he never showed up?"

"That wouldn't happen."

"Why not?"

"Mr. Cohen said he'd let Goldstein know the terms of his will."

"In other words, Cohen told Goldstein to come to you if the almost impossible terms of his will were satisfied."

"That's right, Miss Lanno."

"Laurano. Was this Harold Cohen's first will?"

"Actually, no." He fusses with the knot of his tie. "This was his second. The first he'd made with my late father."

"And when exactly did he make this second will?"

He gives me the hint of a satisfied, smug smile. "Don't have to look that one up. It was odd because he changed his will only two weeks before he died."

Very odd. "How did it differ from the first one?"

"There was no mention of Mr. Goldstein in that one." Rosenwald rises from his chair. "Is there anything else? I'm actually quite busy."

I glance at his desk, which is totally absent of anything that resembles work.

"I have a meeting in about twenty seconds," he says, consulting his wristwatch.

"One more thing. Have you heard from Mr. Goldstein?"

"No. Why would I?"

"What if I told you that someone tried to kill Ms. Rosner?"

His eyebrows twitch. "Is that true?"

"Yes."

"And you think it was Goldstein?"

"A likely candidate, considering, don't you think?"

"I have no way of judging that." He glances at his watch again.

I give him my card. "Should you hear from Mr. Goldstein, would you give me a call?"

I observe that he mentally runs through his ethics folder. "Yes, I suppose I could do that."

I get up, lean across the desk, and offer my hand. "Thank you very much for seeing me."

He's clearly surprised at my agreeableness and takes my hand. "You're welcome."

Back in the waiting room I pass a very angry-looking Janice Blau.

"Ms. Blau, out of curiosity, what place did you finish in the last marathon?"

"Never mind," she says. "You beat me this time but next time watch out. I'm going to hone my skills so nothing like that ever happens again."

"I think you were great even if he doesn't," I say, cocking my head toward Rosenwald's door.

She brightens. "You do?"

"The best. You ever need another job, call me."

She gives me the once-over and says, "Get real, Phillipa. You couldn't afford my coffee break."

What can I say? I have the look.

I have to find Goldstein. I'm positive he's the key. But how? I've already looked up the name in the phone book and there are so many M. Goldsteins it makes me feel sick. And this is in Manhattan. Goldstein might live in one of the other boroughs and maybe doesn't even live in New York City or New York State. For all I know, he could live in New Hampshire or Idaho. Why don't I believe this? Maybe I can get Elissa to do her thing . . . no, that's not the way to go, even if she could or would. Elissa is too freaked out as it is.

My best bet is to go back to see Vitagliano and find out what she was doing, under her maiden name, on the same cruise ship as the Cohens five years ago.

I decide, since it's such a nice day, to walk to SoHo. Soon I find myself about to pass J & R Computer. I smile, thinking about buying my first modem a number of years ago and how stupid and innocent I was. It's then that I get a terrific idea and I do something I've never done before. I pass the store without going in.

At the corner I race down the subway stairs.

The Internet! Why hadn't I thought of it before? I boot up my notebook and take the steps I need to get into Windows and then into NWDC, where I go into the newsgroups and write down the various places I think might be able to help. I end up with forty-seven different Usenet newsgroups. Now I compose my letter.

From: laurenl@NWDC.com
To: All

   I'm looking for a man named Martin Goldstein. He could be anywhere in this country or another. He is related to a man named

Harold Cohen, deceased. The reason I'm trying to find him is
that he's the beneficiary of a large inheritance. If you know where
he can be located, please leave me mail here. There will be a
small reward for the person who comes up with the right Martin
Goldstein.

Now comes the boring part. I have to post it to all forty-seven
newsgroups. I use a forwarding device but I still have to type
in the name of each group.

There's always the possibility that this letter will get me no
information. And I already know it will bring floods of misin-
formation. What if it brings Mr. Goldstein himself? And what
if Mr. Goldstein doesn't like my messing around in his life?

It's a bit risky, I suppose, but on the other hand, I'm in a
risky business. Born to take chances! Maybe I should have that
tattooed across my . . . I've lost my mind. Is this what happens
when you live alone?

I connect to NWDC, then bring up my news reader. After I
connect to the server, I post to all the newsgroups. When this
is accomplished I go off-line, then exit from NWDC.

On my regular phone I punch in Vitagliano's number. I get
a machine and leave a message asking her to call me when she
comes in.

There's nothing to do now but wait.

Vitagliano hasn't called me back by the time I meet William for
dinner at 9 Jones Street, which is both the name and the address
of the restaurant. The bar is near the front and there are two
stairs up to the rectangular-shaped simple and elegant dining
room. The food here is excellent.

"One finds it hard getting used to being alone," William says
when we're seated. "I automatically made reservations for four.
Called back and made it for three and then I realized it was just
us. There's nothing wrong between you and Kip, is there?"

"The truth? I'm not sure."

"That's what I thought. What's going on?"

"We haven't been getting along. At least that's what she says."

"What do you say?"

"That's one of her complaints . . . that I don't say anything anymore."

"Is it true?"

I shrug.

"You're not seeing someone else, are you?"

Inexplicably, I feel a stab of guilt. "No. Why do you ask?"

Now he shrugs. "I guess because of Rick."

"Have you heard from him?"

"No, and I don't want to. I'm glad he's gone. I think it's what I wanted but I didn't know it until it was over."

"You've come to that fairly quickly."

"One is a very quick man."

"True. Are *you* seeing anyone?"

"I'm not that quick. I think I'll enjoy my freedom for a while."

"You'll be careful, won't you?"

"Of course."

He knows that I am referring to safe sex.

"Life is so different than it was when Rick and I got together. I mean, we were all just learning about AIDS. Now, I don't know. I don't think it's much fun out there anymore. Unfortunately, from what I hear, the young men are acting as if nothing can touch them, but we old geezers know better."

William is not a geezer of any description.

The waiter approaches.

"May I tell you about the specials?"

"Please," says William.

"To start we have mdkieid,'sa'd"ffktkykyk;s;s skslkls; jjjjugtt kklll kkkkffgg. slslsldllrremfjuymdl. The soup is kldldolmedf-jhdudejj sdmskk ssisism sksiks skskkekejhfh kslsll. For the entree sksks dkdkdk sklslsl sksk skskiiekeri kdkldl kskemdpo,-dd,dkldkjuemnel xmsjduem. Any questions?"

William and I look at each other. Then he says, "What was that item in the middle?"

"Middle?"

"Never mind, I think I remember."

The waiter gives a slight bow of his head and retreats.

"Do you have any idea what he said?" I ask.

"None. What's the point? one wonders. Is there a special waitpersons' speech school? I mean, are they sent to school to speak like that?"

"I think they are. Just as the cabdrivers are sent to school to learn how *not* to be able to find anything."

"Precisely," he says.

"Are you lonely?" I ask.

"No, are you?"

"I think I might be."

"When do you think you'll know?" he asks.

"What I mean is, I haven't really had time yet to feel lonely but I imagine I will. And then there's Cecchi. I miss him too." I wonder if I should tell William about Cecchi's prognosis.

"I guess he'll be out of commission for quite some time."

I decide to tell.

"How do you think he'll take it?" William asks.

"Not well."

"So, what will he do?"

"I don't think he'll stay on the Job."

"Maybe you should be partners."

I'm startled and begin to protest but William puts up a hand to stop me.

"Don't be negative, Lauren. He might like it. You never know."

"You're right."

"Of course I am." He smiles. "But perhaps *you* wouldn't like it?"

"I don't know." And I don't. I'm so used to working alone. Still, I often work with Cecchi as though we're partners. Maybe it'd be a terrific thing to do. But what if he wanted to be the boss? I express this concern to William.

"I certainly don't know him very well but I don't get the feeling he's that sort of man. Is he?"

"Aren't all men that sort of man?"

"Bossy?"

"I don't mean to be a chauvinist but —"

"But you will be anyway."

"Am I?"

"Of course you are. What if I said, 'Aren't all women that sort of woman?' "

"I see what you mean."

"I had complete confidence that you would. Now, is Cecchi that type?"

"I don't know. I don't think so."

"Well, you'll see. When he's better you can propose the idea to him. Let's order."

We pick up our menus.

I try to see it in my mind: CECCHI & LAURANO. Hate it. LAURANO & CECCHI. He'd hate it. Maybe LC INVESTIGATIONS. Or CL INVESTIGATIONS. Hate. Well, if we can't work out that one, then the writing's on the wall.

"Why do I even look? One always has the same thing here, doesn't one?" William says.

"Speak for yourself."

"I thought I was."

Fourteen

On my morning walk through SoHo I stop at Vitagliano's place, ring the bell, and after ten years, give up. She could be asleep but I feel she's not there. Her absence proves nothing. But it could. Perhaps she's left the country. She might have realized that I'd uncover her passage on Harold's fatal cruise. I still can't picture her throwing him overboard, yet I know there has to be a connection.

On Prince Street between Wooster and Greene I stop to stare at a sculpture placed outside a shop. I assume it's bronze: a woman, perhaps twenty feet tall, with eight sets of breasts. Why? What could it mean? I don't know whether the artist is a man or a woman but I know the sex of the creator is important to the meaning of the piece. Actually, the main thing about it, to my view, is that it's ugly. Of course I don't think breasts are ugly, but *eight* sets are too much for me.

I think of Kip's breasts, then immediately find myself wondering about Alex Thomas's. I'm shocked. Why would my thoughts go in that direction? I turn off my mind, leave the sculpture behind, and pick up my pace as though I can out-walk my imagery. If I keep on this way, I'm headed for BIG TROUBLE.

Back at my office, the amount of E-mail I get is staggering. Obviously, my query has elicited answers, bogus or not. I wade through them. Some are clearly nuts, sending me diatribes, better known as flames in Internet-ese, so I don't need to read more than the beginning, but there are many who claim to know Martin Goldstein.

I make a list.

The New York ones are the most important to me. Some have only phone numbers, others only addresses, some have both.

In the end I have Goldsteins in all five boroughs and I know this batch is just the beginning, that there'll be more mail in the days to come.

I begin with the Manhattan phone numbers, knowing what a horrendous and tiring task this will be. I wish I had a brownie from Once Upon A Tart.

I've been calling Martin Goldsteins for hours and when I look out my office window I see that it's beginning to turn dark. Of those whom I've made contact with, none is the right one. And Vitagliano still isn't home. I feel discouraged, disheartened. I have no one to bounce ideas off, not Cecchi, not Kip.

So this is lonely. This is being alone. I hate it. I phone Jenny and Jill.

Jenny answers.

"What're you doing tonight?" I ask.

"Nothing. You want to come over?"

"Yes."

"You want to eat with us?"

"Yes."

"Good. Come over anytime. We're here and we can decide whether to cook or order in when you get here. If I cook, it'll only be pasta, okay?"

"Fine. Anything's fine with me."

"You're lonely, huh?"

I hate admitting this. "Sort of."

"Yeah. Well, come over."

"Thanks."

I check my E-mail again. There's lots. Most of it is Goldstein material but I don't want to deal with that now. There's also a letter from Alex. This I want to read.

From: athomas@panix.com
To: laurenl@NWDC.com
Subject: Girlfriends
Dear Captain Ahab,

   You're funny. I like that.

   I think I will respond backwards, but first I have to talk about how E-mail correspondence is so different than I imagined. I imagined it to be very similar to the post. Not at all! This is so much more like a conversation. If I mail something, I rarely wait for a reply. If someone writes me back, it is great but I never really think, "Gee, when am I getting my next letter?" But I am checking for E-mail all the time.

   Yes, you are right, I did read about that case. I hope it is going well for you. I guess that would mean that you are getting closer to solving it. I also read about the cop. Of course, I had no way of knowing he is your friend. I am so sorry. I hope he will be all right.

   Okay, okay, I am 32. So what? Do you think I do not know anything about life because I am under 40?

   Yes, I am with someone. Her name is Sally Edwards and she is 41. We have been together for three yrs. How it is going is a good question. There are a lot of things wrong with our relationship but my track record has not been good and I made a commitment to work things out, stay instead of run, for once. I may find out that I should not stay. Time will tell.

   I am so sorry that you had to go through such a horrible experience with your former lover. I do not know how you ever get over something like that. Are you in a relationship now? If so, for how long and what does she do, etc.? Sally is a photographer.

   I really like writing to you. I find it fun and stimulating. Hope you do too.

Yours,

Toots

   I smile at the way she's signed the letter. So she's a lesbian. And she's with an older woman. So what? I don't answer her now. I have to think about this some more. I close up shop to go to the Js'.

On the way to the Js' I make a quick stop at the hospital to see Cecchi. It couldn't be a more crowded time to visit. The hall in front of the bank of elevators is packed, people shoulder to shoulder.

A woman next to me says to her companion, "I came out today without my umbrella. How's that for living on the edge?"

They shriek with laughter of the kind that's laced with nerves; they're probably here to see someone dying. Finally, two elevators land at once, doors yawn open. Everyone rushes to one or the other, jam in, but most of us are left behind. Eventually, I get on one that stops at every floor. What else?

Annette is not at Cecchi's side when I get to his room. But two men stand at the end of his bed. I know at once they're cops, even though I don't know them. They have that worn and jaded look.

"Hi," one says.

I say hello and they introduce themselves: Detectives Donadello and Barber.

Donadello has dark, defeated eyes set against a crowd of black curls and a copious beard. "Heard Cecchi speak of ya."

I nod as though to say Cecchi has spoken of him, but he hasn't.

Barber is shorter, stockier, with a face that almost matches his red hair. He sticks out a square, blunt hand. "Yeah, heard," he says economically.

It inexplicably pleases me that Cecchi talks about me to these men. I wonder what he's said and want to ask, but of course I can't.

I go closer to the bed. Cecchi is out of it. I want to kiss his forehead but don't. He might not like this kind of display in front of his colleagues.

"Cecchi's gonna make it, right?" Donadello asks.

"Oh, sure," I say. Obviously, they don't know the prognosis and it's not my place to tell them.

"I'm sorry about O'Hara," I say, assuming he also was their friend.

They each nod and shuffle their feet in different ways, unable to put words to their feelings.

"Funeral's tomorrow," Donadello says.

Is he telling me this because he thinks I want to, or should, go? Or is it the only thing he can think of to say?

Barber says, "Left a wife and four kids."

"Terrible," I commiserate. And it is.

"Goddamn nigger," Barber adds, and Donadello slams his arm hard with his elbow.

"What?" Barber responds to the poke.

To me, Donadello says, "He don't mean that, he's just upset."

"I understand." I do, but I know the *N* word hasn't been spoken only from a core of sorrow. I know that word is part of Barber's vocabulary, as it is of so many others'. We've become an extremely racist city because so many crimes are committed by blacks, albeit against other blacks. But what we won't face or accept is that we're the ones who've created this mess.

"He don't know 'bout O'Hara?" Barber asks to get the focus off himself.

"No. Not as far as I know. Have you seen Annette?"

"She was just leavin' when we come in. That's good people, Annette."

I agree. We're all uncomfortable, so I tell them I have to go. I shake their hands and we mumble something unintelligible as I find myself backing out the door.

The Js have one of the coziest and most comfortable apartments of all my friends'. As well as building their store, Jenny constructed this too. She's incredible; there's practically nothing she can't create from old or new materials. And both of the Js have style and taste.

And then there's Theo. She's a Welsh terrier. A terrier to the marrow, meaning she's sometimes hard to control even though she's been to school and trained by the best. I have to admit she's come a long way and now responds to commands. She's adorable and I love her as if she were my own. And Thee (rhymes with *bee*), as we call her, seems to have a thing for me! Maybe it's because I gave her a locket for her last birthday.

We sit in the back room, which is part bedroom, part sitting room.

Jenny says, "So what's going on with you and Kip? And don't say 'nothing.' "

"Something," I say instead.

"Well, what?"

I pick at my burrito, which we've ordered from Taqueria de Mexico. "The truth is, I'm not sure."

"What's that mean?"

"Jenny, it means she doesn't know."

"So why did Kip leave?" She grabs a grilled onion, pops it into her mouth.

"She didn't leave," I say emphatically.

"She didn't? What do you call it then?"

"She's a visiting lecturer for one month. Big deal." I consider telling them about Alex but what's to tell?

Jenny says, "So what does it mean when you say you're not sure?"

"You know what you are, Jen . . . you're relentless."

"Yeah, unlike you when you want to know something."

"Obviously, we're not getting along, okay?"

"Obviously. What else?"

"There's nothing else. What more do we need?"

Jill says, "Kip's changed since Tom died."

I want to kiss her. I'm so relieved that someone else sees it. "What exactly do you mean?" I ask.

"Shut down or something."

"Yes, right. It's very hard to be with her, because she's really not there."

"So what do you expect?" Jenny asks. "I don't know what I'd do if my brother died."

I say, "It's not that I *expect* anything; it's just hard to live with."

"So what's going to happen?" Jenny says.

" 'Happen'?"

"Yeah, what d'you think will happen? Will she come out of it, or what?"

"You ask impossible questions. How do I know if she'll come out of it? I mean, eventually she will. She has to. Doesn't she?"

The Js look at each other, trading a glance I can't decipher.

"What?"

No one says anything.

"What?" I ask again. "What does that look mean?"

Jenny says, "It means, what's going to happen?"

I could strangle her. "That's not what it means. Do you know something I don't?"

"Like what?"

"Like, is she having an affair or something?"

Jill says, "Nooo. Are you crazy?"

"And do you think we'd tell you if she were?"

"That's the part I don't like," I say. I actually don't believe Kip's having an affair and don't know why I said it. Yes, I do. My mind flashes on Alex. Uh-oh.

"Are *you?*" Jenny asks out of nowhere.

A snake of guilt creeps along my bones. "No. With whom?"

"With anyone."

"Don't be ridiculous."

"Why do you look like that?"

"Like what?"

"Guilty," Jenny states.

"You're crazy. Let's have dessert," I say, trying to change the subject. I succeed, but not without the two of them giving each other an arcane glance. This is not good.

When we each have our flan Jenny asks, "What's with the case?"

As I explain, I feel on much more comfortable ground. But the conversation has given me a lot to think about.

Fifteen

The Ns are sitting at the door waiting for me when I return from the Js'. There's an immediate wail for food and love, both of which I supply. My answering machine shows that I have two calls. It whirs like a robin redbreast on speed as I rewind. Long.

"Hi," Kip says. "I'm in my room, which is comfy and cozy and even has a fireplace. Guess you're out on the town. I spoke to Annette, so I have the update on Cecchi. My number here is five-one-seven, five-five-five, nine-five-three-oh. Give my love to Nick and Nora. Talk to you soon."

Great. Love to the Ns but not to me. The beep sounds and the next caller comes on.

"Hel-lo, Lauren. Remember me? I remember you and —"

I snap off the machine.

My heart does a dirge and my hand trembles. This is a voice I thought I'd never hear again, but one I'd never forget. Feeling faint, I pull out a chair, sit down. There's no doubt in my mind that I've heard the voice of Charlie West, one of the two men who raped and beat me when I was eighteen. They were released after serving nine years and that was over sixteen years ago. I've never felt completely safe from them, and although I don't think of them every day of my life, I've had periods when I found myself looking over my shoulder. During those moments I've called myself paranoid, kept my own counsel.

And now, all these years later, here's Charlie West on my machine. I know I must listen to the rest of it but everything in me wants to wipe out the tape without ever hearing his voice again. I wonder how he got this number. I'm only listed at my office. Well, West is a criminal and they have their ways, as I do. We are the opposite sides of the coin.

Slowly, hand still shaking, I reach out and turn the machine back on. I have to hit the cue button to get to West's message. I come in on "— remember you and have been thinkin' about ya all these goddamn years, ya bitch. You were a nice piece a chicken, Lauren. 'Member how good it was? 'Member how I fucked yer brains out? Yeah, ya remember, ya little piece of shit. Now I'm gonna finish the job I started. See ya in the comics, bitch."

A click signals his hanging up. A beep and then a day-old message from Susan inviting us to dinner with her and Stan. I tell myself to return the call, then realize I'm focusing on this to block out West's voice, message, threat. I stop the tape and let it run back and reset itself.

Unable to move, I stay seated as Nick and Nora twirl around my legs like walking mops. Suddenly, I'm in motion as I run from window to door to window, checking locks. Upstairs I do the same thing. When I come down, a little out of breath, I race back to the machine to remove the tape. I replace it with another I get from the table drawer, pocket the tape with West's message.

In the kitchen I open the refrigerator and stare, then realize I'm not hungry and ate only hours ago. I close the door. The fact is, I'm not sure what to do. It's ten-thirty. I don't want to wake up Kip, nor do I want to frighten her. And what could she do from there anyway? Normally, I'd call Cecchi.

I could call the local precinct but it seems . . . well, maybe. I punch in the number.

"Sixth Precinct, Sergeant Murray."

"Is Detective Donadello there?"

"No. Can I help you?"

I'm reluctant but I ask anyway. "Detective Barber?"

"No. Who is this, please?"

I hang up.

I'm behaving like a criminal instead of a victim. Should I go back to the Js'? I don't want to go out again and I can't ask them to put themselves in jeopardy by coming here. I flip through my mental Rolodex. William, of course. I get his machine but don't leave a message. Susan and Stan. But I change my mind as I punch in the last digit of their number and hang up. What's the point? Are they going to stay with me until Kip returns? Am I going to stay under self-imposed house arrest or am I going to go about my life as usual? I give up on calling a friend.

Then I think of Jeff Crawford. He was the agent who originally contacted and recruited me. I don't even know if he's still with the Bureau. I haven't talked to him in years. I calculate that he'd be in his late fifties, maybe early sixties, by now. I decide that I'll try to locate him in the morning.

Back to the answering machine. As if I'm a robot, I replace the new tape with the West tape and find myself listening to his horrible voice again . . . listening to his scumbag message. I don't know why I need to do this. I tell myself that this time it's to listen to background noise for a clue to his whereabouts, but I know this is lame. There is no background noise. I listen because I'm compelled, unable not to. I play it over and over until I can hear it without a shudder of revulsion, until I'm inured to its content, as though what I hear has nothing to do with me. It's only then that I can go upstairs to bed.

After I recheck the window locks I do something different. I leave the bedroom door open so the cats can come in. Not that I believe they'll protect me from Charlie West, or anyone else, but for comfort. Usually, they don't sleep with us, because of Kip's allergies. Tonight they will.

And they are ecstatic. Gaining entry to any off-limits room puts them over the top. They sniff the perimeters; check out all furniture, windowsills, and stray clothing before they jump on the bed; examine each inch of it; and finally settle down. I know I can't read, so I turn off the light and stare into the darkness,

Nora at my head and Nick at my feet. They purr in unison and tell me not to worry.

Yeah, sure.

By the time the alarm goes off I figure I've had about three hours of sickly sleep and feel ghastly. I woke up every hour, my guardians with me. I think of West with a thud to my gut.

The cats stare at me, hot fish breath on my face. I roll over.

"Go away."

Nick mews his paltry sound. Nora, on the other hand, lets me have it full force, insistent and annoying.

"All right, all right."

I climb out of bed and we go downstairs to the kitchen. After I feed them I make coffee, sit at the table, and think. It's too early to try to find Jeff Crawford. I have to wait until the normal business day begins. The ring of the phone startles me and automatically I grab the receiver.

"Hello?"

"Hel-lo, Lauren."

I slam the thing into the cradle because it's him. I quaver and tremble. It rings again. If I don't answer, the machine will pick up and he'll leave another filthy message. Timorously, I pick it up, say nothing.

"Lauren?" West says. "Ya there?"

Not sure what I should do, I remain silent.

"Hey, bitch, ya so afraid of me, ya can't speak? I make you speechless, is that it, Lauren?" He laughs cruelly.

Hand over the mouthpiece, I clear my throat, then say, "Who is this?"

West laughs again. "Ya kiddin' me? Ya know who it is, Lauren. Ya never forgot me, did ya? Ya don't need to answer, ya piece of slime. Ya ruined my life. I'm not stayin' on 'cause ya probably havin' this traced. But here's the dope . . . You'll never know when I'm gonna be where ya are, when it's gonna happen or where. But I know every move ya make and one of these fine days I'm gonna fuck yer brains out again, bitch . . . and then I'm gonna kill ya dead. No mistakes this time."

Click.

Funny, how I react. All I can think, as I replace the handset, is I wish caller I.D. were in place. But now it hits me. Charlie West wants to murder me. Rape me and murder me. He knows where I am but I don't know where he is. I'm totally vulnerable and he's safe.

I laugh out loud when I recall his saying that *I* ruined *his* life. I know he believes this, because he's a sociopath. What he and Thomas Bailey did to me is nothing to him. They'd left me for dead and clearly what galls him most is that I survived. Survived and was able to I.D. him, send him to jail, where he should've stayed but didn't, because of our lousy system.

It's still too early to call the FBI directly but maybe I can learn where Jeff is through an old colleague. In my home office I check an ancient phone book. This is where being a pack rat pays off. Maybe. There's nothing to say that Mike Pietsch will still be at this number. I punch it in. After two rings a young female voice answers.

"Hi, is this the home of Michael Pietsch?"

"Daaaaaaad? It's for you."

The sound of the phone being laid down clanks in my ear. A thousand hours pass.

"Hello."

"Mike?"

"Who's this?"

"I don't know if you'll remember me . . . that's ridiculous, sure you will. It's Lauren Laurano."

"Lauren!" he says, sounding genuinely glad. "How the hell are you, kid?"

"Not a kid, for one thing."

"I know what you mean. Boy, do I."

We shoot the breeze for a minute or two, catch up. Finally, I say, "Mike, the reason I'm calling is that I need to get in touch with Jeff Crawford. Is he still with the Bureau?"

"Far as I know."

I realize how relieved I am to hear this. I suppose I'd entertained the possibility that Jeff might be dead. "Know how I can reach him?"

"Not offhand, Lauren. Something wrong?"

I consider telling him but decide against it. Jeff is the one I need. "Not really. I'd just like to speak with him."

"Well, I can track him down for you, tell him to call you."

I smile. He knows where Jeff is. But he can't give me his number. Jeff will have to call me. Fine. "That'd be great. Let me give you my home and office numbers."

I do and he says he'll take care of it. We make idle promises to stay in touch, get together, but both know we won't. FBI employees and *ex*–FBI employees don't have a lot in common.

I decide to get dressed, pick up some breakfast, and go to my office.

At Andy's I get an orange juice, a bagel and cream cheese, and two coffees to go. When I get to my floor I sense it. Or think I do. All the way here, frightened, I found myself looking over my shoulder, scanning faces.

But this is different. I can see that he's not in the hallway. Still, my instinct tells me something's wrong. I open my bag and take out my .38, hold it down by my side so I won't scare an innocent bystander who might come into the hall. When I get to my door I stand still and listen. Nothing. I put the key in the dead bolt. Immediately, I can tell that I'm locking instead of opening it.

My heart thumps the music to *Jaws*. I return the keys to my pocket, move to the side, raise my gun so it's pointing up, turn the knob with my left hand, and throw open the door. Quickly, I step inside and assume the combat position.

The office is empty.

But he's been here.

The place is destroyed.

Sixteen

My small office is crowded with police personnel. You might think there'd been a murder instead of . . . well, it is a burglary — the bastard took my notebook computer. I'm not sure whether I hate him more for that or for trashing my office. Everything is ruined. Gig Price, a cop I've never gotten along with, one who made O'Hara look like Bambi, caught the case. He's young and crude, wears polyester suits, loud ties, and smokes a cigar. His eyes are blue like dead chips of slate, and his brown, crew-cut hair brings the word *militia* to mind.

Price says, "So who'd you piss off, Laurano?"

"Thanks for the sympathy."

"Somebody's got it in for ya, looks like. Take anything else besides the computer?"

"There was a modem in the computer."

"That like a rag for the curse?"

I know he's thinking of Modess and I also know that he knows that's not what I'm talking about. "You know, Price, you're a pig."

"Thanks. Whatcha gonna do now Cecchi's out a commission?"

I don't answer him, walk away, but can't get far.

"Hope you don't think I'm gonna be your boy on the Job?"

"Price, if you were the last cop on earth, I wouldn't work with you."

I stare at my chair, which has been gutted, the stuffing strewn around the floor like cotton balls. I feel sick. The bamboo blinds on the two windows have been wrenched from their moorings and torn, shredded. My desk is on its side. Papers are everywhere, as each drawer of my file cabinet has been emptied of its contents. Much of the paper's been ripped, made unusable.

The small Canon printer I use here lies dead, smashed and flattened in the center so that the sides flip upward like in a cartoon drawing.

"Diskettes," I say to Price.

"Say what?"

"My diskettes, all the backup of my files and stuff. They were in a step cube. I think he took them too."

"You keep sayin' *he* like you know who did it."

"Habit," I say. I don't know why, but I feel I can't tell the police who I think did this until I talk to Jeff Crawford.

Says Price, "You think a dame couldn't do this?"

"A *dame?* You're an anachronism, you know that?"

His ruddy face turns a darker shade of angry. I know he doesn't know what the word means.

"Watch yer mouth, Laurano."

I try not to smile.

"What's funny?"

"You," I say.

He tries to stare me down but I won't look away. Out of my peripheral vision I register a camera flash. I want these dorks out of here so I can get on with the cleanup, call my insurance company, and, yes, go buy new equipment. This last task is not exactly an unpleasant idea.

I watch while forensic dusts for prints. I hate that I'll have to clean up all that black stuff as well.

"I hear maybe Cecchi's not gonna completely recover," Price needles.

"You're hearing things?" I say. "I'd have that checked out if I were you. Maybe it's the beginning of schizophrenia or something."

"Fuck you," he says.

"No, thanks."

"Oh, yeah, right. Forgot yer a dyke."

I have no comeback, and even if I did, I don't want to engage in this particular badinage. I ignore Price by walking to the window, where I look out at Seventh Avenue. But I hear him laughing behind me and I find it infuriating. Feeling impotent is not my strong suit.

Finally, I'm alone amidst the debris of my professional life. Not only has everything to do with my business been taken or destroyed, my letters to and from Alex Thomas are gone. Why am I thinking about her now? It's trivial compared with the rest, but it doesn't feel that way. At least I have some correspondence from her at home.

I don't know where to start. The phone rings and saves me. As I go to answer, I wonder why West didn't destroy this. "Lauren, it's Jeff Crawford."

I could shout with joy. "Thank God."

"No, thank Pietsch."

We both laugh.

"How are you?" he asks.

"Not good. Are you in New York?"

"You want to see me?" he answers in the evasive agent way.

"Yes."

"I think I can arrange that. When?"

"As soon as possible."

"I'm having a cup of coffee at Raffaella's."

I can't believe he's right around the corner. And now I realize he's been waiting for the police to leave. "I'll be there in a minute."

"Good." He hangs up.

I grab my bag and coat and sprint out of the office, not bothering to lock. What's the point? Even so, I close the door so that no one will feel like wandering in. I run down the stairs, out the front door, and bump into a young couple who win my prize for best dressed.

He wears dirty, baggy jeans, one leg cut off close to his crotch, bare top with body paint of daisies running riot, and a two-tone hair-dye job: red and green. Her hair is *black* black with uneven bangs so that part of her face is covered to below her nose. She wears a shapeless patterned dress, filthy slip hanging below, and brown, chunky, unlaced shoes. They give me the once-over, then smile at each other, silently commenting on my hopelessly out-of-date apparel. Once again I'm thankful I don't have kids, then am horrified that I'm reacting like my mother did to my clothes at that age. I excuse myself for colliding with them and continue on.

This is one of my favorite coffeehouses. It's filled with a riff-raff of old tables and chairs, and placed around the big room are standing lamps with fringed shades. At night when the lamps are lit, it's particularly inviting.

I recognize Jeff immediately even though he's aged. He stands up like an unfolding umbrella and puts out his hand, a grin on his handsome face. I push past the hand and give him a hug in which he eagerly participates.

"Lauren, you look great. Haven't changed a bit."

"Liar," I say. "But thanks."

What's left of Jeff's hair is white; strands swirl around his head like unattended weeds. And he sports a beard, basically white, with shots of brown.

"Not lying. You practically could be that young kid I met . . . how many years ago?"

"I'm forty-five," I say.

He winces as we sit down. "Hell, that makes me sixty-two. Nah, must be some mistake. What would you like to drink?"

I tell him a cappuccino. He asks if I'd like something else. Of course, I would and I do. There's a chocolate cake here that's one of the best in New York. And I deserve it after what I've been through.

He orders, then says, "So, what's up?"

"Why do I think you already know?"

He laughs. "You always were shrewd. That's why we wanted you so much. Truth is, I only know about the burglary you had. Somehow I have a feeling it's connected to why you wanted to see me."

"Talk about shrewd. You're right. Charlie West did it."

"No shit."

I tell him the story and give him the tape. He promises to get on it, tries to reassure me I'll be okay. I can't be altogether assuaged but I nod to make him think I believe in his total protection.

My cake comes and I feel almost good. One bite and I *do* feel good. No doubt about it, chocolate's a mood changer.

I catch him up about my life to date, leaving out that Kip and I are having problems. I see no need to go into that. He tells me he's divorced and remarried, and blushes when he tells me she's thirty-five. I immediately think of Alex. I would've been judgmental about the age difference in the past but not now. Even though Alex and I are only thirteen years apart, instead of twenty-seven, she's still a younger woman. WHAT IS WRONG WITH ME? This is an E-mail correspondent; what do our ages have to do with it? Obviously something, or I wouldn't be so laid-back about the difference in Jeff and his new wife's ages.

"Yeah, I know," he says.

"What do you know?" Guilt from nowhere!

"I know it's a big age difference."

"Oh, please, who cares?"

"You had a look."

"Not about that."

He smiles. "Good. A lot of people judge it. But she's not like a thirty-five-year-old, I mean she's —"

"Jeff, you don't have to justify her to me. You love each other, that's all that counts." And it is.

"Thanks."

We talk a little longer, he picks up the check, and we make our way through the café and out into the crisp day. Jeff hails a cab, leans down and gives me a kiss, says he'll be in touch, and then he's gone.

I decide to go back to the house and write a letter and check my mail before tackling the office again.

From: laurenl@NWDC.com
To: athomas@panix.com
Subject: Yesterday When I Was Young

Dear Toots,

A> Okay, okay, I am 32. So what? Do you think I do not know anything about life because I am under 40?

So you're 32. I think I remember what that was like. :) No, I don't think you don't know anything because you're under 40, all right? I'm not judging you on that basis, or any basis, for that matter.

A> Yes, I am with someone. Her name is Sally Edwards and she is 41.

An older woman, huh?

A> Are you in a relationship now? If so, for how long and what does she do, etc.?

Yes, I am. Her name's Kip Adams and she's a therapist. We've been together for 14 years. She's away for a month giving a lecture series.

My office was burglarized last night. Totally destroyed. It's an awful feeling . . . sort of like being raped. I'm pretty sure I know who did it . . . one of the men who really did rape me years ago . . . I told you about this. He's called me and threatened me. This is frightening and something I have to deal with alone, as Kip's not here. I'm not going to tell her when we speak because there's nothing she can do from there and it'll worry her. I've informed the FBI, so to speak. I say it that way because I've been in touch with one person there.

As for the case I'm working on, I've got a new lead but the work it involves is almost overwhelming. Now with Cecchi out of commission, I have to do all of it myself because I don't have that kind of relationship with anyone else on the force.

A> I really like writing to you. I find it fun and stimulating. Hope you do too.

I like writing to you too. Hope to hear from you soon.
Sam Spade

I reread. I see that I've mentioned Kip's being away twice. What message am I really sending here? I almost decide to dump it but don't. So I dial NWDC and go through the drill. There's lots of mail for me, more of the Goldstein stuff and something else. After I send the letter to Alex, I sign off and go immediately to the non-Goldstein one, where the subject is *death,* and when I open it my heart plummets:

From: killerkid@bestbord.com
To: laurenl@NWDC.com
Dear Lauren,

   Yeah its me. Gotcha comin and goin dont I? See I know where you are all the time even here. So your lookin for a goldstein are you. Maybe I know one. Want to meet and chew the fat about it? Ha Ha. I bet you do. Wonder if youll find him before you die.
Killer Kid

Seventeen

After I write a letter asking if anyone knows where bestbord is located, I dial NWDC again and post it to four or five appropriate Usenet newsgroups. I've never heard of bestbord before, but I have a feeling that it could be anywhere, since West probably wouldn't use a New York BBS even though he's obviously in the city.

My next move is to replace my office computer and the rest of the hardware. It's an exciting prospect but the thought of installing all my programs gives me pause. It can be an enormous drag. And then I get a chill thinking about Charlie West using my stuff, reading my mail.

Nick and Nora are mewing at me and I go into the kitchen. Their food bowls are filled, so what do they want? More mewing.

"What?"

"Mew," in chorus.

If only one could decipher mews. And then I see it. An EMPTY WATER BOWL. If Kip knew, she'd kill me. Quickly, I fill it and put it back on the floor. They run to it as though they'd been walking the desert for days. I calculate when I'd filled it last and recall that it had been a while back. Guilt pummels me. Well, I've been on overload. What can these cats expect?

"Listen," I say to them. "My best cop friend's been shot and practically put out to pasture, I'm being stalked by a maniac who once raped me, Elissa's aunt's been murdered, Elissa's been attacked, Kip's away and there's this . . . this woman who keeps writing to me." What in hell does that mean?

"Nick, Nora, cancel the last thing on the list, it doesn't make any sense."

They nod. Yeah, they do.

Time to go shopping. As I enter the hallway, William and another man are coming down the stairs.

"Lauren," he says, grinning in a way that I haven't seen in a long time. "I'd like you to meet Bobby."

We shake hands. Bobby has dark hair worn short, dark eyes with large-framed glasses, and is adorable. He wears a white shirt, sleeves rolled to the elbows, and gray patch-pocket pants. Unless I'm very off, he's much, much younger than William. What's going on? Everybody seems to be dating younger people. Who's *everybody?*

Bobby says, "I'm really glad to meet you. William's told me a lot about you."

How long has this been going on? I wonder. So much for William's celibacy period. Surely, he didn't spend his first date with Bobby talking about me. I smile, reveal nothing.

"Bobby's a city landscape artist."

"I do people's patios and roof gardens, stuff like that," Bobby adds.

"He's very talented," William says.

"He's a bit biased." Bobby blushes.

"I doubt it," I say. "He's a hard marker and wouldn't say anything if it weren't true."

"That's correct," William affirms. "How're you doing without Kip?"

"Aside from being burglarized, fine." I fill him in but don't go into the Charlie West stuff. Later, when I grill him about Bobby.

We all leave the building together but after we say good-bye, nice to meet you, etc., they go toward West Fourth Street and I go toward Seventh Avenue.

I find myself looking over my shoulder, doing a slow 180 to see if anyone's watching me — *anyone* meaning West. It dawns on me that I might not recognize him. As all of us have, West's grown older too. In my mind I try to age him. He could be bearded, bald, anything. Still, the face — eyes, nose, mouth — imprinted on my mind forever, is easy to imagine twenty-odd years older. It's not a pretty picture.

I don't see anyone I think could be West. Now my pressing problem is: CompUSA or J & R? I cross Seventh and walk toward Three Lives. Not that they'll have an answer for me, but I feel like saying hello before I go shopping. Jenny is a big spender too and I know she'll get into it with me, even though computer equipment doesn't turn her on like cars or other kinds of electronics.

When I reach the corner of Charles and Waverly I see that the "Music Man" is doing his thing. Actually, I heard it before I saw him. He's a big guy, although I've only seen him sitting down on his upturned bucket in front of his jerry-rigged drums and other percussion instruments. They consist of white plastic buckets, strips of metal, and wooden boxes. The sounds they emit are astonishing.

"Hey, Music Man," I say when he finishes his rendition of "Keepin' Out of Mischief Now."

"Hello, my friend," he says in a voice that's drunk and smoked its way through more than fifty years.

MM is chocolate-forest-cake dark. His eyes are clear, and even though he lives mostly on the street, his face isn't ravaged but is unlined, handsome. He's also an ex-cop.

"Heard the skinny on your place bein' tossed," he says. "Know which dude done it?"

"Maybe. You hear anything?"

"Not a whisper, kidlet. Don't think it was local talent."

"Why do you say that?"

He shrugs. "Somebody woulda dropped a dime to me by now. Nobody knows nothin'."

"Well, you happen to be right. It wasn't local talent. I know who did it, just don't know where he has his crib."

"How come you know who the mutt is, babes?"

I tell him.

"Whoa, that's heavy shit. You want we should look out for this creep?"

"Sure."

"Draw me a picture."

He means with words and I try.

"Distinguishing marks or somethin'?"

"Could be, but I don't know."

"This makes it tough. So how old this dude now?"

"Around fifty-five or so."

"A youngster, huh?" MM grins, showing salmon-colored gums and yellowish, uneven teeth.

"That's young in my book," I say. "Keep your peepers peeled. See you."

"See you, babes."

I continue down Waverly as MM starts beating out "Just In Time." It's always been one of my favorites but today I feel like he's playing it for me. And fifty-five is a youngster in my book? Hello? Me? Miss Fear-of-Getting-Older? Sure, we were kidding around but suddenly fifty-five honestly seems . . . well, if not young, certainly not old. Could this have anything to do with Alex's being thirty-two? What am I thinking? I'm definitely losing it.

At Tenth and Waverly I go into Three Lives. Tracy, the employee who's been with them the longest, is behind the high wooden counter.

"Hi, Lauren." She has gray/brown hair which she wears in a bun. Her Irish face is freckled and her glasses rest on a small, straight nose. Her conservative clothing is always crisp. "I heard you got burgled. Is it true?"

"Unfortunately, yes."

"So how come you didn't call us?" Jenny says, coming out of the door that leads to the basement. "Were you scared?"

"I wasn't there when it happened."

"I know that," she says. "I mean when you found your stuff all over the place."

I narrow my eyes, give a lame Bogey imitation. "So, how do you know my stuff was all over the place, sister?"

"Well, wasn't it?"

"Yeah, it was but that doesn't get you off the hook," I continue.

"Stop that," Jenny says. "I know if I ever came home, or here, and I'd been burgled like that, I'd freak out."

"You'd freak out over anything," I say.

"Take that back. Go on, take it back."

"Back," I say. "He took my computer and stuff."

The tiniest glint comes into her eyes. "So you need to buy a new one, huh?"

"Right. And I haven't even paid for the stolen one yet."

Jill comes from the back of the store. "You have insurance, don't you?"

"Sure."

She shrugs. "So then?"

"It takes forever to get it."

"What are you buying?" Jenny asks, moving in on me. "And where?"

"I have to get another notebook, modem, disks, printer — everything."

"I think," she says, warming more and more to this, "you should get the newest and the best. State of the art."

"That's up around five thousand," I say.

"So?"

"Jenny," Jill says, "Lauren doesn't have that kind of money."

"So what? Who does? Life is short and she needs it for work. It'll be a write-off."

"I liked the one I had," I say pitifully.

"Yeah, but now it's out of date, right?"

"In a way."

"So get a better one. You're on this case; you'll make money."

Jill shakes her head. "If Cecchi weren't in the hospital, he'd get your old stuff back for you."

"Eeeeuw," Jenny and I say together.

"You two are so bad," Jill says.

Jenny and I discuss the merits of J & R and CompUSA. I finally decide that not paying for six months is the better course to take.

Says Tracy, "I heard that the man who robbed you was somebody you knew."

It amazes me how these things travel so fast. I could ask her, but what's the point? "You have to promise not to tell Kip if you talk to her, because she'll be worried."

"I promise," a tall, lanky man says.

We look at him. He's a customer.

"I do," he says eagerly. "I won't tell Kip."

Jenny says, "Do you *know* Kip?"

"No. That's why you can be sure I won't tell her."

"This is ridiculous. Is there something you'd like?" Jill asks the guy.

He pulls himself together, gives a feeble smile like a small razor cut. "Michael Nava's new book?"

Jill points to the gay male section. "Over there."

Head bent, he shuffles away in faux disgrace.

They all turn back to me and I tell them about Charlie West. They'd known but had lost track of it in their minds, as we all do about such things in the past.

Jenny says, "You're not scared?"

"Of course I'm scared. I only meant I wasn't scared that I'd been burgled until I found out who it was."

"You have to move out of there," says Jenny.

"Why? He knows where I live, what I'm doing all the time. If I get another office, he'll find out. There's no point."

"She's right," Jill says.

"Anyway, people are working on it."

"Hey, wait a minute. If he knows everything about you, then he knows who your friends are, doesn't he?" asks Jenny.

"He's not going to do anything to us."

"How do you know, Jill?"

"He's not, Jen. Don't worry," I reassure her. "But if you want, I won't come in here anymore until he's caught."

"No, don't be stupid. It just hit me, that's all. Yeah, why would he do anything to us?"

"He wouldn't."

"Right."

" 'Course not."

"Never."

"Not in a million years."

"No way."

We look at each other and it's clear to me that not one of us is convinced.

Eighteen

I've cleaned up my office and set up my new equipment, con-
sisting of the newest AST Ascentia notebook, a Megahertz
PCMCIA 28.8 kbps modem, and a Panasonic KX-P6100 laser
printer. I always do what Jenny tells me! The one thing I don't
have is a new chair, but it'll be delivered this afternoon. I sit
on the old one, which is pretty uncomfortable but better than
standing.

The first thing I do is log on to NWDC. I have one piece of
E-mail. It's from Alex and my heart does a dip.

From: athomas@panix.com
To: laurenl@NWDC.com
Subject: Don't Get Around Much Anymore
Dear Sam,
    L> An older woman, huh?
    Yep. As it should be.
    L> We've been together for 14 years.
    I cannot imagine being with someone that long. I have never
made it beyond three. I am so sorry about your burglary

The phone rings and I jump.

"Is this Lauren?"

It's a woman but I don't recognize the voice. "Yes. Who's
this?"

"Alex Thomas."

I stare at the screen and for once am unable to say anything.

"Lauren?"

"Uh, yes. Yes, I'm here." Why is she calling me?

"I'm sorry to call you," she says in a voice like butter, "but, well, I'm scared."

Of me? I wonder. "Scared?"

"I got some strange E-mail."

"Strange E-mail?" I can't stop sounding stupid, repeating everything she says.

"Could we meet? I'm sort of afraid to talk on the phone and definitely don't want to use E-mail right now."

Meet? I pull myself together. "When would you like to get together?"

"How about now?"

I become unplugged. "Now? Where?"

"Wherever you say."

"Let me think." I rule out here, still too messy. "Do you know the Village?"

She laughs but not unkindly. "I live in the Village."

"Oh, I didn't know that."

"No, you didn't."

"How about coming to my house?" I say, as though my words are controlled by a ventriloquist. But I'm sure she won't want to do that.

"Okay. Where do you live?"

Ohmigod. I give her my address and we agree on an hour from now, then hang up. What have I done? What if William sees her? So what? What's wrong with me? This isn't a date, for God's sake. The woman's in trouble and I'm a detective. Right? Right? *Yes, Lauren. Right.*

I return to the screen and finish reading her letter.

I cannot imagine being with someone that long. I have never made it beyond three. I am so sorry about your burglary and all that it means. You must be scared. I know I would be. I understand not wanting to tell Kip (hope you do not mind my referring to her by first name but any other way would seem so formal and strange). I know I would not tell Sally if I were in your shoes. I hope you catch this guy soon.

Is it strange to be with a therapist? I would feel the person was analyzing me all the time. And I would hate that. I like to keep my own counsel. So that is all for now.

Brigid O'Shaugnessy

I'm amazed that she knows the spelling of Brigid's last name. I wonder if she realizes that even though Brigid was a villain, she was also a love interest for Spade, if only for a while. *Oh, stop.* But what does she mean *as it should be* in answer to my question about her partner's being an older woman? I suppose I could construe this as flirting if I wanted to. What's going on here?

It occurs to me suddenly that Alex has invented this need to see me in person. But why would she do that? Face it, Laurano, you're going crazy. I shut down my new notebook, pack it up in my new Targus case. As long as West is on the loose, I'm not taking any chances with this baby. The new lock's been installed but I know if West wants to get in badly enough, he will. Anyway, I like the feeling of locking up.

In the hall I encounter yet another janitor. They don't seem to last very long, for one reason or another.

His name's Deen Nelson and he's young, extremely hand-some, tall, with hair the color of good black leather and eyes that seem to match. When he smiles, long dimples like paren-theses appear in his cheeks. In real life, as he puts it, he's a screenwriter, but then who isn't?

"Morning, L.L., they catch the malefactorater yet?"

Malefactorater? "Not yet, Deen."

"I've put it in my new screenplay. Hope you don't mind."

"Put what?"

"Your burglary. All the hyperbolation that's gone on about it made me see that it fits. See, there's this woman that —"

"Deen," I interrupt, "it's not that I'm not interested but I'm in a big, big hurry."

"Oh, sure. I understand. Got a break in a case, right?"

"Right," I lie. "See you later."

"I'll keep an observerate on things, L.L."

"Thanks."

I think of all the made-up words I've ever heard, *hyperbolation* may be my fave. *Observerate* isn't bad though.

Outside I stop still. Should I run home to tidy up, or should I get a snack or something? But what does she like? She's in the fashion biz, so she probably never eats. No, wait. She's not a model. Maybe she'd like coffee and biscuits or a pastry? But what? And where should I get it? I feel nuts. Nuts. Does she like things with nuts in them? I know nothing about this woman. Calm down. Why *should* I know anything? This is business. Or is it? She said she was frightened and had to talk to me personally. What else would it be besides business? Oh, boy. I decide to go to Lanciani's and get a couple of pastries and if she doesn't want them . . . hell, they won't go to waste.

I keep glancing at my watch, which tells me it's only forty-five minutes since she called. Why don't I believe my watch? Because I know that it was at least two days ago. I look around the living room. As Kip has just left, the place is neat. I straighten some magazines. I straighten them again. Once more.

The Ns are sleeping in a chair, wrapped around each other so that they resemble a huge sweater. I wonder if Ed Wood would've wanted to wear them? But they're not Angoras.

I look out the window. I see the empty street. The magazines don't look right, so I take them from the coffee table and put them on a bookshelf. Nope. Back on the table. The bell rings and I emit such a terrified scream, the Ns jump up.

"Lie down, look gorgeous," I tell them.

As I go to the intercom, I peek in the mirror. I've never looked worse in my life.

"Who is it?"

"Alex Thomas," the voice says.

When I open the door and see her standing there my heart does a rhumba. Alex is a looker, to say the least. I'm surprised to find that we're almost the same height. I'd remembered her being taller. And her hair is different. The last time I'd seen her it was short. But I like this long blonde hair and the wisps that track across her forehead like angels' curls.

Her eyes are brown, as she'd told me, and her nose is small and straight. She has on a tan suede coat, collar turned up.

"Hi," she says.

"Hi." I can tell how nervous she is because her lips, which are full and gorgeous, twitch slightly. "Come in."

"Thanks." She smiles broadly and there are crow's-feet around her eyes.

I'm happy to see them because I'd feared she'd be totally un-lined. A foolish vanity but one I can't shake. She moves past me into the apartment and her arm brushes against mine. It feels like tiny pleasurable shocks.

"This is very nice," she says. "The apartment." And she laughs, again signaling her anxiety, her almost palpable fear.

"Thanks."

I take her coat and hang it on one of the pegs near the door. She wears a black, V-neck cashmere sweater with a white shirt underneath and a brown corduroy skirt that's very short over black stockings. Her shoes are brown leather, almost like a loafer, with a high block heel. Her purse is also brown leather. I can't help wondering what she thinks of my flannel shirt, jeans, and sneakers.

"Would you like something?" I ask.

She looks straight into my eyes, smiles slowly. "Coffee?"

"Sure. Come on into the kitchen."

I can feel the heat of her walking behind me even as I know this is impossible. In the kitchen I stop, suddenly forgetting where anything is: the coffee, the maker, the sugar. What's happening?

"Something wrong?" she asks, behind me.

I turn to face her and we're very close. "No. Nothing." I think I may faint, but recover. "What kind of coffee would you like?"

"What choices do I have?" Now she seems composed, at ease.

"Choices?"

"Of coffee," she says, smiles.

"Oh, coffee." I can't believe what a jerk I'm being. "Well, there's a French roast, hazelnut —"

"Hazelnut's my favorite."

"Fine." I open the freezer, take out the bag, bring it to the grinder, measure out three scoops.

"You own the house?" she asks.

"Yes." I don't see the need to explain that it's really Kip's. I grind the coffee, put it in the maker, pour in water, and click the ON button. Now we wait. I find it hard not to stare at her, because she's so lovely. I force myself to shift into a business mode.

"Want to tell me about the E-mail that scared you?"

"I can show you. I printed it out."

"Okay."

She laughs uncomfortably. "Well, it's in my purse. In the living room," she adds.

"Oh."

"Should I get it?"

"Yes, that'd be good."

I watch her as she turns and leaves the kitchen with a walk that's almost loping but has a definite feminine twist to it. I'm grateful for the moment alone. I feel dizzy and breathless and wish I were anywhere but here. What is this? The terrible thing is that I think I know.

She's back.

Ohmigod, she's so beautiful.

"I got it when I logged on this morning. I thought you'd want to see it."

She hands me a piece of paper and I see that her hand is trembling.

"You're shaking," I say.

She blushes. "Yes."

Quickly, I amend, "It must be very scary." I pretend I mean the note, but I know that's not why she quivers. Her anxious behavior makes me less nervous.

"Very," she says, trying to sound relaxed. But she still blushes.

I drag my gaze away from her and look down at the printout.

From: badboy@aol.com
To: athomas@panix.com
Dear Alex,

So you like the lady dick huh? Are you one too? Wouldnt know it to look at you. Your some kind of sweet meat honey. And Im just the one to buzz you. Stay away from Laurano or you might find that sweet meat hamburger if you get my drift. Ill be watching you.
Badboy

I'm stunned. "Jesus," I say. "And you came here?"

"I thought you should see it," she says again. "Are you angry?"

"Angry? No, of course not. I'm afraid for you." I don't say that I wonder why she thought it less dangerous to do this in person than to read it to me on the phone because I know the answer. "AOL stands for America Online."

"Yes, I know. Do you think it's from the guy who trashed your place, the rapist?"

"Yes."

"I thought so too."

Silent, we look at each other — the only noise in the room, the coffeemaker burbling to a finish.

Finally, she says, "How did he know? I mean, how does he know who I am, that I write to you?"

"He stole my computer. Some of your E-mail was in there. You took a risk coming here, Alex." It's the first time I've said her name aloud and it feels delicious in my mouth. Almost against my will I move closer to her so that we are only a breath apart. She doesn't back up, holds her ground, looks deep into my eyes.

What I want to do is kiss her, it's as clear to me as anything has ever been. What I *do* is say, "The coffee's ready," and turn away to get it.

From behind me she says in a soft voice, "I take milk and sugar. Two."

I get the mugs, fix coffee for each of us, and hand her hers. "Shall we?" I ask, indicating that we go back to the living room.

She nods, flicks me a smile.

I follow her, something careening inside me as if I were a pinball machine.

In the living room we sit opposite each other, proper and perfect.

"Are you on AOL?" I ask.

"No. Just Panix."

"Have you ever gotten mail from a stranger before?" I'm totally in my P.I. mode now and am relieved. Still, I have to be vigilant about looking at her in a strictly professional way.

"I get a lot of mail from strangers. I mean, people I don't actually know except on-line. But that's not what you meant, is it?"

I have no idea what this line of questioning has to do with anything. What difference does it make if she gets mail from a thousand strangers? I'd make a good lawyer in the O. J. case. "Ah, no, it's not what I meant." Please don't ask why I'm asking, I beg an unseen, unknown specter.

"Am I really in danger?"

Oh, thank you, whoever. "You could be. Badboy has got to be Charlie West. And now that you've come here . . . well, he probably knows that too."

She sips her coffee, looks at me over the rim. There's something enchanting about it. *Stop that, Lauren!*

"So," she says, "I'm in the middle of a case."

I can tell she warms to this idea. "Alex, it's not a game. West is a vicious killer. You have to be careful."

"Can I hire you?"

"Me? For what? I'm not a bodyguard."

She smiles in a way that can only be termed seductive. "Too bad. Did you see that movie?"

"Too Bad?"

"You're funny. No. *The Bodyguard.*"

I did see it and know that it's about the bodyguard and the subject falling in love. Am I to make some inference from this remark? "Yes."

"I loved it," she says.

"Well, I'm not a bodyguard. But maybe you should hire someone to protect you. I'm sorry I got you into this."

"It's not your fault. I wrote to you first."

This is true. "Why?" I ask suddenly.

"Did I write you?"

"Yes. I mean, *really*."

She doesn't answer but looks at me in a way that reaches my toes. Am I imagining this? Why would this young, gorgeous woman be interested in me? "What did you mean, *as it should be*, when I asked you about having a lover who was older?"

She quickly jumps to her feet. "I have to get back to work."

I rise too. "Alex, what's going on here?" I move toward her but she starts for the door. "Alex?"

She puts on her coat, her back to me. I come up behind her, put a hand on her shoulder. She whirls around to face me and suddenly my lips are against hers. I feel like I'm going to pass out. In fact, we both lose our balance a bit and I have to steady myself with an outstretched arm, hand against the wall. This leads to Alex's arms around me and our bodies press together. I feel that magic, that unexplainable thing that happens, like surging waves and jagged shocks, when you kiss someone new. I know I should stop but I can't. I want to drown in this feeling, never take my lips from hers, sink into them, maybe die right now.

Finally, we pull apart, our faces almost touching as we look into each other's eyes.

I say, "I can't do this, Alex."

"You've already done it," she whispers, accurately.

"I know. But I can't do it anymore." I move away from her.

"I'm sorry," she says.

I don't know if she means she's sorry I can't do it anymore or that it happened at all, so I say nothing.

She opens the door and I let her leave without a word.

Nineteen

===

I can't believe I kissed her.

I can't believe *she* kissed *me*.

But most of all, I can't believe I forgot to serve the pastries.

From my office window I stare down at Sheridan Square. Everything looks out of focus, as though I've used eyedrops. My mind, too, feels blurred.

I leave the window and sit on my crucified chair. Alex's coming to see me made me forget that I was expecting a chair delivery. A note was on my door saying they'll try again tomorrow. I don't care. I can't seem to care about anything at this moment: not Charlie West or Ruthie's killer or my own safety. All I can think about is the kiss and then, Kip.

I've been unfaithful. Something I never thought I'd be. Still, I remind myself, it was only a kiss and how unfaithful is that? Unfaithful. I haven't kissed anyone that way for fourteen years, except Kip. But if that's all that happens, then I can forget about it, can't I? Yes. There's no need to tell Kip, because basically there's nothing to tell. I must make sure that there doesn't become something to tell. I have to stop writing to Alex, and never see her again. But she's in danger and it's my fault. I can't simply abandon her, can I?

The phone rings and saves me from answering the question.

"Lauren Laurano, private investigator," I say.

"Hi."

One word and I know immediately that it's Alex.

She says, "I'm sorry I ran out of your house like that."

"It was my fault. I shouldn't have —"

"Yes. You should have. I mean, I wanted you to."

Oh, God. "Look, Alex —"

"I know, I know. It won't happen again."

How can she be so sure? I wonder.

"We won't let it," she continues. "But I hope we can go on writing to each other."

"Sure," I say, as though I have no control over my response.

"We'll forget it ever happened. Okay?"

"Okay."

"Well, that's all I wanted to say. Except, is there anything I should do or not do regarding Charlie West?"

"Be careful. Don't go out at night alone. Lock your doors and windows. Meanwhile, I'll track the bastard down."

She giggles. "You butch thing."

I assume she's making fun of me. "You got it, sister." What am I saying? I laugh to show her it's all a joke.

"You're killing me."

"Huh?"

"It's just an expression."

"Oh. Well, it's an odd one to use with a detective."

"I never thought of that."

We don't seem to want to hang up but I can't think of anything benign to say. Everything that comes to mind is suddenly suspect or could have a double meaning. We're silent, breathing like a couple of obscene callers. I will myself to speak.

"I don't want you to feel unsafe. I really will catch West, I promise."

"I believe you," she says.

"Good." *Good?* What the hell does that mean? *Get off the phone, Lauren.* "I better get to work if I'm going to protect you." Oh, no. I shouldn't have said it that way. This is confirmed by the sweet laugh I hear on the other end.

"Thank you," Alex says. "Okay, I guess I'd better say good-bye. I'll be typing to you."

"Right. Bye."

I force myself to cradle the receiver and not listen for her to hang up first. This is crazy. I need to work. I need a therapist. I need Kip.

After calling many Martin Goldsteins and reaching none who knows Harold, I decide it's time to try the other two people I still haven't made contact with on the list of Ruthie's friends. They're Lisa Stein and Harriet Weiss. Amazingly, I reach Stein and she tells me I may come see her. This means a trip uptown, which automatically entails a subway ride. Not my favorite sport.

Stein lives in the Sixties. I take an uneventful ride to Forty-second Street, where I get the shuttle to Grand Central. And there I wait for another uptown. My luck has been too good to last, so when a man wearing a Santa Claus suit — even though this is not the Christmas season — approaches me, I'm not surprised.

He grips a cup with a grimy white-gloved hand. "For the orphans," he says.

"What orphans?"

He peers at me over a squalid beard that looks like mice have made it their lunch. *"What orphans?"* he repeats, shocked.

"That's what I said."

"What difference does it make? Orphans are orphans."

"And you're Newt Gingrich."

"I certainly hope not." He waves the cup under my nose again. "So then?"

"Look, this isn't Christmas, you aren't Mr. Claus, and there aren't any orphans, so take your cup before I make it runneth over."

"I'm aghast," he says with an outraged sniff. "The disregard for those less fortunate than you is staggering."

"Are you an out-of-work actor?"

"English teacher," he says candidly.

"Sorry about that but I'm still not giving you any money. Why don't you be honest about it, stop wearing that stupid suit, and say it's for you?"

"Pride," he says.

"So, it *is* for you?"

He sighs. "Yes."

"Do you know what you're doing is illegal? Dressing up like that and asking for money for bogus orphans?"

"It is?"

"Of course. You could be arrested."

"My God." He whips off the beard, removes the hat. "Thanks for telling me."

It seems odd that an English teacher wouldn't know this. I hear a train in the distance.

"You may have saved me a jail term."

"Right." I take out a dollar and hand it to him.

"That's very nice, very generous. One question?"

I see that it's my train arriving and I'm relieved. "What?"

"Does the same go for a Batman costume and money for Bosnia?"

I want to snatch back my dollar.

He starts to cackle as he moves away from me. "Or how about the Easter Bunny and money for polio? Love your hat, see ya Thursday, honey." His mouth opens wide and I know he's howling with laughter even though the screech of my train drowns out the sound. I stop myself from running after him, board, and continue to watch him dance around the station, holding his sides as my train pulls out.

The ride is slow but no one tries to accost me in any way. I get off at the Hunter College/Sixty-eighth Street station, go up the stairs to the street, and head east. I've always considered this a fairly boring neighborhood. Not as bad as farther up, but less than interesting. Lisa Stein lives on Seventieth between First and Second. It's definitely clean in this area, I have to give it that. Still, the fact that I don't have more to say about it tells the tale.

Stein's building is a brownstone, four floors. Her bell indicates that she's on two. I ring once and she answers immediately, as though she's been waiting for me.

"Who is it, please?"

I announce myself. She rings me in. The stairs are carpeted in a pale blue and Stein stands on the first landing, hands on hips.

"It's about time," she says.

I'm taken aback. "I got here as fast as the subway would carry me."

"No. I don't mean that. I've been waiting for you since Ruthie was killed."

Lisa Stein's apartment is neat and small. And so is Stein. In fact, she's shorter than I, a disconcerting feeling for me. Her black hair has wavy gray strands that shoot from her head like broken watch springs. She's dressed in a polyester green blouse, cut low to show ample cleavage. Stein is wide at the hips and thick thighs hide under dark green slacks. Matching mules complete the ensemble.

"Sit down," she instructs, pointing to a couch draped with a well-worn canvas drop cloth.

"Thanks."

Stein, who appears to be well into her sixties, sits opposite on a dilapidated bentwood rocker. Her head is much too big for her body, the features large, as though she's been drawn by a cartoonist. Big blue eyes under plucked eyebrows blink at me. She uses heavy makeup, green eye shadow, carmine lipstick, and a layer of pancake.

"What did you mean, you've waited for me since Ruthie's death?"

"Well, maybe not you. But somebody." She opens the drawer of a spindle-legged walnut table, takes out a pack of unfiltered Camels. "Want one?"

I tell her no.

"My only vice." She lights up, using a gold Dunhill. I recognize its rectangular shape because I had one like it in the days when I smoked.

"I *have* tried reaching you before," I say. "You were never home."

"I lead a busy and exciting life." She laughs ironically. "I suppose you think I should have an answering machine."

I shrug.

"My *darling* children are always after me to get one."

"You don't like the children or is it just the answering machine?"

"Both. The answering machine I don't have to have; the children I'm stuck with. You have any?"

"No."

"Smart girl."

I'm tempted, because of my natural curiosity, to pursue the reason Stein doesn't like her children but I know that whatever the grounds they're not pertinent to the case.

"How long did you know Ruthie?"

"All my life."

"No kidding?"

"No kidding.

"We went through school together, from kindygarten, mind you. We were more like sisters than friends. Her own sister, Sylvia, was *meshuggenah*."

She's referring to Elissa's mother.

Says Stein, "You know about Sylvia?"

"I do."

"You're a friend of Elissa's?"

"Right."

"Then you know when I say *meshuggenah*, I mean *meshuggenah*."

"I do."

"Of course, Ruthie liked to rewrite history. To hear her tell it, Sylvia was a saint who had some bad breaks."

"I know." This drove Elissa up the wall about her aunt.

"Sylvia didn't have any worse breaks than Ruthie, who made a life — even if it wasn't a life I would of wanted for her."

This surprises me. "But she married well, didn't she?"

Stein rolls her head on her short neck from side to side as if to say maybe yes, maybe no. "It's the eye of the beholder, like always."

"Didn't you approve of Harold?"

"In a word, no."

I've never heard anyone say anything negative about this man and I'm intrigued. "How come?"

She squints at me, leans forward, propping a plump hand on each knee. "Never trusted him."

"Really? Why not?"

As she leans back into her chair, she blows a stream of smoke that rings her head like a crown. "Did you know about him and Sylvia?"

"Harold and Sylvia?"

"Not Harold and Maude, girlie. Harold and Sylvia. They had a thing. Ruthie never knew about it, as far as I know. At least, she never told me if she did. But the neighborhood knew. You couldn't keep secrets in the Bronx. I think denial was what Ruthie was in, only back then we called it 'head in the sand.' If the truth be known, Ruthie was blind about the whole crazy family. The sister was a saint, the nephew a genius, the parents from heaven, and the husband, perfection. Phooey." She spits smoke.

"Tell me more about Harold and Sylvia." I wonder if Elissa knows this.

"It was when Ruthie and Harold were first married, like in the second year, maybe. Under the guise of helping Sylvia with her finances, such as they were or weren't, he'd meet with her and they'd . . . what do the kids say? Oh, yeah . . . get it on."

"You mean they had an affair?"

"What's wrong with you, you don't speak English?"

"It's just that I can't imagine . . . Harold seemed so proper, so straight and narrow."

"*Seemed* is the operative word here, girlie. That was what he wanted everybody to think. But I saw through him for what he was. A snake. And the snake doesn't change his stripes, you know what I mean?"

"Tiger."

"What?"

"It's a tiger that doesn't change his stripes." Why am I doing this?

"I find it hard to think of Harold as a tiger."

"Whatever."

"Anyway, what I'm trying to bring out is, if a man cheats with his sister-in-law in the first two years of his marriage, do you think he'll be faithful later on?"

"Doubtful, I guess."

"My point precisely. You're wise for your age."

"Thank you. Now let me get this right . . . are you saying that you know Harold had other affairs?"

"Know? No. Maybe you're not so wise. How could I know? Things changed. They moved away and Harold became this big stockbroker. I couldn't keep tabs the way I did when they lived in the Bronx. But like I said, a weasel doesn't change his spots."

I use control and don't say *leopard*. "Did you continue to see Ruthie after they moved?"

"Of course. We never lost touch. Each week we'd go to a different Chinese for lunch. First, wonton and egg rolls. Then I'd have egg foo yung, she'd have chow mein, and we'd share. Rice came with. White rice, not this *farkocta* brown."

"And did Ruthie seem happy?"

"What else? Does an ostrich look and act unhappy? No, it puts on a happy face. And that's what my Ruthie did. On the other hand, if she didn't know, maybe she *was* happy. What am I, a doctor?"

"So she never even hinted that Harold might be seeing other women?"

"Not a *bissel* of suspicion. But he didn't fool me. I know the type. I should. I married one myself."

Oh, boy. Were these the ravings of a woman scorned?

"I know what you're thinking. You think I see all men as liars and cheats because of Jacob. That was his name, Jacob. Well, I don't. Just ask Myron."

"Who's Myron?"

"My boyfriend. Now *he* is a gentleman. You want to see his picture?"

"Maybe later," I say gently. "I need to know more about Harold right now."

"Naturally. Sorry to go off on a tangent. So, it's true that I was cheated on by Jacob but that doesn't make me a bra-burner."

"They never burned their bras." I've lost control.

"Who?"

"The feminists who were accused of that. It never happened. The media made it up."

"*Ach,* the media. Don't get me started."

"I won't." I don't tell her I have enough of that at home. Suddenly, I remember that for the moment I don't have it at home. Do I miss it? "Harold," I prompt.

"Harold. Most people thought he was a nice, quiet man, but not me. He never fooled me."

"So what are you getting at?"

"This is the trouble. I don't know what I'm getting at. I only know what I know."

"Which is?"

"Something stinks."

And something does.

Twenty

I sit next to Cecchi's bed. He's sleeping. Annette is taking a coffee break. The room is filled with flowers. The biggest and most beautiful arrangement is from Ruby Packard.

I always carry a book with me and I have Ellen Hart's latest open in my hand, but I can't concentrate. I keep thinking about what Lisa Stein told me about Harold.

Is it true that Harold had an affair with Sylvia, Elissa's mother?

Did Ruthie know?

Does Elissa know and should I ask her?

This last is the most troublesome, in a way. What if she doesn't know? If I ask, she *will* know, because Elissa's no dummy. I suppose I could disguise it somehow, be general in my question. But if she does confirm Stein's story, so what? Does it mean that possibly Harold was a regular Senator Packwood and there were other women in his life besides Ruthie and Sylvia; maybe a woman around the time of his death and . . . and what? An unknown woman killed Harold? Why?

I pick up Cecchi's phone and dial Elissa.

After checking on her state of mind I ask, "How well did you really know Harold?"

Says Elissa, "How well does anyone know anyone?"

I immediately think of Alex and the fact that Elissa has no knowledge of her in my life. No idea that I've kissed a stranger. Guilt, guilt, guilt.

"This is true," I say. "But you know what I mean."

"Why don't you just ask me what you want to ask me, Lauren?"

"Right. Did you ever hear anything about Harold's having affairs?"

"Of course."

I'm flabbergasted. " 'Of course'? "

"Yeah. What's the big deal?"

"And Ruthie?"

"What about her? They both had them."

"They did?" My chin almost hits my knees. I can't believe this, especially how casual Elissa is about it.

"Well, only together, I think," Elissa adds.

"Together?" Then comes the light. My mind goes immediately to a movie title: *The Catered Affair* . . . 1956, Ernest Borgnine and Bette Davis. There's a notion that Jews call events *affairs*. Maybe they do, I think.

"Elissa, I'm not talking about a bar mitzvah."

There's a thundering silence. And then a tiny "Oh."

"You get what I'm asking now?"

"I do."

"And?"

"Did Harold have affairs with women? *Harold?*"

She doesn't know, or it isn't true.

"I can't imagine that he did," she says. "Why?"

"Nothing really. Just an idea I had. Stupid." I'm not about to get into this, mention her mother, suggest that what Stein said is true. There are some things people don't have to know. If it's true, Elissa's having this information about her mother and Harold will do nothing to solve the case. Sometimes you have to make an ethical call.

"Did Harold have a double indemnity clause in his life insurance policy?" I ask her, without knowing why.

"He did. That's why there's so much money."

My heart does a conga. I thank her and hang up. If the policy was the usual, then an accident like Harold's would fit the double indemnity requirement. So what? So, maybe the woman Harold was having an affair with killed him. And maybe that woman was Vitagliano. So? She gained nothing by his death and only some jewelry by Ruthie's. Nothing adds up. I wish I could discuss this with Cecchi. Like magic, he opens his eyes.

"Lauren."

"Cecchi, you're awake."

"I am?" He smiles.

I laugh. "Annette's getting coffee."

"How am I?" he asks.

"How do you feel?" I skirt the issue.

"Look, I know I'm in trouble here. Tell me the truth," he says raggedly.

"What do you mean *trouble?*" I stall.

"Ah, Lauren, you were never good at this. Except when working. I mean, I'm hurt bad, right?"

I hate this. I don't want to be the one to tell him. But I hate lying to him more. "Yeah, you are," I say.

He shuts his eyes, says, "Finished? I'm finished with the Job?"

"No," I say truthfully.

Cecchi opens his eyes again, painfully turns his head to look at me. "Really?"

"You can go on working."

He waits a moment. "Desk?"

Now he has me. "Probably," I whisper.

"Shove that."

He turns away and closes his eyes, pretends to sleep. I know he's awake but I also know he doesn't want to talk about this or anything else. I close my book, push it into my purse, get up and leave. Right then, Annette returns.

"He woke up and asked me," I say.

She knows what I mean. "And?"

"I couldn't lie."

She puts a hand on my sleeve. "I understand. What did he say?"

" 'Shove that.' "

Smiling, she says, "I thought it would be along those lines."

I wonder if I should tell her my idea about Cecchi working

with me, then decide I ought to tell him first. "Something will work out," I say.

"Always does. How are you?"

"Fine. I miss being able to talk over my case with him."

"I miss being able to talk over my life," she says.

Of course she does. "He's on the mend, I think."

"Yeah. I guess."

What we both know is that the worst is yet to come. Cecchi out of it was bad, but Cecchi's awake and immobile is going to be horrendous. I kiss her cheek good-bye.

"So what have you been up to?" Kip asks from Michigan.

I feel myself flush and quickly tell her about meeting with Stein and about Cecchi's waking up. As I'm talking I'm positive she knows about Alex, even though this is impossible. "And you? How do you like it there?"

"It's okay. You sound funny."

"Funny?" Oh, God.

"Something wrong? . . . I mean, something more than the something we already know about?"

There's a moment when I don't know what she means and my entire body vibrates as though I'm in a Cuisinart. Guilt is a powerful thing. I could tell her about Charlie West to deflect what she might be thinking, but then she'd worry and I don't want that. Or she might come home and I don't want that either. This last thought takes me by surprise.

"Nothing," I say. "What do you mean, it's *okay* there?"

"I guess I miss you."

"You sound surprised."

"I am, you little runt. I thought I'd be glad to get away from you."

"Yeah, me too." I hope this is as ambiguous as I mean it.

"You too, what?"

Nothing gets by her. "Thought I'd be glad."

"Oh."

No wisecrack. Hmmm.

"Lauren, I think when I get home we should see a couples counselor."

"You do?" I'm stunned. Therapists never want to see therapists.

"Yes. We need help, darling."

Oh, God. Hideous guilt. "I guess we do."

"I'm glad you can see that. I know I can get a good recommendation but that might feel inequitable to you, so if you want to look for someone, you can."

"No. I think it's fine for you to look into."

A bump from above the living room startles me and I gasp.

"What?" Kip asks.

The sound came from our bedroom. My gun's in my purse on the chair. I walk over to get it.

"Lauren? Are you there? It sounded like you gasped or something."

"Sorry, honey. I just had a frog in my throat."

"Oh. Hope it doesn't turn into a princess."

"What do you mean?"

"Joke."

I fake a laugh. "Oh, right. Frog . . . princess. Very amusing."

"I can tell you're rolling on the floor."

Another bump. Louder this time. I jump. I need to get off this phone. "Kip, I have an appointment I have to get to."

"Really? Who is she?"

What is this? "I'll never tell."

"Just remember, toots . . . I'll be watching."

Jesus! "How could I forget?" I say, playing along. "I've really got to go now, Kip."

"I'll talk to you soon."

"Okay."

"Love you," she says.

"Me too. You. Bye."

I hang up feeling so guilty that I almost hope it's Charlie West upstairs and that he'll kill me. OHMIGOD. Maybe it *is* West.

Another thump. Now I'm really scared. I put my hand on the phone and pick it up. But wait. Where are Nick and Nora? I laugh out loud. Of course. It's one of them, or both, jumping off the bed. God, my guilt has me thinking . . . "Hi, Nick," I say as he saunters into the living room, looking macho. "Where's Nora?"

He opens his mouth and the usual squeak comes out.

"Upstairs, huh? Jumping on and off the bed, you say?"

Another squeak and then in comes gorgeous Nora. She meows normally.

THUMP!

"Liar," I whisper at Nick. It's evident that someone is upstairs. Someone who wants me to know that he's there. In my quaking heart of hearts, I know it's West. I have to call for backup. Quietly, I pick up the phone and put it to my ear.

"Hel-lo, Lauren," he says. I slam it down.

It's West on the upstairs phone. I cross to the door. I know I can make it out before he gets to me. But what about the cats? What if I leave and he hurts them? Now I don't know what to do, one hand holding my gun, the other on the doorknob.

I turn and walk to the bottom of the stairs to the second floor. Trying to think like a sociopath isn't the easiest thing I've ever done, but I know a little about how that kind of mind works. If I go up, he's got the advantage. If he comes down, I have the advantage. And he has all the time in the world because I can't use the phone in this apartment. I suspect that he knows I won't chance going up. West is probably counting on me to leave. And that's what I'll have to do.

Fortunately, the cats' carrying case is in a hall closet. As silently as possible, I go get it. The minute I have it out and open its door, Nick runs inside. Bless him, he's always been like this because he knows the case means he's going with me. Nora, on the other hand, hides. I close the carrier door, should Nick change his mind while I search for her. Seven hours later, inside the open back of a wooden magazine rack, I find her curled into a ball, her eyes the size of jar lids. When I pick her up to take her to the case she meows.

"Shut up."

She bites my arm and I stifle a scream. It doesn't actually hurt but it surprises me. I open the carrier's door and try to shove her in but she bends in the middle like a rag cat and the front of her is out again. We struggle while Nick sits at the back of the case purring. I love him so! After a lot of pushing and pulling, she's finally in and I snap the door in place.

Quietly, I make my way to our front door, open it, go out in the hall, and climb the outer stairs to William's apartment. I can see that the place is dark. I don't want to knock, because West might hear it, so I take out my key and hope I won't frighten William or find him in a compromising position.

When I put the key in the lock it sounds to me as if it's in Dolby sound, while Nora imitates the MGM lion. My hand trembles and I have difficulty with the key. I set the case on the floor, steady one hand with the other, and finally get the lock to open. I turn the knob and push slowly. Quiet. I pick up their case and go into William's, softly close the door behind me, and lock it. Relief floods me like soothing sun.

"William," I call in a loud whisper.

No answer. I snap on a light and walk toward the bedroom. I call his name again — still no answer, so I turn on the bedroom light. No one, thank God.

Back to the living room. I pick up the phone, punch in the number of the Charles Street police station, put it to my ear. It's not ringing. I turn it off, then on. Nothing. No dial tone. It's only then that I realize there hadn't been a dial tone on my phone either when West spoke to me. Sometime between my call with Kip and when I picked it up again, the bastard cut the lines.

Twenty-one

The outside phone lines are in a box next to our bedroom window, where there's also a fire escape. When West entered that way he must've seen them. I wonder why he didn't cut the lines then, before Kip rang me. I assume it was a mistake and her call, which he undoubtedly listened to, alerted him to his error.

What I must do now is clear: I have to leave the building to get help. Do I leave the cats here or take them with me? If West comes downstairs and finds me gone, will he think to come up here to William's? I doubt it. I decide to leave them.

After I turn out the lights, I slip out, lock the door, and tiptoe down the steps. Every creak sounds thunderous to me. When I get to the front door of the building I turn the knob slowly until it clicks open, then squeeze through and close it behind me. I do the same thing with the exterior door. To get to the sidewalk, I have to go up three steps. Once I'm there, if West is looking out the window, he can see me.

Incredibly, there's no one on the street. Where are all the creeps when you need them?

So that I'm not in view, I need to make my way to the corner by going over the iron fences that separate the houses. This is not my idea of fun or exercise. Every fence post has a pointed top, like a miniature spear, and if I fumble . . . well, I don't want to imagine what could happen. My purse is slung over my shoulder and across my chest, my gun within, so my hands are free. I grab hold of two of the hideous spikes and hoist myself up to a ledge, then jump. When I land on the other side the sound is earsplitting. I never thought two feet could make so much noise. After a moment, I start across the front of this house and the door opens. Neighbor. All I have to do is tell him what's happening and call the police from his phone.

"Whatcha doing?" he shouts.

"Shhhh." I put my finger to my lips.

"Huh?" Gallagher, a man in his sixties, has a hairline so far back that his head resembles a marble egg. Small eyes crowd the bridge of his colossal nose. We've been neighbors for years but we don't actually *know* each other except to say hello, which he doesn't do now.

"There's someone in my house," I whisper. "I need to call the police."

"Oh." He seems perplexed.

"My lines are cut," I explain.

"I have a date," he says.

This can't be happening. This man can't be saying this. "There's a killer in there. I have to use the phone."

"How do you know he's a killer?" Gallagher bellows.

"Please keep your voice down. I'll explain later."

He actually looks at his watch. "Hot date," he explains.

"Mr. Gallagher, please, I beg you. Let me use your phone."

"Okay," he says grudgingly. "But make it quick."

Once inside, he snaps on a light to reveal a living room overflowing with papers, magazines, cartons, and unidentifiable debris. I suspect this is why he stalled, not his "hot date."

"Maid didn't come this week," he mumbles.

I smile and nod. "Where's the phone?"

He looks around the room, then at me, puzzled. "Got to be here somewhere."

"Where is it usually?"

He points to the corner of the room. I go there, move aside some boxes to find the jack, then follow the cord, which is under an inordinate number of newspapers. Eventually, I uncover the phone and punch in the Charles Street Precinct's number. When it's answered I explain my situation and instruct them not to use sirens, because it might scare West away and I don't want that to happen.

Gallagher, who has overheard everything, says, "How come you got this killer in your house?" as though I'm depraved or have issued an invitation.

It's almost impossible not to answer this remark with a wisecrack, but the man did let me use his phone, so I control myself. "It's a long story."

"You said you'd explain," he whimpers.

"It's a guy thing," I say, irritated by his tone.

He stares at me. I pity him.

"Long time ago I put him away. Revenge."

"Put him away?"

"I worked for the FBI."

"You did?" His beady eyes grow as round as Lifesaver holes.

"Yes." I start toward the door. "Don't you want to go on your date?"

"I have time. I don't want to miss this," he says, following me.

Outside we stand close to the door, to remain unseen by anyone in my building. In a minute I hear them. Why doesn't it surprise me? They round the corner of Perry, sirens screaming. A blue-and-white and a prosaic Ford pull up in front of my house. I go to them, Gallagher at my heels.

A uniformed cop jumps out of the first car.

"You call?" he asks. Three others and two plainclothes detectives join him.

"Yes."

"You got a perp on the premises?"

"He's on the second floor." *Or was,* I think, *before you dorks turned on your sirens.*

After I unlock the doors they draw their guns as they enter. Gallagher brings up the rear.

"You can't come in here," I say to him.

"Why not? I let you in my house."

His petulance continues to amaze me. "Just wait here."

He does. But so do I after one of the cops orders me to stay in the hall while they go into my apartment.

Hours later they return without West. Surprise!

"Nobody in here."

"I told you not to use the sirens."

"Didn't tell me," a blonde cop says.

"I told the desk man."

"Cornwell? That dipshit. Hey, guys, she told Cornwell no sirens."

They laugh.

"Cornwell's a moron. Doesn't listen to anything. Sorry about that. But whoever was in there is gone. Let's go back in and you can tell me what was taken."

I follow her inside. "What's your name?"

"Detective Lent. And this is my partner, Gold."

He nods.

Says Lent, "I've seen you around, haven't I? You a friend of Peter Cecchi's?"

"Yes."

"I like him, he's a great guy. My name's Michele." She extends her hand to me.

We shake. She has wavy hair and skin as pale as a stripped stick. Her skirt is tan, her jacket blue with white buttons, a lighter blue blouse underneath.

"Yeah, Cecchi never gives me a hard time about being a woman. Those guys out there, phew. Not him though," Lent says, a nod toward Gold. "How's he doing, Cecchi?"

"He knows now how bad he's hurt."

"I sent him flowers," she says.

"That's nice."

"He'll be coming back, won't he?" she asks, a trace of anxiety in her voice.

"His call," I say ambiguously. "I doubt if this perp took anything."

She gives me a strange look and briefly I explain.

"Well," she says, penetrating blue eyes looking directly into mine, "we better see anyway."

"Fine." I lead them through the house to the upstairs. We

check out both bedrooms and the bathroom and, as I suspected, nothing's gone.

"You want me to get forensic in here? Check for prints?" Gold asks.

"I know it was him. I heard his voice when I picked up the phone."

"Yeah. Okay. You live here alone?"

"Not usually. Right now I'm alone."

Lent says, "Your husband away?"

"My partner, yes. She's gone for a month."

Neither detective bats an eye at my reference to a woman. This is the Village, after all.

"Maybe you should get somebody stay with you," Gold suggests.

My mind jumps to Alex. I can't believe my own chain of absurd thought. "I have friends in the building. Oh, God."

"What?" Lent asks, her hand to her gun.

"The cats. I forgot about them. They're in my friend's apartment."

"Gee, you had me going there." She removes her hand from the butt of the gun. "You want us to go with you?"

I'm about to say no but then realize West may've gone into William's instead of disappearing out the window and down the fire escape. "Okay, if you don't mind."

"Hey, that's what we're here for. To protect you." She gives me a big smile and if I were a different kind of person, I might think she was flirting with me. Then I realize I am a different kind of person and I *do* think she's flirting. I'm disgusted with myself.

"Thanks," I say, not flirting, and we go off to retrieve the cats.

A new list of Goldsteins, Martin, in New York City blinks at me from the fabulous screen of my new Ascentia 810N. With a sorting program I arrange them in the order of their addresses, beginning downtown, which means Battery Park City. I decide that phoning them will tell me little, and what

I should do is review each one in person. This is going to be one helluva job. The worst part will be looking over my shoulder all the time, West Watching.

Before I leave I check my E-mail and get this letter.

From: athomas@panix.com
To: laurenl@NWDC.com
Subject: Won't Rain On Your Parade
Dear Lauren,

I wish I could turn back the clock. What happened at your house was all my fault and I apologize. Yes, I know we already talked about this but I cannot stop feeling guilty. And I know we said we would continue with E-mail but I think we must stop because I cannot be responsible for what I might say. Maybe in another life.
Yours,
Alex

Am I crazy or is there a double message here? She apologizes for what happened but won't be responsible for what she might say? Puhleeze. And what does *maybe in another life* mean? Maybe in another life she'll write me? Maybe in another life we can be together? Maybe in another life what?

From: laurenl@NWDC.com
To: athomas@panix.com
Subject: Takes Two To Tango
Dear Alex,

I'm not sure why you're blaming yourself for what happened. It takes two people to kiss, you know. There, I've said it: kiss. Big deal. So it happened. So what? Aside from the fact that it was very enjoyable, I don't think we should make so much of it — especially not call off our writing to each other, which we both enjoy and agreed to continue. Are you into punishment or something? Why don't we just see what happens? I mean, let's continue to write. I hope you'll reconsider.
Best,
Lauren

I realize I've given her some double messages as well, but I send it anyway. I think about not seeing her again.

I hate it.

By one-thirty I've crossed off seven Goldsteins and put an NA next to six. I find myself in the Gramercy Park area and need to stop for lunch. This is a neighborhood I'm not totally familiar with. It houses the Gramercy Hotel, a park, and lovely brownstones which surround it.

On First Avenue I pick a restaurant that looks like it's been in business for a while. The inside is charming, wainscoting and wooden booths, and I hope the food matches the ambience. I take a small table near the back, look over the menu, and order a burger from a phlegmatic waitress with blonde hair heaped on top of her head like a sand castle.

My investigation so far today has been discouraging and I begin to question whether I'm going about this the right way. My thoughts of the Goldstein dilemma quickly shift to thoughts of Alex.

I realize that if she doesn't respond to me through E-mail, I have no way to find her. No real address. No phone number. I know she lives in the Village but that's it. What if she disappears from my life? This is ridiculous. I know where she works and I am a detective. I know ending this would be best, but I'm not ready to give up this flirtation, or whatever it is. I know damn well what it is: DANGER AND BIG TROUBLE.

The kiss we had lingers on and I can recall it anytime I want. As I think of it now, a feeling shoots through me that makes my body warm and tingly.

"You sleeping?"

I hadn't realized my eyes were closed. "Resting," I say.

"Here's your burger. I onct knew a guy could sleep anywheres, any position. Standing up, middle of traffic, ringside, didn't matter."

"Did he have narcolepsy?"

"Hell no, he never stole nothing in his life. Why would ya ask that? Sheesh." She walks away in a huff before I can explain.

My burger's done exactly as I like it: very rare, cheese melted, pickles on top. I dab on some ketchup, salt, and pepper and take a bite. Delicious. Then I think of Kip and the food doesn't taste quite as good. It's not the thought of Kip that turns it, but rather my guilt about her.

I've never cheated and I don't think she has either. I know this fascination with Alex is because Kip has been so absent, so uninterested in me. How long has it been since she's sent me flowers, taken me out to dinner, looked at me as though she cared? But why should I expect that from a long-term relationship? Romance diminishes, sex cools off — it's the way of the world. At least we haven't been casualties of Lesbian Bed Death. Oh, really?

It's then that I calculate the last time Kip and I made love, and realize it's been more than two months. This is unusual for us, as we've been on guard against LBD and have never gone longer than a week. Are we headed into LBD? Is this why I'm so interested in Alex Thomas? Or is it the fourteen-year itch? I have to face the truth . . . some part of me wants to have an affair with Alex. A big part of me. In fact, only a small part doesn't. That's the guilt part. But if I do, what will happen to me and Kip?

I've never known any lesbian — hell, any woman my age, who could have a sexual fling and leave it at that. We always fall in love, or think we do. If I believed I could make love with Alex, and have it be that and only that, I'd be tracking her down now. But I can't be sure that it wouldn't taint my relationship with Kip, that I wouldn't think I was in love. I'm already obsessed by Alex's kiss. What makes me think I can cross the sex line, make love with her, then go back to Kip? What makes me think I can't?

"Excuse me," the waitress says, slapping my check on the table. "I just have to say, I don't think it's right, you going around saying a person — or even asking if a person — you don't know is a thief."

"You're absolutely right," I say. "I was way out of line."

"Oh." She looks deflated. "Well, then, okay."

I laugh to myself. Maybe I'm growing up, defusing something before it begins by not explaining. Is this a first? I pay my check, leave her a nice tip, and go back out on the street. My next Goldstein is on Nineteenth, between First and Second Avenues.

It's a small building, four floors. This Martin Goldstein is on two. I ring.

"Yes?"

"Mr. Goldstein, my name is Lauren Laurano and I'm a private investigator. I —"

"I don't want any."

"Any what?"

"Whatever."

"I'm not selling anything. I'd like to speak with you, that's all."

"What about?"

"Ruth and Harold Cohen."

There's a long silence and my heart does a shuffle. I have a feeling I may have found my man.

"Do you know them?" I ask.

"Ruth and Harold Cohen?"

He's stalling and now I know I'm on target.

Silence.

"Mr. Goldstein?"

"Yes?"

"Do you know them?"

"Yes, I do."

Be still my heart! The words I've longed to hear. I want to dance, sing, shout. This is what it's all about, why I do this work. The rush I feel is unbeatable.

"May I come up and talk to you, Mr. Goldstein?"

There's an odd sound that comes over the intercom, as though he's speaking in the background to someone. Then his voice comes through to me.

"All right."

The buzzer rings me in. It's a well-kept building, azure blue carpet in the hall and on the stairs. A basket on a table holds the mail. I check through it very quickly and see names like Halm, Scully, Roberts. No Goldstein. Maybe he's already gotten his. I hear a door open above. I drop the mail and start up the stairs.

Martin Goldstein is waiting for me on the first landing. It's almost impossible to tell what he looks like, because most of his face is covered with a black beard and mustache shot with gray. Large, thick, tortoiseshell-rimmed tinted glasses hide the color of his eyes. He wears a black toupee which looks ridiculous.

Goldstein is a smallish man. He's dressed in dark gray slacks and a yellow cardigan over a light green shirt, buttoned at the neck. His shoes are brown Hush Puppies.

"What's your name again?" he asks, without greeting me.

I tell him. He nods and motions me into his apartment.

The living room is small and neat, furnished simply with couch, reading chair, television, and an upright piano. There are three closed doors off this room and at one end is a kitchenette with the usual half fridge, stovetop, and a wall-mounted microwave. Cabinets presumably house dishes and pots.

We sit across from each other, Goldstein in the chair.

"They're dead," he says flatly.

"Yes."

"So what can I tell you you don't already know you're an investigator?

"Are you aware that you're a beneficiary of Ruth's will?"

He raises sparse eyebrows. "No, I'm not. I mean that arrangement is only if the niece is deceased."

"Yes. Someone tried to kill her the other night."

"You think it was me?"

"You're the only one with a motive."

"And I look like a killer to you?"

"What do killers look like?"

"Not like me, this I'm sure."

"Actually, they might look like you. You or anybody. People always say that, 'Do I look like a killer?' and the answer is, there is no special look."

He crosses his legs, wipes off nothing from his knee, glances absently at one of the closed doors. I look in that direction, then quickly back to Goldstein.

"You're aware, of course, that Ruthie was murdered."

"The Granny Killer."

"So they say."

"But you don't think so?"

"Could be, but I'm not convinced."

He shrugs. "I only know what I read in the papers and see on the TV. That's what they said, the Granny Killer."

"When's the last time you saw Ruth?"

"Never," he answers promptly. "Harold never introduced us."

"Didn't you find that strange?"

Again, he shrugs bony shoulders.

I don't know what it is but there's something familiar about this guy. It's not that he looks like anyone. Maybe it's more to do with the way he shrugs. I can't quite get it.

"You did or you didn't find it strange?"

"Harold was strange, so nothing he did ever seemed odd to me."

Here we go again. "Like what?"

"Well, look at the way he died. That was strange, wasn't it?"

I find this a peculiar example. "But in life, Mr. Goldstein. What was strange about him?"

"I can't put my finger on it now."

This guy is holding something back. And he's nervous. Not only does he keep a steady rhythm with his right foot, almost toppling a stack of paperbacks on the carpet, but he glances over his shoulder again, then quickly at me.

I can't help but believe that there's something behind the middle door that Goldstein doesn't want me to see. Or *somebody*. I stand.

"May I use your bathroom?" I ask, walking directly to the door in question. But as I'm about to turn the knob, he stops me.

"That's not the bathroom," he almost shouts. He points to the right door with a quavering finger.

Inside I take a quick inventory. Towels, linens on a shelf; in the cabinet below the sink are extra rolls of toilet paper, soap. Carefully I open the medicine chest. It holds the usual, including vials of medication. But the name on one of them clobbers me:

M. Narizzano.

Twenty-two

I stare at the name on the bottle and stare and stare as the whole puzzle puts itself together. Maggie Vitagliano, née Narizzano, and Martin Goldstein killed Harold and Ruth. Goldstein was on that ship with Vitagliano (I need to check the passenger list again to see whom he signed on as) and threw Harold overboard.

Then they bided their time so it wouldn't look as though there were a connection, and when the moment presented itself, one or both of them killed Ruthie. Now they're trying to kill Elissa. And I'm in this apartment with one, maybe two (if Vitagliano is in the bedroom, as I suspect) killers.

I flush the toilet. I mustn't give Goldstein any reason to think I've copped to his plan or that I suspect him in any way. I'll behave exactly as I would if I hadn't seen the name on the pill bottle. Oh, sure. And how would that've been?

When I come back into the living room Goldstein's standing at his sink drinking a glass of water. He turns to look at me.

"So where were we?" I ask.

"You're the shamus," he says.

Shamus. "Read a lot of mysteries, huh?"

"They're a good escape."

"From what?"

He shrugs.

I let it go. "I think we were talking about how strange you thought Harold was." I force myself to sit on the couch again, although all I want to do now is get the hell out of here.

"Were we?" he asks absently.

"You said you thought everything about him was strange or something like that."

Goldstein puts the glass in the sink and walks toward me. I feel slightly apprehensive and, as surreptitiously as possible, put my hand under the flap on my purse.

He stops in front of me, then moves to his chair, where he plunks himself down with a grunt and a sigh. Again, I experience a sense of familiarity but can't identify it.

"Perhaps," Goldstein says, "that was somewhat of an exaggeration. Marrying Ruth Edelman was strange, we all thought."

This was Ruthie's maiden name. "Why, and who is *we?*"

"*We* is the Cohen/Goldstein families. Why, because she came from a different kind of background. They were Russian Jews. We were German Jews."

"I guess I don't understand the difference, other than the countries."

"No, you wouldn't, being an Italian. Or maybe you would. Are you Sicilian by any chance?"

"No." I see what he means because the Lauranos, who come from Rome, are all very snobbish about Sicilians. "Are you talking about a class difference?"

He sniffs. "Don't like that way of putting it."

"But that's what it is, isn't it?"

"They're just different from us, that's all. Look, is there anything else you want to know?"

Plenty, but this is my chance to get out of here. I rise. "No, thanks. I appreciate your cooperation. There are a few names I'd like to run by you, though," I add, unable to control myself. I dig in my purse, bump the cold comfort of my gun, and bring out the list of Ruthie's friends, including Maggie Vitagliano. I read the list to him. "Know any of those people?"

He pretends to mull it over. "No. No, I don't recognize any of them. Who are they?"

"Friends of Ruthie's."

"I told you I never knew her," he says, irritated. "Why would you ask me about her friends?"

"Just cross-checking," I answer, trying to make it sound sensible and important.

Goldstein looks annoyed, cranky. . . it's time to go. I hold out my hand to shake his. "Thanks again."

When he takes my hand I feel that the fingers are soft, the palm uncalloused. "Oh, what did you say you do, Mr. Goldstein?"

"I didn't. I'm retired. I was a businessman. Very boring."

I know he won't give me more than this, so I nod as if I sympathize with the inanity of his life's work.

He walks me to the door, opens it, and watches while I go down the stairs. He's still there as I exit to the street.

I want very much to look up at his windows, see if either he or Vitagliano is watching, but don't — because if I do and they are, this might be enough impetus for them to put me on their hit list. As it is, I'm not entirely sure I'm not there anyway.

I start toward Second Avenue. Funny, he never once asked whom I was working for. Almost everyone does when you question them. Is it because he assumed it was Elissa, or maybe he *knew*? Has Elissa told Vitagliano she hired me? I think it's time to have another talk with my client.

Elissa says, "Now I know how Benazir Bhutto felt."

"Meaning?"

"What else can you call this but house arrest?"

"You want to go out? We can go out."

"Oh, perfect. With my jailer I can go out."

"I'm not your jailer. I'm trying to keep you safe. You're a huge target right now."

"Is this a trick way of saying I'm fat?"

"Stop."

"But I am, right?"

"What?"

"Fat."

"You're always the same."

"Fat."

"Don't use that word or the PC Fat Police will get you. *Woman of size* is the term, I believe."

"That's what I am? A woman of size?"

"Elissa. I didn't say that. I'm just saying, no one's allowed to say *fat* anymore."

"*Fat?* You can't say *fat?* Can you say *thin?*"

"Good question. I don't know, but if you can't say *fat* you shouldn't be able to say *thin* and I bet nobody's PC about the word *thin.*"

"I like the idea of the Thin Police. But it would never happen. Don't you think things are getting a little crazy . . . I mean all these words you can't say anymore. It's like food. One day you can't eat things with fat, excuse the word, another day that same unspeakable word is good for you."

"I know. Can we change the subject now?"

"I didn't realize we were on a subject."

"Have you told anyone you hired me?"

"It's a secret?"

"Not necessarily. It's a secret for me . . . ethically, I'm not supposed to say whom I'm investigating for. You can tell anyone you want. So, did you?"

She thinks. "I probably told anyone I spoke to."

Great.

Suddenly, she begins to cry. I go to her, put my arm around her, and wait until she's ready to speak.

"I can't believe Ruthie's dead, Lauren. I know I used to complain about her sometimes, but I loved her."

"I know you did."

"She was more than my aunt."

"I know. She was like your mother."

"God forbid."

"I don't mean it that way."

"Yeah. I'm just trying to be funny."

"So you won't cry?"

She nods.

"It's okay to cry."

"There's so much death lately," Elissa says plaintively.

And this is true, so I have no response. It's not just Tom or

AIDS. Breast cancer, car accidents, heart attacks, mysterious deaths like our friend Diane's: she thought she had the flu on Sunday and was dead on Monday . . . the reason still not clear except that it was bacterial or viral.

But in my world it's mostly murder and for a moment I wonder all over again why I choose to do this. It can't simply be that I wish to make order out of chaos; there must be more to it than that. Even though this way of life, this career, was in some ways formed by circumstance, not every rape victim becomes a crime solver. I suppose if I went back into therapy, I'd discover the root of my chosen profession in the refuse of my childhood, but living with a therapist is bad enough. I don't want to think about Kip now.

Instead, I say, "Did you think you were going to breeze through Ruthie's death without mourning?"

"No, of course not. I'm really an orphan now. My brother doesn't count."

This is true. Even though Andy is still alive, with the way she feels about him, he might as well not exist. Ruthie was the last of the Edelman clan. Elissa never speaks of anyone on her father's side.

My mind jumps to my parents, damaged and alcoholic. Still, they are there and, as annoying and impossible as they sometimes can be, I don't feel alone in the world, as Elissa is feeling now.

"You do have Martin Goldstein," I suggest stupidly.

"I don't even know him."

"You want to meet him?"

"No. Should I?"

"I've met him," I say for an answer.

"Really? And?"

"I don't trust him." I decide it's unwise to tell her that I think he's trying to kill her.

"Meaning?"

"You haven't been in touch with him by phone or anything?"

"No, I told you I don't know the man."

"Have you told anyone about me who might have some connection to Goldstein?"

"Not that I know of."

"How about people who might know Maggie Vitagliano?"

"I don't know who she knows, but I told Maggie I'd hired you."

Of course she did. Why not? Naturally, this is the connection because Goldstein and Vitagliano are in this thing together.

"Have you heard from Maggie lately?"

"This morning. She's coming over" — she looks at her watch — "in about an hour for coffee."

"Why the hell didn't you tell me that?" I snap.

"Excuse me for having a life and not letting you know every breath I take."

"I'm sorry. It's just that . . ." I don't know what to tell her. And I'm also surprised, remembering Vitagliano told me she thought Elissa was guilty, that she'd call her and make a date. But the probable truth is, she didn't really think Elissa was guilty because she knew who was.

"Just what?" Elissa asks.

I don't want to alarm her. "I've been trying to find Vitagliano and she hasn't been at her loft."

"No. She said she's staying with a friend because she's too nervous to be alone."

Goldstein. "She didn't mention who, I suppose?"

"No. Why would she?"

"True."

"What's going on, Lauren? You know something?"

I have to tell her a little bit; she is my client. "I don't trust her. I have reason to believe she might have had something to do with Harold's death."

"Harold's death? How?"

This is not good, having your employer be your friend. My need to protect her is in direct opposition to my duty to reveal what she's entitled to know. "It's too complicated to explain now. Look, I want to be here when she comes over."

"You mean here here, or hiding here?"

"Hiding here."

"Not unless you fill me in."

"Do you want me to solve this thing or not?" I take an indignant stance.

"I thought you were trying to solve Ruthie's murder, not Harold's accidental death."

"I am. But I think they're connected."

"And Maggie had something to do with both?"

"I think so. Look, Elissa, when I first interviewed her she said she thought you were guilty, so why is she coming over now to make nice with you?"

"She thought *I* was guilty?"

"She said a lot of stuff, like Ruthie didn't approve of you and Deanna, that you stood to inherit, that —"

"Ruthie loved Deanna."

"I know. I didn't believe her but I didn't know why she was saying this stuff. Now I think she was involved in both Harold and Ruthie's deaths."

Says Elissa, "Wait a minute. You think Maggie is coming over here to kill me, don't you?"

"Could be."

"No way are you leaving here. Get in that closet."

"Elissa, she's not coming for another forty-five minutes or so."

"You can never get too prepared for a thing like this."

Elissa plans her Fourth of July parties on New Year's Eve.

"I don't have to get in the closet until the bell rings."

"Okay. But what if when I open the door she shoots me? Maybe you should open the door."

"Thanks."

"Well, you know what I mean. Maybe you shouldn't be in the closet, maybe you should be right next to me, behind the door. No, that wouldn't work, she could still shoot me. I think I should call her back and tell her not to come."

Something occurs to me. "She give you a number where she could be reached?"

"No."

"So how can you call her?"

"I can't."

"I don't think it would be her style to cold-bloodedly shoot you."

"Cold blood, hot blood, who cares? I think we should get the hell out of here."

"No."

"Bait. That's all I am to you. Nothing but bait."

In a way, this is true. "I promise you won't get hurt. It'll help to see what she does."

"Help? How can it help if I'm a corpse?"

"I'll be right here."

"You'll be in the closet."

"With the door ajar. She tries anything, I'm out of there like a bat."

"I don't know, Lauren." She wrings her hands.

"And I have some questions for you to ask her."

"Are you crazy? You think I'll be able to remember anything you tell me?"

"They're simple."

"It's my life that's on the line here."

"I know, but there are certain things I need you to help me with."

"Like what?"

"Like —"

The bell rings and we both scream.

"Who could that be?" Elissa says.

"One way to find out."

She tiptoes over to the intercom as though that way her caller won't hear her. "Yes."

"Hi," the voice comes back. "It's Maggie, darling, early I know, but I was so anxious to see you. Hope you don't mind."

Elissa looks at me, her eyes wide. I nod.

As she rings her in, I go toward the closet to secure my hiding place.

Twenty-three

I wait inside Elissa's closet, gun at my side. The door's open slightly so that I'm able to watch as well as hear.

Elissa ushers Vitagliano into the living room. She wears skintight black jeans, a pink shirt, and a tweed jacket.

They start with small talk and Elissa makes sure to seat Vitagliano where I can see her.

"Darling, how're you doing? I know *I'm* still in a state of shock. You must be a mess."

"*Mess* is a good word for it," Elissa says.

She's out of my field of vision, so I only hear her.

"You said you're staying with a friend. How come?"

Says Vitagliano, "As I told you, dear, I feel a little scared myself. Since you were attacked, there's always the possibility that this killer wants to get all of Ruthie's friends."

"I suppose. But it's more likely that whoever it is wants me out of the way for money reasons."

"Oh? You mean somebody stands to gain if you're dead?"

What a phony this babe is. She knows because I told her.

"If I die, then a cousin of Harold's inherits."

"Oh, that's right. I forgot for a minute. Your private detective paid me a visit and told me about that."

Hmmmm.

"It seems like a waste of money to me. What's wrong with letting the police handle this?"

"In case you've forgotten, they think I did it."

"Oh, that's ridiculous. I'm sure it's because you're convenient."

Elissa says, "Even though they haven't charged me with it, I'm their prime suspect. Where's Helen Mirren when you need her?"

"Who, dear?"

"Nobody. Never mind."

I have to keep myself from laughing.

"You want the truth, I think it's this cousin of Harold's who did it," Elissa says.

"Did you tell the police that?"

"Sure," Elissa lies. "And I told Lauren too."

"And where is he, this long-lost cousin?"

"I don't know. Never met him. Name's Martin Goldstein. Ever hear of him?"

"Why would I have heard of him?"

"Then Ruthie never mentioned his name to you?"

"Never."

"It's all very peculiar," says Elissa.

"I suppose it is. Funny that Ruthie didn't talk about this man."

"Actually, she didn't know him. Harold told her not to look for him or try to meet him. The lawyer who's handling the will explained that Goldstein will inherit if I die and somehow he'll know to come forward to claim the money. You knew Harold, don't you think that's weird?"

She pretends to think. "It's not like the Harold I knew."

"I'm confident Lauren will figure it all out."

"Has she found this mysterious Goldstein?"

"Yes."

Legs crossed, Vitagliano bobs a well-heeled foot. Alex would probably know the brand. *Stop.*

"Did she tell you anything? I mean, what did she think of him?"

"Nothing much. An ordinary guy, apparently."

Vitagliano gives an almost audible sigh of relief. "So she doesn't think he's the one who shot at you then?"

"I didn't say that."

"Well, what did you say, darling? I mean, what does your friend think?"

"I don't know if I should go into that, Maggie. So who're you staying with?"

I can't believe how well Elissa's doing.

"Oh, someone you don't know." She rises. "I guess I'd better get going."

Not too subtle.

"Want to leave me a phone number where I can reach you?"

"You won't believe this, darling, but she doesn't have a phone. Can you imagine such a thing? Drives me crazy but she's an odd creature and doesn't like, as she puts it, 'this modern world.' "

"And she's a friend of yours?"

Vitagliano laughs falsely. "I know. But we go back to high school."

She walks out of my sight, though I can still hear.

"I'll be in touch with you," Vitagliano says. "I'm sure your little detective friend will crack this thing."

This description makes me boil.

"I hope so. She's all I've got."

Oh, boy. Now they'll try to kill me too. There's more small talk, the sound of cheek kisses, and then she's gone. When I hear the door close I come out of my hiding place.

Elissa says, "So what was that all about?"

"She's checking to see how much we know."

"How'd I do?"

"Terrific. I have to go because I want to follow her. See you later."

"Am I still under house arrest?"

"It'd be better if you stayed in but I can't force you."

"Can I go out with Deanna, at least?"

"Daytime only."

"She works, you know."

"She's a therapist. They don't work." I'm out the door.

On the street I see Vitagliano cross Fifth Avenue and head uptown. When I get to the corner I stay on the west side, walk close to the buildings as she makes her way north. She doesn't seem the type to walk anywhere, so I'm surprised by this. At Eighth Street she takes a right. I cross and stay on the north side, slightly behind her.

Even this part of Eighth has changed: not junky like the block between Fifth and Sixth, but it's still lost some of its panache. The mutation of Eighth from an upscale, jazzy shopping street to a mall manqué is a microcosm of the whole city.

Vitagliano walks at a fast clip, as though she has a purpose. We cross University and at Broadway she crosses again, turns downtown. When she takes a left at Astor Place I understand. You can't get through directly, so the only choice is to go up to Eighth or down to Waverly. Either way, if you're going to Astor Place, it's a matter of doubling back.

I watch as she goes into the big Barnes & Noble. Although it's large, it isn't suitable for safe surveillance, so I check the time and wait across the street. Sometimes I go in B & N to see what's new, have a cup of coffee, read magazines for free, but I never buy anything, in deference to the independent bookstores in general, Three Lives in particular.

I don't believe that B & N, or the other superstores that are trying to crowd out the small guys, will create new readers. Although some might shop for the discounts, those who go to drink coffee and pick up people won't suddenly become book buyers. My feeling is that these stores are going to crash and burn. I only hope it won't happen *after* they've buried the independents.

A new wrinkle to living in NYC is the street smokers. People have always smoked on the street, but this is a different breed. These are the office workers who have to come outside to get their nicotine hit. You see them everywhere, huddled in the doorways of their buildings like outlaws. Puffing away next to me are two women, one with a high baby voice, the other modulated. I listen while I keep my eye on the door of Barnes & Noble.

HIGH VOICE: So I go, Larry, whose life is it anyway? And he goes, my mother's.
MODULATED: He's got a point, Daneva.

DANEVA: What kind of point?

MODULATED: It *is* his mother's life.

DANEVA: Whose side are you on, Cindy?

CINDY: Your side, naturally. I always hated Larry, you know that.

DANEVA: You never told me you hate Larry.

CINDY: Sure I did.

DANEVA: Why? I mean, what did Larry ever do to you?

CINDY: He lives. That's enough.

DANEVA: Oh, this is very interesting, Cindy. This is something I never knew. Something you never divulged before.

CINDY: I thought I told you. Larry, to my way of thinking, is scum.

DANEVA: Scum? Larry is scum to you, Cindy?

CINDY: What I'm trying to bring out is that he's not good enough for you, Daneva.

DANEVA: I can't believe this. Larry's your brother.

CINDY: So who knows better that he's scum? We gotta go back up.

DANEVA: Why didn't you tell me this before I married him?

The response is lost to me as they go into the building. It occurs to me then that if Cindy and Larry are brother and sister, then Larry's mother is Cindy's mother too. So the life that Cindy was referring to . . . what am I doing? Do I care?

This is what happens when you have to wait around. I hate surveillance. It makes you stupid. I check my watch. Vitagliano has been inside the store ten minutes. She's probably having coffee, eating a piece of cake or something.

Envy creeps over me at its petty pace. I have visions of brownies, blackout cake, even blondies — and then there she is coming out the door, a B & N bag dangling from her right hand. She walks east and I follow on my side of the street. At the corner she hails a cab.

I hate it when they do this, because of what I have to do. She gets her cab and I flag the next one.

When I get in I say, "Follow that cab." This is what I hate.

"You're serious?"

He isn't moving. "Yes, go."

"Is this *Candid Camera?*" He eyes me in his rearview mirror.

"That went off the air years ago. Now get going."

"Are you from *Sixty Minutes?*"

"No. You're going to lose them."

"*Eye to Eye* without Connie Chung?"

Vitagliano's cab has taken a turn and I know the game is up. I open the door.

"Hey, where you going?"

"You lost it."

"I put the meter on, you owe me."

"Tough." I slam the door.

He's out of the cab and in my face. I reach into my purse, pull out the Smith & Wesson.

"Do whatever you had in mind," I say. "I'd like a change."

His eyes widen. "You some kinda nut?"

"Yeah. Hazel. Now get back in your cab and beat it." I try to sound like Clint.

If this were a cartoon, steam would come out of his ears. It amazes me how quickly people get angry. "You owe me," he says, grits his teeth.

"Good-bye," I say.

Fortunately, he has the sense to see I have the power here. He doesn't like it but he gets it. When he pulls away, burning rubber, I replace my gun, walk back to B & N, and go in.

Only three cash registers have clerks. The second one I try remembers.

"Oh, yeah, just checked her out. Lemme think."

"Can't you look it up?"

"Nah, it's in the computer and I'd have to get permission. But I have a photogenical mind, so I don't need no computer to tell me what I already know."

"So what do you know?"

"Ummm. Lemme think."

I do.

A fortnight later, she brightens.

"Oh, yeah, she the one who bought a whole bunch of mysteries. Paperbacks. You want to know the titles?"

"Lemme think," I say.

"Huh?"

"Never mind." I don't need the titles. I know where Vitagliano's taking them. The stack of paperbacks next to Martin Goldstein's chair is *photogenically* in my mind.

Back on the street, as I walk toward my office, I have to dodge the latest craze. Rollerblades have overtaken New York. They skate on the sidewalk, while the bicyclers rule the street. There's no safe haven. Navigating here has become an art form.

The one that barrels toward me is a large man, sleek in all his protective gear: knees, elbows, helmet. And me? I'm here, nothing to protect me, ready to be a casualty. To lunge left or right — that's the question. It's up to the pedestrian because these bladers don't care any more than the bicycle brats.

He's almost upon me when I dart to the left. He goes by unscathed but I've bumped an older woman.

"Are you crazy?" she yells.

"Yes."

She looks at me from suspicious, shiny, cerulean eyes, white hair in tiny ringlets. "Yes? You're saying *yes* you are crazy?"

"Yes."

"Then you're not. You're just insensitive and rude." She twirls away from me and continues on.

When I finally get to my office building I take a long look around to see if West is anywhere to be seen before I go in. If he's watching, he's well hidden.

My office is the way I left it. I sit at my desk and think while I boot up my computer. So what do I have?

Suspicions.

It's almost certain that Vitagliano and Martin Goldstein are romantically together. There's the vial of pills in his bathroom with her name on it and the circumstantial evidence of the bunch of books she bought. But this is not proof of anything. Still, why is Vitagliano lying about knowing Goldstein?

Then I remember the passenger list for Harold's fatal cruise. I take it out of my desk and go over it. No Martin Goldstein. This doesn't mean anything, because he could have used any name. I put a red dot next to all the males who weren't with women who shared their names. There are only fourteen. *Only?* I could check out the names and eliminate people but I don't think it's worth the time. Not yet, anyway. I put the list away in my backup folder.

Then I dial into NWDC and when I connect I launch my mail program.

"Go fetch," I say.

I have mail. It's from Alex. My heart thonks. I log off, go back to the mail reader, and click open her letter.

From: athomas@panix.com
To: laurenl@NWDC.com
Subject: Isn't It A Pity?
Dear Lauren,

    I got your letter. I have to tell you that I am very glad you do not want to stop writing. I know I would miss it. Well, that is all I want to say. I am going to Lanciani's for a cup of coffee now because I cannot concentrate on work.
Yours,
Alex

I happen to know the words to "Isn't It a Pity." The time stamp shows that the message was sent only twenty minutes ago. Yes? No. Yes? No. I do it.

Lanciani's is on West Fourth between Perry Street and Bank. When I get to the storefront, which is all glass on either side of the door, I see her. She's reading a magazine, a cup of something on the table.

I still have time to leave, since she hasn't seen me, but even as I'm thinking this, I know that's not what I'm going to do. I like looking at her without her knowing.

Today she wears a dark blue jacket with a gray V neck underneath. It's all I can see from out here. Her long blonde hair touches her shoulders, one side almost shields her face from me. And then she looks up.

I jump.

She smiles.

I wave.

She motions me in.

I enter.

"Hello, you. Sit down," she says in a sweet voice.

I do. "You were expecting me, weren't you?"

She blushes. "I hoped."

"I shouldn't be here," I say.

"No, I guess not. So why are you?"

Something propels me to speak the truth. "I wanted to see you."

"Me too."

We're silent, neither of us knowing what to say. The waitress saves us. I order a cappuccino, no chocolate anything, because I know I couldn't eat in front of her.

She says, "What the hell are we going to do?"

I don't have to ask what she means. "I'm not sure."

"Have you ever done this before?"

"Done what?"

"Well, I guess that's the wrong way to put it. You've been with Kip for a long time and I was wondering if you've ever cheated."

"Is that what we're doing?"

"Almost."

When my coffee is set before me the foam spits and burbles and looks like a volcano to me because everything is magnified at this moment.

"I've never cheated on Kip, no." *But I wish to now* is what I want to say.

"I've never cheated on Sally either. But, of course, we haven't been together as long as you two."

"Do you want to cheat now?" I ask.

"This minute, you mean?"

"In general."

"It's not that I want to *cheat*, it's that I want *you*."

My heart does a trampoline jump, blood rushes to all my extremities because I want her too.

"Come home with me now," I hear myself say.

"All right."

I think I might die.

On the guest room bed we face each other, fully clothed. I can't remember this kind of fear but I move in and kiss her anyway. I experience the same excitement I did the last time. I let my hand stray over her breasts, down her body, between her legs. She groans and reaches out for me. Her touch is electric because it's new, because it's her.

Little by little we explore each other through our clothes until the moment comes when we can no longer stand it and begin to undress each other.

She's beautiful.

She makes me feel wonderful.

I love her skin, her body.

Fearful as I am, I ease into the moves I know so well, and then we're making love as if we've done this a hundred times.

Lying in my arms, she says, "I didn't know I could feel that way. You have no idea what passes for sex out there."

"What do you mean?"

"Well, no one has ever made love to me like that."

"Really?"

"Really."

"What about Sally?"

"We haven't had sex since the sixth month of our relationship."

"You've got to be kidding."

"No. And when we did, it was nothing like this. Do you still make love with Kip?"

"Yes. Let's not talk about them." Guilt hovers.

"You're right. I knew it would be wonderful with you. I've thought about it for so long. Ever since we first met."

"You mean years ago?"

"Yes. I've had a crush on you forever. But I never thought anything would happen."

"You're incredibly beautiful," I say.

"So are you."

She turns, her lips a moment from mine, and the next thing I know we're again in the magic of new lovemaking. My mind gives over completely to my senses, my body. Nothing else matters but Alex and me, me and Alex.

Twenty-four

She's gone home to Sally and I'm alone.

Hello.

What did I expect?

She didn't let me walk her to the door, so I lie in the guest bedroom, bereft. How can I feel like this about Alex? Still, there's a pain, an emptiness inside and it's familiar. I can't identify it, and why do I think it's more than meets the viscera? Because this longing is too soon. I hardly know her. Is this what Kip and Deanna, the therapists, would call *historical?* If so, we all know what that means: M-O-T-H-E-R.

I have a doctor friend who told me that when people are dying, no matter what their age, they do two things: grab their genitals and call for their mothers. I asked her whether anyone called for their fathers and she said she couldn't remember ever having heard that.

I'm almost tempted to phone Deanna (since I can't call Kip with this one) to ask her why I feel like this. But that wouldn't be too discreet. I suppose I could get in touch with Alana, my old therapist, and ask her. What would I say?

"Hi, Alana, I've just made love with a young woman I hardly know and she had to go home to her partner and I feel like my world has come to an end. Can you explain that?"

And she'd say, *"Lauren, you know your mother was never there for you, even though she was physically present. My guess is, for some reason, this experience mirrors one or more you had with your mother."*

Pyuck! Alex Thomas is NOTHING like my mother. I put the pillow over my head to block out these thoughts but, of course, it won't work. I know that Alex doesn't have to look like my mother, or have her personality or anything obvious. The fact is, she's unavailable. And it doesn't matter that I'm unavailable too. Actually, I'm not. At least, not at this moment. I hate this. It's a situation I've steadfastly avoided all my adult life, never knowing exactly why.

I move my hand under the pillow and feel something. It's soft. Fabric. I pull it out, hike myself up, and in the fading daylight see that it's a tiny garment of some kind.

"The Lindbergh baby lives!" I say to no one.

On the night table next to the bed, there's a black gooseneck lamp. I reach over and click the switch. What I hold in my hand is a small white cotton item of clothing. A T-shirt, but not a T-shirt. It has three white buttons down the front. The label is DKNY. Even I know this is Donna Karan New York. And I know it's Alex's because I'm one helluva detective!

I sniff it. Perfume, soap, something. Her smell. Again, the ache of abandonment dissects me and tears threaten. I curl into a ball, the shirt in both hands tucked against my chest.

It's the middle of the night when I awake, still clutching Alex's shirt. The mewing outside the guest bedroom has reached an all-time crescendo. I realize I've forgotten to feed them. I jump out of bed and say, as if to Alex, "Thank you for starving my cats!" Hey, whenever I can blame somebody else, I see no reason to take it myself.

On the opposite side of the street from Goldstein's apartment, I'm staked out in my car. Last night I finally went to sleep in my own bed with the Ns. And, though I hate to admit it, still holding Alex's shirt. Now I tussle with incredible, increasing guilt. What have I done? For one thing, I've crossed the sex boundary and don't know if I can cross back. Now that I've made love with Alex, will I be able to make love with Kip again? Will I want to?

Will I fall in love with Alex? Will I leave Kip? I can't imagine this. Alex and I have so little in common but I never thought I could make love with someone I wasn't in love with. Still, I don't want to lose Kip. Oh, shit.

Vitagliano comes out of the apartment building with a suitcase and stands, waiting. I'm glad I brought my car for cover, even if it is red, because it's hard to run a covert operation in the Gramercy area. Moments later Goldstein follows, also with a suitcase. My hand on the key, I watch, ready to roll.

They walk halfway down the block and stop next to a new black Saab. He clicks something in his hand and the car squawks, flashes its lights, and presumably unlocks.

The windows of my car are tinted so it's hard to see in. I had this feature installed for purposes of surveillance. I turn the key, the engine engages.

They pass me and I wait for another car to come between us before I pull out. The Saab turns uptown at First Avenue. Traffic is bearable and I'm able to keep them in sight without giving myself away. . . . I hope.

I suspect they're heading toward the Midtown Tunnel, which will take them to the Long Island Expressway. From there they can go to either La Guardia or Kennedy Airport.

We stop at a light at Twenty-eighth. Now I'm three cars behind them. From the cassette I've put in, Michael Feinstein sings "You're Mine." All I can think about is Alex. Images of our lovemaking pop up in my mind as though in a slot machine. I realize I can't listen to music, so I turn off the tape, switch to the radio and the news at 880. I will myself to concentrate on this chase, such as it is. The light changes.

When they turn right at Thirty-sixth I see that my suspicion is correct. Cars feed into the line from three sources, but eventually we are underground and the radio fades.

I hate being in tunnels, always afraid that the water will break through, even though I know this is impossible. I wonder what I should do if they *are* taking flight. If only Cecchi were with me or even on call. I suppose I could alert another detective but what would I say? I have no solid evidence to go on.

Six months later I see the proverbial light at the end of the

tunnel and we're out, threading our way onto the expressway. To concentrate better, I turn off the radio. After we pass
the La Guardia and Kennedy turnoffs, I'm relieved. Wherever
they're going, it's not by plane — unless, of course, it's a private
airfield. Somehow I doubt it.

I keep well behind them and try not to think my thoughts,
feel my feelings.

An hour and a half later (literally) we take the exit for the
Hamptons. There's traffic, I suppose because it's such a bright,
sunny day. This is good, as I remain hidden behind two cars.

Eventually, we drive through the towns and when we reach
Ridgehampton they take a right on Mecox Lane. I can't follow, because I would be the only car behind them, so I keep
going.

I pull up and park in front of a place called The Dandy
Kitchen.

The place is neither old nor new and has a counter with
stools and some leatherette booths. When I go to the phone in
back I'm amazed and thrilled to find a current book. I don't
know why I think this is going to be so easy, but I'm right. It's
under Narizzano. Seventy-four Werthem Lane.

If I go there now, I'll be seen as they unpack. Best to let them
settle in before I pick my stakeout spot. Automatically, I lift the
receiver to call Kip and tell her where I am and that I don't know
when I'll be home. Then it hits me. She isn't there. I don't need
to call her. Feeling dizzy, I replace the phone and take a stool at
the counter.

I haven't always called her in the past. Sometimes the situation has made it impossible, but when I can, I do. I think the
reason this hits me hard is that it makes me cognizant of what
life without her would be like.

I try to imagine calling Alex at our home. It doesn't play.

The man behind the counter, who is tall and large, with
a belly that spills over his belt like a laundry bag, asks me
what I want. I haven't looked at the menu on a board behind
him.

"Don't know yet," I say.

He grunts, moves away. I peruse the menu. Nothing much appeals. But I know I must eat something because there's no telling how long I'll be at this. I make a decision and keep my eyes on the counterman, trying to engage his glance. No small feat.

Although there are only three others seated here, and the counterman doesn't appear to be doing much but cleaning things, it takes about four hours before he comes back to me.

"I'll have a cheeseburger very rare and —"

"Whatcha mean by *very rare?*"

I want to ask him which word he doesn't understand, but don't. Still, I'm at a loss to describe what I mean. I want to say *very rare* over and over but know this won't get me anywhere. I try the negative.

"Not well done. Not medium. Not rare."

He stares at me, eyes like burnt bits of coal, uncomprehending.

"You know what I mean," I insist.

"Blue in the center?"

He even knows the terms, so this behavior must be because I'm a stranger. I don't like it blue in the center. "Not quite."

"Pink?"

"Between pink and blue," I try.

"Anything else?"

"Are the fries homemade?"

"Whatcha mean *homemade?*"

I can't believe this. "Are they frozen?"

" 'Course not."

"Then I'll have them. And a Diet Coke."

A snatch of a smile snakes over his lips. "Only have Diet Pepsi."

"Fine."

I can tell as he moves away that he's disappointed I'm not upset they don't have what I want. I can't believe summer customers are treated this way.

I hear the strains of music and then the unmistakable voice of Tony Bennett with the first words of "Just In Time." I swivel around and note the jukebox near the back, a woman in her fifties feeding it quarters.

Just In Time. Is that what's happened to me? Has Alex come into my life just in time? For what? To ruin my life? Or to bring me back to life? Because, of course, that's what the song's about. Was I dying? Perhaps wilting?

Alex Thomas's happening at this time in my life is no accident. But what is? Now if I can only remember that she's something I need, like a Band-Aid or a pick-me-up drink, instead of falling in love with her, this might work. Why am I so doubtful that I can pull this off?

The counterman slaps down my burger and fries and I think I should introduce him to Ruby Packard. I smile, thinking what a great couple they'd make.

"Something funny?" he asks aggressively.

I'm startled. "No, nothing," I say, as though I've been accused of stealing.

He grunts and adds the Pepsi to my fare.

I take my first bite and am surprised to discover it's very good. I glance at the exposed burger where I've bitten off what I'm chewing. A perfect very rare! And the fries are thin and dark, the way I love them. If it weren't for Barbra Streisand singing "How Long Has This Been Going On?" and the Pepsi instead of Coke, lunch would be a ten.

Werthem Lane looks sparsely populated. I decide to backtrack and hide my car in a copse of trees I passed on Mecox.

After I park and make sure the car is suitably camouflaged, I decide to stay off the actual road and make my way back to Werthem as surreptitiously as possible. There are spots along the way where I'm totally exposed and I pray that neither Goldstein nor Vitagliano drives by.

My luck holds and when I turn at their street, I'm able to continue in the same manner. Seventy-four is about a quarter of a mile in. I spot the number on the mailbox, which is in the shape of a barn. From my side of the road I can't see if it has names. What I can see is a dirt driveway that twists out of sight and is bordered on either side by trees. This is great for me, even though I don't know what I'll find at the other end.

I wait, listen for oncoming cars, then dash across the road to the right-hand side of their driveway. As I pass the mailbox, I note there aren't any names.

I hide behind the trees and check my ankle holster to make sure my gun didn't fall out during my sprint. Still there. It's quiet except for the sounds of birds and insects. I can't imagine how people live like this year-round. I'm overtaken with a longing for city noises, then immediately think of Alex. Funny, how almost anything can make me think of her. I push her from my thoughts, return to the job at hand.

Slowly, behind the trees, I make my way up the twisting drive. At times the growth is so dense that I can't see the road but I keep going, listening for signs of human life.

At last there's a collision of sparkle and gloom, a break in the trees where the house becomes visible. It's new and large, made of wood and lots of glass. I'll be easy to spot if I'm not careful. I hear the murmur of voices. They seem to come from what is the front of the house, the part not facing me.

I continue along the driveway but when it turns toward the garage I keep going straight until I find myself adjacent to what is clearly a front lawn. I peer through the trees.

Martin Goldstein is sitting in a white webbed lounge chair, reading a paperback book. Undoubtedly one of the mysteries Vitagliano bought him. He wears a tan canvas hat, a long-sleeved brown polo shirt, khakis. Sunglasses blank out his eyes. On his feet are dark brown boat shoes.

A door slams. A woman carries a tray and walks toward Goldstein. It's not Vitagliano. This woman is young, maybe in her twenties. She has hair the color of carrots and wears a bright patterned blouse and skirt. On the tray are two glasses. She offers them to Martin and he takes one, puts it on the table beside him. The woman moves to an identical chair, puts the second glass on the table next to it.

As she starts back toward the house, I hear the door slam again. Vitagliano comes into view. She holds the hand of a child, not more than three or four and of indeterminate sex.

Wordlessly, the women pass each other. Goldstein looks up, sees Vitagliano and the child, a smile cracking his face. He puts down the book, holds out his arms.

"Come to Daddy," he says.

Vitagliano lets go of the hand and the child rushes toward Goldstein.

"That's right, Billy," he says, "come to Daddy."

Billy hurls himself into Goldstein's arms, cuddles up.

Goldstein kisses the head of Billy, beams. He says to Vitagliano, "Did he have anything to eat?"

"Oh, Martin," Vitagliano answers as she sits in the other chair. "He just woke up. Venetia will bring out his snack in a minute." She sips at her drink.

The door slams again and Venetia appears. She carries what is probably the snack and starts toward Billy.

"No, Venetia," Vitagliano says. "I'll do it."

Venetia takes the plate from the tray, puts it on the table next to Vitagliano, and leaves.

"Billy, want your snack now?" Vitagliano asks.

"Yes," the boy says.

"Then come over and get it."

Goldstein says, "Go ahead, son. Go get your snack from Mommy."

Twenty-five

As I make my way back to my car, I reflect on the discovery that Maggie Vitagliano and Martin Goldstein have a child together. They have kept hidden not only their relationship, but the child as well. Why? If all were innocent, why the secrecy? But I know it's not innocent.

The fact that Vitagliano even knows Goldstein is suspicious. She must've known the terms of the will from Harold. Or perhaps from Ruthie. No. I have to remember that Maggie was onboard the ship from which Harold disappeared. And that she was booked under her maiden name, Narizzano.

Goldstein is going to inherit a fortune if Elissa dies. The motive for killing all of them is no mystery. I don't know which one did what, although I think Vitagliano had something to do with Ruthie's murder. And probably the attack on Elissa. I believe that both Goldstein and Vitagliano were responsible for Harold's death.

Vitagliano worked for Harold. She was probably privy to the terms of his will, sought out Goldstein, and enlisted him in this rather serpentine plot. Obviously, they had great patience, but not patience enough to wait for Ruthie to die a natural death. Certainly, they have to kill Elissa before she can write her own will, and not take any chances that she'll be convicted of her aunt's murder. At least, I think this is how it goes.

But there are holes. The biggest one is why Harold would've

left money to a man he didn't even want his wife to contact. This has to be meaningful, and I feel I know the reason but can't quite grasp it — as though it's the tail end of an elusive dream.

Thinking about their house and property, recalling the turned earth in a large garden, I now know why Vitagliano had a blister.

When I reach my car I decide there's no point in staying here in the Hamptons. I undo my ankle holster, throw it and my gun on the passenger seat, put the key in the ignition, start the car, and pull out from the group of trees onto the road.

Back on Mecox I head for the main road and the L.I.E. What's more important than anything is protecting Elissa. And, let's face it, I want to see Alex again.

Around exit 62, as I'm about to turn on the radio, I hear a familiar noise behind me. It's the unmistakable sound of a gun's being cocked.

"Don't turn around," a man's voice says.

My first thought is that somehow Goldstein and Vitagliano have found me out and have hired someone to do this.

"Even though I'm on the floor," he says, "my gun is right behind yer brains, so do what I tell ya."

Then I know, and something like a cold steel spike rends my gut. I recognize the voice from the phone, from over twenty years ago. Charlie West.

"What do you want, West?" I hear myself say, as though my voice is coming from a great distance.

"I want you, little girl," he says.

"I'm not a little girl anymore."

"Yeah, I noticed. Yer a big old dyke-whore now."

His words ping off the back of my head like poisoned darts. He's as crazy as ever and I know he's going to kill me. Funny, but I'm not scared in the way I thought I'd be if it ever came to this. My limbs feel light but my heart doesn't thunk or beat rapidly, it simply taps out my life as usual. Still, there's a watery feeling in my bowels and my breathing is ragged.

"Yer gonna do what I tell ya, understand?"

"Yes," I say, calmly. Because I *am* going to do what he says. I have no choice.

"Get off at the next exit. And don't try nothin' stupid, like reachin' for a gun, because I have nothin' to lose, get it?"

"Yes, I get it." I've never felt quite so serene, as though I'm in someone else's dream.

"I got a mirror down here, so I can see everything yer doin'. I see the exit comin' up, take it."

He's correct about the exit and I do take it. A million thoughts collide and I can't get ahold of any one thread. Within my feeling of helplessness, there's an odd sense of freedom.

As we get to the light, he says, "When it changes take a right."

Has he planned all this? How did he find me? Does he have someplace in mind where he's going to take me? And then what? Will he effortlessly put a bullet through my brain? Instinctively, I know it won't be that simple, that easy, that kind. Charlie West is not a kind man.

"Keep goin' until I tell ya to turn."

"All right," I say.

"You never thought I'd getcha, did ya?"

"No, I didn't," I answer.

He laughs, a sound like an assault weapon. "I knew I would someday. I been waitin' a long time for this, bitch. Okay, take the next left."

There's no doubt in my mind now, as we turn into a more residential area, that West knows where he's going, that he has some elaborate plan, some scheme that he's been hatching for years.

"At the end of this street, take a right and then another quick left."

I take note of the street names out of habit: Carlson Place, Wallace Avenue, Dunlap Street. I'm resigned to the idea that I'll never have a chance to remember and use them, but my training refuses to release me.

"Okay, halfway down this block yer gonna see number seven-seven-seven. Pull in the driveway there."

Out of obligation more than anything else, I say, "Whatever you're going to do, West, you'll never get away with it."

He laughs again. "Ever occur to you that just maybe I don't care about that part?"

Exactly what I thought and why my resignation has come so easily. Getting caught doesn't matter to him. It's the violent act that is paramount.

I see the number 777 on a small white house with green shutters and flip my signal even though there's no one behind me.

"Pull all the way up to the garage," West orders. "Turn it off."

I do.

"Just keep lookin' straight ahead."

I hear movement behind me as he rises from the floor.

"Stay put."

He opens the rear door and gets out. Idly, I wonder why I don't do anything. Is this what the Jews felt like in the camps? They knew what was coming but couldn't bring themselves to take any action, because maybe what they feared wasn't going to happen after all.

Is that what I actually believe? It is. I'm not resigned. I believe that somehow I'm going to escape this: I'll talk my way out, I'll outwit this maniac, I'll get rescued. Then, as quickly as I think these things, the other side takes over and I entertain doom.

He slams shut the rear door and opens mine. "Put yer arms in front of you and get out."

It's awkward, but I do as he says. I could kick myself for having taken off my ankle holster and gun. I'm unarmed and the bastard knows it.

"Keep yer back to me."

I don't understand why he doesn't want me to see him. If he's going to kill me, what difference does it make? And then it hits me. Maybe he's not going to kill me. Maybe he's going to torture, rape, and set me loose. I'm not sure whether I can handle this.

I think of Kip. I've never wanted her more than I do at this moment. Although I know it isn't true, I feel that she could save me if only she were here. Oh, Kip, I'm sorry. I love you so.

I'm disgusted with myself. My thoughts are those of someone about to die. But I *do* love her. What happened with Alex had nothing to do with my love for Kip. It was something else entirely. I shouldn't be thinking about this now; I should be trying to make a plan, find a way out — something.

"Okay." West interrupts my stupid contemplation. "Walk toward that back door. I'll be right behind ya, so don't try nothin'."

Is this where West lives now? Once I'm inside that house, all is lost. What if I make a run for it? But run where? There is a small backyard surrounded by a chain-link fence with no obvious egress. The only way out is to turn around and run through West to the street, and that's impossible.

But how can I let him march me into the house, into my coffin? It occurs to me that if I refuse to move, he probably won't shoot me right here in the open driveway, with another house to the right. And if he does, it will be a matter of sooner rather than later, so why not take a chance?

"You hear me?" West growls.

He doesn't nudge me with the gun, so I figure it's in his pocket or by his side, but he leans his body close to mine and I feel his fetid breath ripple my hair.

"Yes, I hear you," I stall.

"So move, bitch."

And I do.

I whirl on my left foot as I lift my right and bring my knee up hard into his crotch. He yells and doubles over as I chop the nape of his neck with the side of my hand.

West goes down and I run toward the street. I don't look back. When I get to the avenue I take a right, keep running until I come to another street, where I turn right again. In the movies people can run forever but I begin to feel the inevitable pull on my lungs. I try to ignore it and keep on. Two more blocks until I have to stop. I look behind me. He's not there. I'm in front of a house that has a brick bottom and a white shingled top. I take the five steps to the stoop and lean on the bell.

The door flies open and a woman says, "What the hell?"

"Please let me in. I'm being chased by a maniac," I beg breathlessly.

She stares at me. "How do I know *you're* not a maniac?"

"You don't, but please believe me. Look," I say, holding out my hands, "I don't have a weapon. I don't even have a bag, because he has it. Please let me in."

She bites her lower lip, thinks. "Oh, God, I know I'm being stupid, but all right." She pushes open the screen and steps aside.

I scurry in. "Close the door, quick."

She does and stands with her back to it, flattened like a cartoon character. "What now?"

"I need to use the phone."

With a trembling hand she points.

"Thanks." When I get to the phone I'm not sure whom to call. Normally, it would be Cecchi.

I dial 911.

A male voice answers.

I say, "There's an emergency at seven-seven-seven Dunlap Street. Please send a car there immediately."

"What's the emergency?"

"A man is trying to kill a woman. I'll meet the car and explain."

"What's your name?"

I tell him.

"Phone number?"

I tell him. "Look, send a car now or he'll get away." I hang up before he can ask me anything else and hope they do what I requested. I punch in the number for the Charles Street Precinct.

"What now?" the woman asks.

I take her in for the first time. She's probably my age but looks older . . . she does . . . and has pineapple-colored hair piled on top of her head like tropical vines gone crazy. Her face is crimped, creased like an old bedspread, and she wears a pink polyester exercise suit.

"Who're you calling now?"

"My local precinct. They know about this case."

"Case? It's a case?" she says, frightened.

"It's okay." I hold up a hand when the call connects. I realize I don't know whom to ask for and then I remember Michele Lent.

Surprisingly, she's in, and I tell her my tale.

When I finish she says, "I think you should stay where you are and I'll come out there with my partner. Give me the address."

The thought of waiting with Pineapple Head is not my idea of how I want to spend my time. "I'm at some woman's house," I whisper softly.

"Gotcha."

"And I've called nine-one-one," I add. "They're sending cops to the site. I said I'd meet them there."

"If we're not there when those guys leave, go somewhere else and we'll pick you up. Now what's the address of the crime scene?"

After I give it to her she says, "Ask the woman for the name of some public place for us to rendezvous."

The woman gives me the address of a coffee shop, which I give Lent, and we hang up.

I say, "Could you drive me to the Dunlap address? The local cops should've arrived by now."

"But what if the maniac is still there?"

"He won't be. And if he is, he'll be arrested."

"What if the police haven't come yet?"

"I think — excuse me, but what's your name?"

"Susan. You can call me Susie."

"Thanks. Susie, I don't want you to be afraid, because we'll be in your car and when we get near I'll put my head down and you can see whether the police are there. If they're not, we'll keep going. If they are, there's nothing to worry about. Okay?"

She mulls this over. "If they're not and we keep going, where will we go?"

"We'll go to the coffee shop. Susie, trust me."

"This is the worst thing that's ever happened to me in my life," she says.

If this is true, I wish I had her life. On the other hand . . . "Susie, get your keys and let's go."

She does and we do.

Twenty-six

My car is gone and so is West. The local police would not let me into the house at 777 Dunlap. However, now that I've met up with Lent and her partner, we're going in. Lent has had to argue with the area's top cop, but she's prevailed.

Inside, it is a veritable nightmare. Especially for me. There are pictures of me all over the walls. They range from ten years ago until the present.

The idea that West has been watching me all this time is so unnerving, so devastating, I feel faint. And I'm not a fainter. Lent puts her arm around me.

"You okay?"

"I guess."

"Want to sit down?"

We look at each other and start to laugh because the living room is empty, with the exception of a dirty mattress on the floor.

"I'll pass," I say.

"Don't blame you. Want to go back out to the car?"

"No, I'll be okay." My P.I. instincts overcome my personal trauma and I want to see the rest of the house. Lent has put in a call for a forensic team and we're careful not to touch anything. There's also an APB on my car and West. I hope they find the car but doubt West'll be in it. They're also checking where I'd been parked, to see if they can find anything to lead them to West . . . perhaps his car.

The kitchen is filthy. Dirty dishes, pots, and pans are everywhere. The fridge has little in it, but what's there is growing mold, and a half-full milk carton gives off the sharp smell of dead fish.

A third room is barren. We go upstairs. There are two small bedrooms, both empty except for accumulated dust, and a bathroom with a sour stench and yellowed sink, tub, toilet.

Back downstairs I can't keep from looking at the pictures of me again. Some are with Kip, some with Jenny and Jill, one with William and Rick, two with Elissa. It occurs to me then that West might have killed Ruthie, and tried to kill Elissa, the whole Goldstein-Vitagliano connection a red herring. But somehow I can't buy this; it's too complicated, too impossible, for him to orchestrate.

One of the pictures of Kip and me was taken about nine years ago and it shocks me to see how young we looked. A kind of longing invades me and I'm not sure whether it's for Kip or for my younger self. And how much does this have to do with Alex? Alex. I can't think about her now.

The forensic team arrives and we're able to leave. I'm glad to get out of this dank place, this depraved lair.

I sit at my desk and stare at my computer screen as I read the letter from Alex.

Dearest Lover,
    Where are you? I have been trying to reach you all day. I am afraid to leave any messages, because you never know. Are you regretting what happened between us? I hope not, because you made me feel so wonderful. I do not think I have ever felt like that before. I know I have not. Where are you? I still feel your touch on my skin, your kiss, your mouth. Please do not cut me off now. I need you and I think you need me. Where are you? I want you. I must have you. Please call me.
Yours,
Alex

There's no denying that her words thrill me. And no matter what, I have to write back or call her. I don't know what to say, what to do. I'm afraid if I speak to her, I'll see her again. I'm afraid I'll never see her again. I need to talk to someone about this. Elissa's the obvious candidate but I don't want to burden her. On the other hand, it might give her something to think about besides herself and her situation.

Still, telling anyone is a total betrayal of Kip. Or is this some stupid lesbian law, like taking off my wedding ring when I made love to Alex? I could tell Jenny and Jill. No, this would be an even worse betrayal. William's no good either. Suddenly, I know the perfect person.

Cecchi is awake, and although he's weak, he can think and talk. I've told him everything. His hound-dog eyes look sadder than ever but I know it's due to his condition rather than mine.

"It doesn't have to mean the end for you and Kip, Lauren."

"She'd never forgive me," I say, not sure this is true.

"You want to see this Alex woman again?"

This Alex woman. It sounds so odd, almost out of a forties film. "I do want to, Cecchi, that's the problem."

"I don't see the problem. You already did it with her, so what difference does it make if you do it again?"

I weigh this. "It doesn't, I guess, but it seems like it does."

"Like a bigger cheat?"

"Exactly."

He laughs lightly, because it hurts. "Lauren, once, twice, a hundred times. You already cheated. You think Kip's gonna ask you the number?"

"She might. And it could make a difference."

"I don't think that's what you're afraid of."

"What then?"

"I think you're afraid of getting more involved with this Alex."

He's right, of course. I nod.

"Is she really competition for Kip?"

"We don't have much in common."

"Then it's a sex thing?"

I'm a little embarrassed talking to him about this. "Women don't have sex things."

"Who says?"

"I never have. I don't have any friends who have."

"Maybe this is a first for you."

"It's hard to believe."

"You feel in love with her?"

"No. In lust."

"There. See?"

"But I'm afraid if I go on with it, I'll fall in love. You know the joke about 'What do lesbians do on the second date?' "

"No. What?"

"Rent the U-Haul."

He smiles. "Well, the way I see it, you have two choices: you see her or you don't."

"Oh, thanks, great wizard," I say.

"Look, you say you don't have much in common and she's, what, ten years younger than you?"

"Thirteen."

"Thirteen. I can't see you setting up housekeeping with a kid like that. I still think it's a sex thing."

"You don't understand. Women just don't have sex things."

"Yeah, they do," he says, a plaintive air to his words.

"Why do you sound like that?"

Cecchi presses his lips together for a moment, then says, "I know up close and personal that they do."

"You had that with a woman?"

"No. Annette had it with a guy."

"Before you were married, you mean?"

He slowly shakes his head. "Nah. Two years ago."

I'm shocked. "How do you know?"

"I'm a detective," he says. "And she told me. I already knew but she told me when it was over. Said it was pure sex."

"Weren't you jealous?"

Cecchi says, "You bet. I wanted to kill the guy. But she explained to me that I'd been sort of ignoring her and she met this bozo and he turned her on and made her feel wanted again."

"You believed her?"

He gives me a look. "Shouldn't I?"

"Sure. Of course," I reassure.

"See, I think it's the same with you. Kip's been out of it since Tom died. You don't feel wanted, needed."

"That's true."

"I know it's true."

"How?"

"You told me plenty of times, one way or another."

"I guess."

"And this Alex makes you feel desirable. *Desirable* is the word Annette used."

I say, "It's the right word. Alex makes me feel that way. Says and does things that Kip used to."

"See?"

"But any long-term relationship changes. Nobody can sustain that honeymoon feeling, those romantic impulses."

"Not true. You need to make an effort, that's all."

"Is that what you've done with Annette?"

"I try."

It occurs to me that if Kip knew . . . maybe . . . no, not a good idea!

"And everything's okay between you now?"

"Yeah. Good as these things go. I try not to let my feelings go underground now. We talk more and stuff." His eyes close.

"You tired, Cecchi?"

"Yeah, a bit."

"God, I'm sorry."

"Hey, no. I'm glad you told me. Makes me feel useful."

"You'll always be useful to me."

"They told me official, Lauren."

I experience a frisson of fear, say nothing, wait.

"Yeah. Desk duty for this old warhorse if I stay with the department."

"I'm so sorry, Cecchi."

"Yeah, well. Guess I'll have to find a new career."

It's time to present my idea to him. "Cecchi, it's occurred to me you might want to do just that."

"'Maybe I can be a brain surgeon.'"

"Not enough thrills and chills. How would you like to be partners with me?"

He opens his eyes, turns his head, stares at me. "A P.I.? Me?"

"Why not? My requirements are different from the NYPD's. You could be on the street as much as you want. And we've always been great together."

"It'd never work."

"Why not?"

"What about the billing?"

I laugh. "I thought about that. We wouldn't have to call it either 'Cecchi and Laurano' or 'Laurano and Cecchi.' We could come up with something else."

"Like what?"

"I don't know yet. But think about it. Think about joining me and a name."

"You serious?"

"Sure."

"I'll think about it," he says grudgingly.

"Good. I better go now, you need some sleep."

"Yeah."

"And Cecchi, thanks for the advice. I really appreciate it."

"Anytime. Don't worry about betraying Kip with me; I betrayed Annette with you. Mum's the word on both."

"Right."

I lean over and kiss him on the forehead. "I love you, warhorse."

I start for the door but he stops me by saying my name. I turn and look at him.

"Love you too."

I phone her from the street.

"Alex?"

"Hello, you."

"Sorry I worried you. I've been on a case."

"I guess I should get used to that, huh?"

"Yes," I say. "Get used to it."

Twenty-seven

I have spent the morning with Alex. I think I'm obsessed. I know this can't be love. When Kip comes home, I'm sure I'll give up Alex. I don't tell Alex this but I think she knows. Besides, she's in her own relationship which, though dissatisfying, she doesn't want to leave. We both know that whatever we have together is finite: one or both of us will suffer when it's over, but it will come to an end.

I think Cecchi's right. This is a sex thing. Something I didn't believe I was capable of, but see now that I am. I like Alex, find her charming and funny but not someone I could build a life with. Besides, I have my life with Kip and though it may be in tatters now, I know we'll work things out. Why is it that I don't believe this completely? Why am I afraid I've crossed some line and won't be able to cross back? This is based on past behavior — but I'm older and wiser now, so who knows what will happen? Anyway, I live in the moment, or try to.

Nick and Nora are sitting on the kitchen table staring at me as if they know.

"Why are you looking at me that way?"

Nick opens his mouth but no sound comes out and Nora flops onto her side in a fetal position.

Thank God they can't talk.

"Keep your opinions to yourself," I say. "We shouldn't even

be thinking about her when we have something far more serious to think about."

Nick gives the tiniest of squawks.

"That's right. Charlie West."

My mood plummets. How am I going to go about my daily life with him on the loose? He's gotten into my house, my car, and my office without being caught. And am I afraid? In a word, yes. I could get out of town, but what good would that do? I know West would find me. Besides, I have a job to do and Alex to see. Alex. Am I putting her life in danger? Probably. But she knows this and has made the choice to see me.

It's my life I have to worry about. I think of any possible precautions I can take and come up empty. With the exception of going out armed for battle and keeping my eyes on double alert, there's not much else I can do. This is a nightmare.

The phone rings and I'm afraid to pick it up, because it might be Kip. So I let the answering machine take the call. It turns out to be Michele Lent.

Lent says, "Screening your calls, huh?"

"Yes. I'm afraid it might be West," I lie.

"I have good news and bad. Which do you want first?"

"Good."

"We found your car."

"Bad?"

"It's been totaled."

"Oh, Christ. And West?"

"He wasn't in it. In fact, it looks as though he purposely wrecked it, probably jumped out at the last minute." She gives me the details but all I can think about is how I'm going to tell Kip. She loves that car and the insurance will never cover the cost of a new one. Money will rear its head again and we'll be into one of our things.

"What're your plans today?" Lent asks. "You gotta be careful, you know. West is still out there and he's gonna try to get you again."

I feel her words like a skewer in my belly. "I know that. I was just thinking about it, but I can't stay home."

"No, I'm not suggesting that. Unfortunately, I can't give you any protection, but be aware."

"I will be; I always am."

She's silent, because as we both know I hadn't been aware yesterday, when West hid in my car and captured me.

"I'll be extra vigilant," I assure her.

"Good. Well, we're still looking for him. I'll let you know. And if you need me, call."

I thank her and we hang up. I have to get to work. There's still one friend of Ruthie's I haven't interviewed and although I don't think it'll be meaningful or helpful, because I believe the answer lies with Goldstein and Vitagliano, protocol says I should at least try to meet with Harriet Weiss.

Weiss lives on Sullivan Street between Prince and Spring. This makes me happy because it's lunchtime and I'm ready for a sandwich from Melampo Imported Foods, the little shop of horrors.

I've given it this sobriquet because of its owner, Alessandro Gualandi. When one thinks of him, Mussolini comes to mind. He runs his shop with an iron *focaccia*. Entering this SoHo store is to take your life in your hands. Still, the sandwiches are worth it.

A small line has formed leading up to the counter where Gualandi presides. Vivaldi plays in the background. I'm not afraid. I know the rules: don't touch the wares, don't get out of line, and don't ask for things not on the menu. But others aren't so lucky, don't know the drill. Like the woman who is two in front of me.

She steps slightly out of the line and touches a bottle of sauce. Two out of three mortal sins.

Gualandi, who is tall and bearded, with a long nose and big eyes, comes from behind the counter and grabs the woman's arm.

"You want to touch the merchandise?" he screams at her. "Huh? You need to feel it up?"

She stares at him as though he were a lunatic, which, in his way, he is.

"Out," he says. "I want you out." He takes her by the arm, pulls her to the door, opens it, pushes her through, then closes the door, locks it, and goes back behind the counter, continuing to make the sandwich he'd begun.

The rest of us are all cognizant that we've experienced a Melampo moment, deli dread, and each is glad he/she is not the expelled woman. In fact, we feel privileged, as though we're the best kids in class.

Even though I've been fully trained in ordering here, I experience a tiny amount of apprehension when my turn comes. I ask for a Roxie. This is a chicken breast and sun-dried tomato sandwich on *focaccia* bread. I would love some eggplant dressing on it but I know this doesn't go with the sandwich, and requesting it would definitely get me expelled.

Gualandi wears a dark-blue billed cap and a full blue apron over his white shirt, and while he builds my sandwich he looks at me with a strange little smile as though he knows a helluva lot more than I know. I wonder if he knows who killed Ruthie and where Charlie West is and what will happen with Alex and me and me and Kip.

We make our transaction and I leave without incident. My feeling of accomplishment is enormous. I walk over to a bench on Spring where I decide to eat and people-watch.

These are some of the people who go by during my repast: two teen boys who wear baseball caps backwards, jeans so large that the crotches come to where their knees must surely be, enormous sweatshirts with FUCK YOU on one and EAT MY SHIT on the other (very nice); a tall man with hair dyed platinum, a pierced nose, ears, and tongue (which I see because he licks an ice cream cone) who is dressed in a T-shirt that says DON'T BLAME ME, I VOTED FOR BUSH (hard to believe) and skintight purple leggings; three women speaking French; a woman who reads *The Bridges of Madison County* while she walks; a black woman and a white woman holding hands; someone dressed like a chicken; a woman with blue hair in serious spikes, jeans so shredded that the amount of remaining material is negligible, a yellow T-shirt that says DENIAL IS NOT JUST A RIVER IN EGYPT (love this); and three local ladies who are all shorter than me, all wear black dresses, all talk at once. I won't bother to list the weird ones.

The building Harriet Weiss lives in is a tenement and I guess she's lived here for many years. The name on the bell says ARTHUR & HARRIET WEISS. I bet with myself that Arthur is no longer alive. I push the bell and am surprised that it works and that there's an intercom system.

After I explain who I am and what I want she lets me in. I climb three flights to Apartment 4C. A woman, who I assume is Harriet, stands in the doorway.

She's small, frail-looking, and wearing what used to be called a housedress. It's shapeless, with pink diamonds on a field of yellow. As I get closer, I see that she must be in her seventies, her skin's loose and mapped with lines like a system of estuaries. Two dabs of rouge adorn her cheeks, her lips bright red. And she's black.

"So you're a detective?" she greets me.

"I am." I extend my hand. She takes it. Hers is dry and warm. "Thank you for seeing me."

"Why shouldn't I see you? Ruthie was my friend. Come in, come in."

I follow her into the kitchen, which is typical of these apartments. A yellowing Formica table is centered on four plastic and chrome chairs, one on each side. In the middle of the table is a bowl of fruit. It looks so perfect, I wonder for a moment if they're wax, but instinctively know that Harriet Weiss wouldn't have fake fruit on her table.

"Sit," she says. "You want something to drink, eat?"

"No, thanks."

"So let's get the black bit over with, all right?"

I feel myself flush.

"Oh, don't be embarrassed, it's a natural thing. With a name like Harriet Weiss, you wouldn't expect an old black lady. The thing is, I was named for Harriet Tubman. But then I met Arthur Weiss, who was, of course, a Jew and white."

"Have you been married a long time?"

"We were. He's dead."

"I'm sorry."

"Thank you. I loved him. But as you might guess, neither family was happy about our union. Today it happens; back then it was very unusual."

"I guess so."

"So shall we get down to the business at hand?"

I smile at her.

"I know, I know. You think I talk funny. I mean for an old black lady who married a Jew."

"Well, I —"

"I graduated from Howard University at the age of eighteen. I was a prodigy. Bet you didn't know there were black — I guess I should say *African-American* — prodigies, did you?"

"I have to admit, I've never thought about it."

"That makes sense."

"Did you know Ruthie for a long time?"

She nods and her face grows sad, like a closing flower.

"How about Harold?"

"I knew them both since about 1954."

"How did you meet them?"

"We were all Communists back then . . . so it was at a party meeting. That didn't last long — the communist thing, but we stayed friends."

I know about Ruthie and Harold's fling with communism through Elissa, so this doesn't come as a surprise. "Then when Harold's accident happened, it must have been a loss for you too?"

"The thing is, I don't think it did."

"What do you mean?"

"I don't think it happened."

"You don't think *what* happened?"

"I don't think he fell overboard. The man didn't die."

I feel woozy. This is what I've been holding beneath the surface, and to hear it verbalized is heady stuff. Still, there's a lot left to be explained.

"So if Harold didn't die, then what?" I ask.

"He lived."

"But how?"

"Wits. By his wits. No one ever said Harold was dumb."

"But they searched the ship."

"So?"

"They didn't find him."

Says Harriet, "Did I say he took up residence on the ship? He didn't die. He lived. And he still lives."

"Are you saying that somehow Harold got off the ship to safety?"

"That's what I'm saying. And I'm saying more."

"What else?"

"I'm saying he killed Ruthie."

"Harold killed Ruthie?" This is too fantastic even for me. "But why?"

"You're the detective, not me."

"What is . . . was there about Harold that makes you think he'd do something like that?"

"The philandering."

So here it is again. Harold and his women. But even so, what Weiss is suggesting is quite complex and byzantine.

"I don't quite get it, Mrs. Weiss."

"Call me Harriet. I know it seems bizarre, but I'd bet my savings — which are considerable, believe it or not — that Harold killed Ruthie." Her eyes fill with tears.

"But if he's still alive, what would he gain by killing Ruthie? Not money. Her will states that Elissa inherits."

Slowly, Harriet Weiss looks up at me, wet shaggy lashes blinking. "And if Elissa dies?"

"Martin Goldstein."

"And who, pray tell, is he?"

"A cousin of Harold's."

"A cousin nobody ever met or heard of. Ruthie had no idea who he was."

"What're you getting at, Harriet?"

"You know anybody who ever laid eyes on Martin Goldstein?"

I contemplate my answer, then decide to go with it. "Yes. *I've* seen him."

"You have?" She's visibly surprised.

"Do you know Maggie Vitagliano?"

"Wait . . . tell me about Goldstein."

"I've met him and talked to him."

"You mean he really exists?"

"Yes."

"I have to admit, I'm shocked. This makes things confusing, to say the least."

I ask her about Vitagliano again.

She nods. "I met her over the years. I won't pretend I liked her."

"Any special reason?"

"A feeling. I always thought she was Harold's mistress and after he supposedly died, she seemed too solicitous of Ruth. Now, this Goldstein, can you describe him?"

I realize that this interview is turning around, as though Harriet's the detective. Still, I do as she asks.

"A beard," she says, almost to herself. And then smiles and looks me in the eye.

"Yes," I say, "a beard," and smile too, because I know that Harriet Weiss and I are thinking the same thing. But most of all, I can't believe I didn't make the connection sooner.

"You know what, Harriet? You're a genius."

"I know," she says.

Twenty-eight

Telling someone that her uncle is not dead, when for the past five years she's believed he was, isn't easy. But I feel it'll be improved by a cappuccino and a piece of mud cake. Let's face it, most things are.

I arrange this by having Elissa and Deanna meet me at Raffaella's. I know that Elissa'll be safe because no one will try to kill in broad daylight with Deanna.

When they arrive, Elissa looks radiant. I've told her nothing except that she's temporarily released from house arrest.

"A free woman. I can't believe that I'm at large . . . no, I didn't say I *was large,* I said *at large.*"

I laugh. "I know what you said."

Deanna says, "You have some news, don't you, Lauren?"

She always knows things like this. "I do. But why don't you order something first?"

"Who could eat at a time like this?" Elissa asks.

"*You* could," I say.

"You're right. I'll have a cap and a piece of cheesecake. Deanna?"

"Regular coffee, nothing else."

I hail the waiter and give him the order.

"One thing," Elissa says. "Is this a celebration?"

"It depends on how you want to look at it."

"How I want to look at it is that I'm not going to jail."

"You're not going to jail."

"And I'm not going to be killed?"

"Not that either."

"Then this is a celebration, kid. See, Deanna, did I hire a smart P.I., or what? How'd you do it, Lauren?"

"Is there a happy ending here?" Deanna asks.

"Me not dying or going to jail isn't happy enough for you?"

"Of course. But I don't think it's that simple."

"Deanna's right."

"What now?"

The order arrives and we wait as the waiter sets things down. While this happens I make a change in my plan. It's not exactly fair to Elissa but I feel it's the best way.

I say, "Will you excuse me a minute? I have to make a call."

"What're you doing, trying to torture me?"

"I'm sorry but I just realized . . . I'll be right back."

I go to the phone, dial Detective Lent, make my plan with her, and return to the table.

"So tell," Elissa says.

"I'd rather show," I say.

They look at each other, then back at me.

"I know I said I'd tell you something but it occurs to me now that I'd rather show you something and have *you* tell me."

"Games? You want to play games?"

"No. It's not that. Have your coffee and cake." To Deanna I say, "Could you get your car out of the garage and pick us up here?"

"Why not?" When she finishes her coffee she leaves.

Elissa says, "You wanted to speak to me alone, is that it?"

"No."

"Lauren, please. Now that I'm facing you, I see that you look different."

"Different how?"

I pray she doesn't use her ESP, or whatever she has, on me. She might just come up with Alex.

"More alive or something. I was beginning to worry about you."

"Meaning?"

"I know I've been self-involved, but not too much gets past me, you know."

I blush.

"What's that?"

"What?"

"The red face."

I shrug.

"You think I don't know?"

Ohmigod. "Know what?"

"Aha! So there *is* something to know."

"Now who's playing games?" I recover.

"It's not a game. I know you and Kip are in trouble and I also know that isn't all. So who is she?"

"Who is who?" For this reading, I should win an Oscar. Inside, my heart's cascading.

"You're seeing someone, aren't you?"

"You mean, like a girlfriend?" I ask, incredulous, and hope Elissa's not viewing a name on my forehead, as she did once with another person.

"Not *like* a girlfriend. A girlfriend."

"Are you crazy?"

"No. So, who is she?"

"There's no one."

"That's who you called before, isn't it?"

"No." At least this isn't a lie.

"No? So who'd you call then?"

"Oh, look, there's Deanna in the car."

Saved. For the moment. I know it won't end here, because when Elissa thinks she knows something, she's relentless. Like Jenny. Why are my friends like this? At least William's not that way, and even if he were, he's preoccupied with Bobby.

I pay the check and we leave. Elissa sits in the passenger seat, I'm in back.

"What now?" Deanna asks.

"Get on the L.I.E. and I'll direct you from there."

Elissa says, "We're going to the beach?"

"Right."

"Why?"

"Wait and see. And don't try to read my mind."

Elissa turns to look at me, with an all-knowing, all-irritating expression.

"No, that'd be too dangerous, wouldn't it?"

I pretend I don't understand the reference. "It's not a matter of danger, it's the element of surprise that's important."

"Yeah, well, I know somebody who's going to be surprised," she says, not too arcanely for me.

Deanna says, "I'm lost."

"We're not even out of the Village and you're lost?" says Elissa.

"I meant in this conversation."

"Drive," Elissa says. "So we're going to the beach. Tell me this much: North Fork or South?"

"South."

"Well, anything's better than sitting around that house."

I've had Deanna park where I parked the day before. Then I've led them, grumbling and stumbling, to the spot behind the trees, where we have a good view of the yard at 74 Werthem.

I know they're home because the car's in the driveway but there's no one in the yard. We've been waiting half an hour or more.

"This is a nightmare," Elissa whispers.

"It'll all make sense in the fullness of time," I say.

"How full does it have to be?"

"Trust me."

"Nightmare."

Seven days later Vitagliano comes into the yard with the child.

Shocked, Elissa says, "That's Maggie."

I put a finger to my lips. "Wait."

"Who's that kid?"

Deanna says, "Be quiet."

And then Goldstein joins them.

Elissa claps a hand over her mouth, her eyes wide with disbelief, and I know I've hit a home run.

"What is it?" Deanna whispers, taking in Elissa's expression.

I shake my head at her. We turn back to watch the scene in the yard. It's totally domestic, sweet if you didn't know the truth.

I whisper into Elissa's ear. "Are you willing to go into the yard and confront them?"

Her face is white, like sailcloth. "I can't," she says.

"We're safe, trust me."

Deanna says, "I wish you'd tell me what's going on."

"You'll see soon enough," I tell her. "What do you say, Elissa?"

"I can't believe this. All right, what the hell? I owe it to Ruthie."

"And yourself," I add.

I push through the bushes and they follow. We're in the yard before either Vitagliano or Goldstein notices. When they do, he jumps to his feet and she clutches the child to her.

"What're you doing here?" he demands. "Get off my property." I can tell that when he sees Elissa he knows he's in trouble.

"You have no right," Vitagliano says without conviction.

We walk closer to them. I suspect they're unarmed, but I'm not. I keep my hand inside my purse.

Goldstein stares at Elissa as he pulls down his sunglasses from atop his head.

Elissa says, "That won't help, Harold."

Vitagliano chokes back a gasp.

"Who?" Goldstein tries.

"You think I don't recognize you?" says Elissa.

Says Deanna, "Harold? This is Harold?"

"Who are *you*?" he asks.

"Your niece and you know it."

"Maggie, call the police," he says.

She doesn't move but looks at him with a mixture of fear and contempt.

Billy pulls away from his mother and runs toward us.

"No, Billy, wait," Goldstein/Harold says.

I grab the kid and hold him in front of me, my arm loosely draped over his small chest. "Don't be afraid," I say to him.

"I'm not," he says.

"Good."

Elissa says, "Harold, who's this boy?"

"This is Harold?" Deanna says. "But Harold's dead."

"Who is he, Harold?"

"My son," he answers with pride, unable to help himself.

"And Maggie's his mother," I say.

"She is? Is that true, Maggie?" Deanna asks.

Vitagliano nods.

"I can't believe this," Elissa says. "You didn't die on the boat. What happened?"

Deanna says, "Then where did he die?"

"He didn't," Elissa says firmly. "This is Harold right here. This person who says he's Martin Goldstein is Harold Cohen."

"He is? I don't get it."

"Deanna, you don't have to get it. Just be quiet."

Harold says, "Let Billy go. Let him come to us." His voice quavers.

"I don't think so," I say.

We watch as Maggie sinks back into her chair. It's then that Harold pulls a gun from the small of his back. He's faster than I.

"Let Billy go," he demands.

"Drop the gun." It's Detective Lent, who's been hiding behind her own tree with her partner.

"Thank God," Elissa says.

I say, "I told you it was safe. Thanks, Lent."

"No problem. Goldstein, or whoever the hell you are, drop the gun."

He does.

Detective Gold says, "Now walk away from it, go closer to the woman."

Again, he does what he's told, his shoulders in a dispirited slump. When Harold is standing next to Maggie, Gold goes over, picks up the gun.

"You have to understand, Elissa," Harold says. "Ruthie could never have children."

"And you have to be kidding," she says righteously. "To think I actually sat shiva for you, wept, comforted my Ruthie. I despise you, you putz. You killed her, didn't you?"

"Why don't you shut up, Harold?" Maggie spits out.

"And you," Elissa says. "You've been in on this from the beginning, haven't you? It wouldn't surprise me if it was you who got Harold off that boat."

"Nice going, Elissa. She was on the boat, and her husband, Orlando Vitagliano, just happened to have a big yacht where they put Harold. By the way, Maggie, whatever happened to that husband?"

"He went back to Italy," she says.

"How strange that he'd do that after you promised him a third of the money. Actually, I heard he met an untimely death."

"You don't know anything," Maggie says.

"Guess what? I know everything." I don't, of course, but I will. They were good guesses.

"Let's go," Lent says. "I don't want to cuff you, because of the kid."

Harold says, "What about Billy?"

"We'll take him to a shelter," says Gold.

"No," Elissa says. "We'll take him."

"We will?" Deanna says, horrified.

"Yeah. I think we'd better."

"We'll work something out," I say. "Let's go home now."

"Billy," Elissa says, "you come with us, okay?"

His mouth puckers and his eyes fill. "I want my mommy."

Oh, Christ, I think. The four words that never end. *I want my mommy.*

Vitagliano, who has to accept what's happening, says, "No, Billy. I'll see you later. You go with these nice ladies for now. You do that for Mommy. Be a good boy, all right?"

He presses his lips together and nods fast, the way children do.

Harold, head bowed, says nothing.

Elissa holds out a hand to Billy, who first eyes her with suspicion, then cautiously takes it. "We have a bit of a walk," she says to him.

Deanna says, "I'll get the car and bring it here."

"Oh, right."

Says Lent, "I'll fill you in later. Good working with you, Laurano."

"You too." I get the feeling she'd like to take Cecchi's place with me. This is okay because I'm going to need a liaison, with or without Cecchi as a partner. But it's certainly not Gold's idea of heaven. He gives Lent a scathing look.

Elissa says, "Billy, you want to play a game until the car gets here?"

"No," he says. "I hate you."

And Elissa thought it was a nightmare before.

Twenty-nine

We all sit around William's living room. Elissa and Deanna, Susan and Stan, Jenny and Jill, Annette, Bobby, and, of course, William. Billy is asleep in the bedroom.

William tends bar, dispensing drinks as though this were actually a party. Maybe it is. Anyway, he always likes a party, so he enjoys it. When they all have what they want and William's seated, they look to me.

"I feel like I'm in a detective novel," I say.

William says, "Should we call you 'Poirot' or 'Marple'?"

"You're so retro," Jill says.

"One doesn't read all the modern things you do."

"Well, we *have* gotten beyond Agatha Christie," I say.

"Oh, don't fight," Bobby begs.

The rest of us laugh.

"This isn't fighting," Jenny says.

"This is having fun," says Susan.

Stan, Susan's husband, says, "You'll get used to them, Bobby. It took me a while, but I finally caught on to the insult-as-love syndrome."

"God, we sound awful," Annette says.

"We sound terrific," says Jill.

"Could we have the explanation?" Elissa asks.

"Give her the envelope, please," Susan says.

"Okay, okay. It's complicated and devious, but simple."

"Oh, great."

"Swell."

"No, really. This is what happened: Harold fell in love with Maggie and he also wanted children, which Ruthie couldn't have."

"And," Jenny says, "he had no money."

"Yeah, right. I guess nobody ever has enough money," I say. "The thing is, he knew that an accident would mean double indemnity and Ruthie would inherit everything. So he, Maggie, and her husband, Orlando, planned the whole thing. Harold, with Maggie's help, got off the cruise ship and onto Orlando's yacht. Of course, Orlando didn't know about his wife's relationship with Harold, or that she was pregnant with Harold's baby. And he thought he'd be cashing in too."

"But Harold and Maggie had other plans for him," Jill says, getting into it.

"Exactly. It was easy to get rid of him — read, kill him — and then say he went back to Italy."

"What if someone checked?" Bobby asks tentatively.

"Good question."

He beams, feels part of us.

"In case someone did," I say, "Harold took a trip to Italy using Orlando's passport. So there's a record of his leaving the U.S."

"And you knew this?" Deanna asks.

Oh, how I wish I could say I did. "No. Not that part. Not until now. Meanwhile, before all this took place, Harold planned for it by telling Ruthie about this fictitious cousin and how he wanted his money to be left to him. He knew he'd be taking on the identity of Martin Goldstein."

"And, Ruthie being Ruthie, Harold knew she wouldn't ask him a lot of questions," says Elissa.

"Right."

"Are you saying that Harold killed Ruthie?" Deanna asks.

"I'm afraid so. When the Granny Killer came to light he and Maggie saw an opportunity even though Ruthie wasn't quite the right age. It seems Maggie has a cousin on the NYPD and she got details about how the guy killed his victims."

"And Harold tried to kill me too?" Elissa asks.

"No, that was Maggie. And that's it. See what I mean? Simple."

"But how'd you figure it out?" Bobby asks.

"I have my ways," I say.

Everyone groans in unison.

"Okay, okay. I had my suspicions. I never thought Ruthie's killer was the Granny Killer and I knew Elissa didn't do it. So who'd have a motive? Only Martin Goldstein. Then there was the business of Harold's falling off the boat, which I also never bought. When I found out Maggie was on that trip under her maiden name, well, I knew they were my prime suspects, but I couldn't put it together.

"Then there were Ruthie's friends whom I interviewed. One of them made me see that Harold wasn't the person everyone thought he was.

"When I finally found Goldstein and went to his apartment, I was pretty sure he was involved with Vitagliano and that made me concentrate on them. I followed them and saw them together with Billy and I knew they were lovers, or married, and had this kid."

"And are they married?" William asks.

"No."

"I always knew Maggie was a tramp," Elissa says.

We laugh.

"Harlot!"

"Strumpet!"

"Trollop!"

"Hussy!"

"Very funny," Elissa says. "Go on, Lauren."

"I still didn't know Goldstein was Harold, although something nagged at me. Then when I interviewed the last of Ruthie's friends, she said things that brought my buried thoughts to light. In fact, I was almost positive at that point.

"Taking Elissa to see him was the final piece. The rest is history."

Elissa says, "Thank God those detectives were there."

"I wouldn't do anything like that without backup. I told you it was safe. That," I say pointedly, "was the phone call I made from Raffaella's."

She looks properly chagrined and I pray this puts her off. "So why couldn't you tell me the police would be there?"

Deanna says, "The element of surprise. Right, Lauren?"

"That was one reason. Also, if I'd told you cops were going to be there, you would've freaked out."

"No, I wouldn't."

"Yes, you would," says everyone but Bobby.

"That's what I said, I would've freaked out," Elissa says.

"I thought if Goldstein really was Harold, you'd know," I say.

"I'd know him anywhere. Beard, glasses, mustache — nothing could fool me. Oh, poor Ruthie."

We are silent, contemplating the horror and sadness of it all.

Bobby breaks the silence. "I guess the motive is always money or sex, isn't it?"

I say, "Almost always. Just the way it is in relationships that go bad."

Suddenly, I feel everyone looking at me. "What?" My heart takes a dive.

No one speaks.

"One wonders," William says, "if those two elements, or one of them, might be the cause of your trouble in paradise."

"I thought we were talking about the case."

"Is there more?" Susan asks.

"No. Except Elissa is a very rich woman."

"We know that," Jill says. "What about Kip and you?"

"What about us?"

"What's going to happen?" Jenny asks.

How can I answer this? With lies and deceit, naturally. "She's going to come home and we're going to go on with our lives."

Deanna says, "I think you should go into couples counseling."

"So does Kip. But I think we'll be fine. We have a few problems and we'll work them out."

Silence.

"Well, at least the murder's solved. Everything pales by comparison, doesn't it?" says Bobby, who knows nothing — and why should he?

"Exactly," I say.

"Cecchi and you are going to be partners and you and Kip are going to work things out, so there's nothing to worry about," Annette states.

"Nothing," I concur.

Right. Nothing except Alex, the mess of my fourteen-year relationship, and not least of all, Charlie West . . . and the fact that he wants to kill me.

Thirty

When I come downstairs from William's, gun drawn, I carefully inspect every inch of our apartment. Charlie West, unless he knows of a hiding place I don't know, is not in residence. There are three messages on my machine.

I play them back:

"Hi, you," says Alex. "Give me a call if you come in before nine. Bye."

It's after eleven. I'm both sorry and relieved. The second call:

"Lauren," says Kip. "It's about nine-thirty. Haven't talked to you in so long. You're never home, so I guess you're having an affair. Just kidding. Call me when you get in, no matter what time . . . well, as long as it's not two in the morning. Love you."

I feel faint. *Just kidding,* she said. But I know her. Some part of her thinks this is true. Third call:

"Hel-lo, ya disgusting dyke," says West. "Ya got away once but yer not gettin' away the next time. And there *will* be a next time, don't think there won't. See you in the funny papers, bitch."

It's amazing but I prefer his message to Kip's. Almost. I sit there for a while contemplating whether or not to call her back. If I don't, she might continue to have suspicions. If I do, she might ask. This is ridiculous: she'd never ask.

I punch in her number.

"Hi," I say when she answers. "I didn't wake you, did I?"

"So, are you?" she asks.

"Am I what?"

"Having an affair."

I try to play it as I would if I were innocent. "How'd you figure it out?"

"I live with a detective," she says. "So who is it? Do I know her?"

"No. I don't even know her. I found her in the subway. She lives there."

"Eeeew. Hope you cleaned her up before bedding her."

"Naturally." Enough. "So how are you?"

"I'm okay. I miss you though."

Guilt, guilt, guilt.

"Guess I'm lonely here," she says.

"So I could be anyone."

"Oh, Lauren, do you still think that?"

I used to say this to her because when we met she hadn't been with anyone for a few years, having been left and devastated by her former lover. "Of course I do."

"You're so crazy."

"Never said I wasn't. I caught Ruthie's killer." I want off this topic.

"Oh, that's great. Tell."

I do. This takes about ten years. When I've finished and Kip's said all the appropriate stuff, she adds, "I can't believe how rich Elissa's going to be."

Money. I don't like this topic either.

"Yeah, she'll be a millionaire."

"Maybe she could give you some," Kip says.

I hate this. "Let's not start the money message, okay?"

"Sorry. Did you ask Cecchi about joining you?"

"I did and he's going to."

"Oh, good. I think it's a great idea."

"I like it too."

"What are you going to call yourselves?"

"Spenser and Warshawski."

"No, really?"

"We haven't decided yet. But it won't be our names. See if you can think of anything."

"Okay."

I say, "I have a new contact on the force."

"Who is he?"

"She."

Silence.

"Is that who you're having the affair with?"

Oh, God. "No, I told you, she's a homeless person."

"What's her name?"

I glance at a computer magazine and say, "Micra Gates."

"Micra Gates is the cop's name?"

"Oh, the cop. No. Her name is Michele Lent."

"Who's Micra Gates?"

"My affair." This is getting out of hand.

Silence.

"Kip?"

"What?"

"You don't really think I'm having an affair, do you?" I can't believe how easily this disingenuous question rolls out of my mouth.

Silence.

"Kip? Do you?"

"Are you?"

"Of course not."

"Good. Because I love you, you know."

"I love you too." And I do.

I ask her about her work and she tells me but there's an odd sound in her voice and I know she knows on some level that I've been lying. Why wouldn't she? No one's ever known me better than Kip. Once she's filled me in, we try to wrap up the call but it's not comfortable.

"So I'll be home in about two weeks," she says.

I feel glad and awful at the same time. "Can't wait," I say.

She laughs. "Why is it I don't believe you?"

"Please, Kip, don't."

"Well, I'll talk to you before then. If I can ever find you at home. Stay out of the subways, darling. Bye." Abruptly, she hangs up.

I sit there with the receiver in my hand until I hear a taped operator's voice telling me my phone is off the hook. Thank you, I didn't know that. I put it back in the cradle and almost immediately it rings.

It's Kip. "I hate this," she says.

"What?"

"Fighting."

"I didn't know we were fighting."

"Oh, please."

"Well, I didn't." I don't know what to say anymore.

"You love me, don't you? Oh, God, I feel so pathetic having to ask you," Kip says.

"I told you before that I love you. You're falling into your mother thing." When Kip was five she made her mother tell her she loved her every day for about a year.

"I guess," she says. "There's no question that I'm feeling vulnerable. I don't know why, but I keep thinking there's something you're keeping from me."

I make a completely selfish decision. "You're right. I am. I didn't want to worry you, but Charlie West has been stalking me."

"Oh, my God."

Now she'll worry but she won't ask about my having an affair anymore. What a little shit I am. I tell her about West but not about the really scary stuff, not that he almost had me in his clutches.

"Are the police giving you protection?"

"Of course," I lie.

"I knew there was something. Funny, but I'd rather it was that you were having an affair."

"Not too funny," I say. "One is life-threatening, the other isn't."

"That's true. Oh, Lauren, you'll be careful, won't you?"

"Kip, please don't worry. Nothing's going to happen. The cops will get him if he tries to get near me." I suddenly remember the car. Well, she doesn't need to know about that until she gets home.

"I don't know what I'd do without you," she says.

My heart does the guilt dirge. "You aren't going to have to know," I say. And this is true. I must get Alex out of my life.

"Good. Well, I guess we'd better hang up."

"Okay. I *do* love you, Kip."

"Lauren?"

"What?"

"If you were having an affair, would you tell me?"

I can't believe this. "I have no idea. Will you stop it?"

"I don't think you would."

"Kip, you're putting me in a no-win situation. Would you tell me?"

"Yes."

"Well, don't. I wouldn't want to know. What I don't know won't hurt me." Maybe she is having an affair and all the accusations and questions are pure projection.

"Okay," she says.

"Okay, what?"

"I won't tell you."

She is. I want to know but I don't. "Good."

"I wouldn't mind as long as it didn't interfere with us."

"Kip, please."

"But I don't think women can do that, do you? Could you do that?"

"I have no idea."

"I don't think I could," Kip says.

"Can we drop this?"

"Sorry. Okay, please be careful. I'll talk to you tomorrow, all right? Now that I know about West, I think you should call me every night."

"Fine."

"I don't want you to feel that I'm checking up on you."

Oh, sure. "I don't. I understand. I have to go to bed now."

"Okay. I love you, Lauren."

"I love you too. Talk to you tomorrow."

We hang up. I feel horrible. I've never lied to Kip like this . . .

over and over. Certainly nothing of this proportion. First thing in the morning I'll call Alex and end it. I can tell I hate this idea. Still, I can't see any other way around it.

"Nick, Nora, come on, we're going to bed."

Me and my shadow and my cats, we climb the stairs.

Thirty-one

When I awake there's something hard and cold pressed against my temple. I don't have to be Einstein to know what it is or who's holding it there. The room is dark, so I know it's still night. I hear him breathe. I'm convinced these are my last moments alive. Again, there's an absence of fear. His presence produces shock, which numbs me.

"Okay, dyke," West says, "sit up real slow."

This is easy, as I lie on my back. The top of my head brushes against one of the cats, probably Nick, who has taken to sleeping above me on the pillow.

"Put yer arms in front of you, hands on yer thighs."

I do as he says.

"Swing yer legs out to the side."

I do.

"Now get up."

I do this carefully, as I don't want to give him any reason to pull the trigger.

West stands at my side, the gun pressed hard against my head.

"Let's go downstairs."

"Can we put on a light?" I ask.

"Yeah."

"By the stairs," I tell him. I shuffle forward as though my ankles are chained together. He flips the switch.

"Now go down. My gun's aimed at the back a yer head, so don't try nothin' stupid. I ain't forgot the last time, ya know. I'm ready for ya."

"I'm sure you are."

"Shut the fuck up."

He prods my head with his gun as we slowly make our way downstairs.

"Living room," he commands.

Light from the hall illuminates our way. When we get into the room he tells me to sit on the couch, perches on the edge of a chair across from me, gun trained on my chest. Next to him is a table lamp he snaps on.

This is the first look I get of him. He's aged, but who hasn't? West has lost most of his hair and his small eyes appear watery and red-rimmed, as though he spends a lot of time crying. Lines crosshatch his face like screening and the long fleshy nose almost obscures his upper lip. He wears a dark sweatsuit and black sneakers. He's put on weight: paunchy and flabby, like someone who doesn't move around much.

"You got old," he says arrogantly.

I bite my tongue.

"So you got a new girlfriend, huh?"

I'm not sure whether he means Kip or Alex. "What do you mean?"

"The new one, the tot."

" 'Tot'?"

"Well, she sure looks a lot younger than you."

My ego screeches. "Whom do you mean?"

"Alex Thomas, who else?"

"She's not my girlfriend," I say, worried for her.

He laughs. "Sure, she's not. What should I call her, yer cunt? Yer pussy?"

"We're friends, that's all."

"Yeah, right," he sneers. "That why I saw her hanging around here earlier?"

"What's that supposed to mean?"

"It means when I was watching this place, so was she."

God, Alex, no.

"That what friends do?"

"I don't know anything about that."

"I shoulda knocked her off then but I didn't wanna create any kinda mess that might interfere with our meetin'. This meetin'. Don't worry, I know where she lives, I'll get her after yer dead."

The word *dead* reverberates.

"And Kip too."

"Look, West . . . there's no point in that. They haven't done anything to you."

"Yeah, but they do *it* with you."

"I'll be dead, you just said so. It won't mean anything to me."

"Tell me somethin', Laurano. I make ya a dyke?"

I know he'd like me to tell him that he did, but it no longer matters what he wants. Why should I give him that satisfaction? "No, West, you didn't. I've been a dyke all my life."

His brow furrows and the small eyes become slits. "What about that boyfriend we wasted?"

"He was for show."

"Fuck you, you lyin' bitch."

I almost laugh. Instead, I shrug as though I don't give a damn what he believes, which I don't. But his anger brings me out of a languor and I recognize the need to concentrate on escape. I won't let this creep kill me! Still, this time it's not going to be so easy.

"Ya tellin' me you was always a queer?"

"That's what I'm telling you, West." Again, I want Kip. I see that whenever I'm in trouble it's her I think of, not Alex.

"Summa bitch." He looks upset, as if he hadn't accomplished his life's mission. Good.

"What do you want?" I ask him.

"I wanna kill ya. I thought I done it back all those years ago but ya got lucky. Ya got away and then ya put us away, me and Bailey. Know what happened to him in the slammer?

Somebody stomped his head in. Real messy, bloody." Recalling this, West gets an expression on his face that could pass for
enjoyment. "Yer fault," he accuses.

"My heart's breaking," I say. Can't help myself.

The eyes bead again. "Watch it, bitch. Ya know what I think
I'm gonna do? I think I'm gonna kill everbody ya know. All them
snooty friends a yers. And I know about ever one a them. You
think yer hot stuff, don't ya, 'cause ya know all them big shots
from the movies and such."

I say nothing.

"Huh? Whad ya say, didn't hear ya?" He waves the gun at me
as though it's a magic wand that'll make me answer. "Lissen,
dyke, ya better talk when I say."

"What do you want to talk about, West?" I want to keep him
occupied until I can come up with a strategy.

"Wanna talk about the Granny Killer?" He snickers.

Jesus. "What about him?"

"Maybe I know who he is."

"Do you?"

"Wouldn't you like to know?"

"Yes, I would. What difference will it make if I know? You're
going to kill me anyway. Is it you, West?"

"Me? Ya gotta be kiddin'. What I want with a buncha old
broads? I like 'em young, like you was. So you was cherry when
I nailed ya, right?"

"Right. Who's the Granny Killer?"

"Hey, won't mean nothin' to ya. Name's George Bastable. I
call him Geo."

I don't know why I believe he's telling the truth, but I do. God
let me get out of this, so they can get this Bastable bastard as
well.

"Can't believe you was cherry. Hot shit, man." Pride lights
up his stupid face and it gives me an idea.

"You know what I remember about you, West?"

"This a trick?"

"Is what a trick?"

"What're you up to?"

"I'm not up to anything. Just thought you might like to know what I remember about you."

He weighs this carefully, as though my words might wound him, which is what I hope they'll do. "Okay, what?"

I brace each hand flat on the cushions on either side of me. "What I remember is that you had a tiny little dick." As the last word leaves my mouth, in a move I didn't know I had in me, I push myself up and backward, feet over head, plunge and crumple behind the couch.

"Hey," he yells.

The horrible loud report of a gunshot hurts my ears, and the smell of powder permeates the air. But I don't feel hit.

"You okay, Lauren?" It's a woman's voice, one that I know but can't identify.

I peek around the couch. The first thing I see is the soles of West's sneakers as he lies on the rug, unmoving. And then Michele Lent, coming through the door, bending down to offer me a hand.

I get up, look past Lent, and see immediately that West is dead, a hole in his chest.

We both stare at him and then I notice her hand holding the gun. It's shaking.

Says Lent, "Shit. Oh, shit. I never . . . oh, my God."

Her voice cracks and I know what she's trying to say is that she's never killed anyone before.

"You had to," I say. Small comfort.

"Yeah, I know. But shit. Christ, it's a big hole, isn't it?"

"Michele, you saved my life."

"No. Not me."

I'm confused. "But you shot him."

"Yeah. Oh, God."

"It's all right. You had to. He was scum."

"I should've brought Gold with me," she says. "Then maybe he would've . . ."

She trails off but I know what she's thinking.

"I better . . . better call in. Oh, Christ."

She doesn't cry but she's in trouble emotionally. "Michele, what did you mean, you didn't save my life?"

"Friend of yours called me."

"Friend?"

"Yeah. Said she saw some guy entering your house. Gal named Alex Thomas."

"Alex Thomas," I repeat stupidly.

"You know her, don't you?"

"Yes, I know her."

"I'd say she's the one who saved your life."

Thirty-two

━━━━━━━━━━

I've spent the last seventy-five years at the Sixth Precinct. When you're involved in a killing, especially when it happens in your home, there's a great deal of paperwork. Plus you have to tell your story over and over and over.

I stop at Lanciani's to get some coffee before I go home. I've been told that the body's been removed and so has the rug where West fell and leaked his last blood.

In actual time, a day and a half has passed since the West killing, about two since I talked to Kip, and ten hours since I saw Alex at the station house, where I thanked her profusely for saving my life. The first thing I have to do when I get home is call Kip, then Alex.

Alex. The timing of ending our affair couldn't be worse. But even though I'm walking these streets because of her help, I must do it.

I get my coffee and a brownie and drag myself home. When I reach the door, I hesitate even though I know West is dead. He's managed to make entering my own house an uneasy experience. *How long will this last?* I wonder.

Nick and Nora are waiting at the door for me. They try to pretend that they haven't been fed, that they've been abandoned. But I know the truth: William's been feeding and watering them.

Nora does her usual fainting goat act and Nick opens his mouth but nothing comes out.

"Hey, guys," I say. I lean down and pet them. Nick takes his position on his back and with each hand I rub a stomach. I like to give them this attention, but I'm aware it's a stall. I don't want to look in the living room. Sooner or later I'll have to, so I might as well get it over with.

It looks as it always has, except the white rug is gone. Crazily, I think about Kip's coming home to no car and no rug. I'd rather dwell on that than remember what took place two nights ago. I can't stay in here anymore and I can't shake the feeling that someone's watching. There are five messages on the answering machine. I hit the button and play them back.

Two are from Kip, who's a little hysterical that I haven't called, one from Alex, one from Jenny, and one from Elissa. I call Kip but get her machine. I leave a message, telling her I'm sorry I didn't call, but that everything's fine and I'll try her tonight.

I check my watch. Alex will be at her desk. I punch in her number. Her secretary answers and puts me on hold. I sip my coffee and take a bite of my brownie.

I have no idea how I'm going to tell Alex it's over. She picks up.

"Hi, you."

I feel it to my toes. "Get over here," I say.

While I wait for her I resolve to end it. I know by what I said on the phone, she's going to assume that everything is okay between us, that we're going to continue the affair. Why did I say that?

I'm the most undisciplined, selfish, incredibly stupid person I know. Okay, so even though I've made Alex believe that nothing's changed, I have to tell her it's over. She'll hate me and call me cruel and she'll be right. Still, it has to be done.

Kip will be back soon. I don't want to end my relationship with her or jeopardize it in any way, so I don't have a choice. But maybe once more with Alex? Can I do it without telling her that it's the last time? But if I tell her, it will be awful, even if she agrees to it — and I don't think she will.

The bell rings and I scream. Yeah, I'm okay.

As I go to the door, I glance in the mirror. I'm a mess: tired, old, and crazy. Maybe Alex will end it for me.

I open the door. She looks gorgeous. Today she wears a blue miniskirt and a gray long-sleeved sweater with another, lighter gray one tied over her shoulders. She smiles at me and when those brown eyes light up, I feel helpless and hopeless.

We don't say anything. She follows me into the apartment and when I turn to face her she seems anxious, twitchy.

"You okay?" I ask.

"Nervous," she says.

Does she know? "Want anything to drink or eat?" What a stupid question.

"No, thanks. How're you?"

"Still a little shaky."

"Why wouldn't you be?" She reaches out a hand and touches my cheek. I take the hand, kiss the palm, then lead her to the couch, where we sit. Kissing her hand was not a good advertisement for what I have to tell her.

We face each other, and we're much too close.

"Alex . . . ," I say softly, unable to go on.

"You want to end it, don't you?"

"Kip's coming home soon."

"I could point out that Sally's, being here in the city hasn't stopped me," she says.

"But you won't."

She smiles and my resolve dims.

"We could meet in a hotel," she says.

"We could, but we're not going to."

"Lauren, I don't think I can give you up so easily. What makes you think you can give me up?"

"I never said it was going to be easy."

"Can we be friends, at least? Have lunch?"

"You could do that?"

"Well, it's better than not seeing you at all."

"I don't think I can do that. I mean, go from being lovers

to friends without any time in between. But you think you can?"

She shrugs. "I'd like to try."

"Alex, that's so naive."

"Has this just been sex for you?" she asks.

I think it has, but I do care for her, about her. "No. That's why I can't make that kind of transition overnight. Has it only been sex for you?"

"I think you know it hasn't."

"Well, then, that's my point. You might think you can be my friend, just like that." I snap my fingers. "But I don't think you can."

"I'll miss you so much," she says plaintively.

"When we can be in a room together without wanting to kiss, then we can be friends," I say.

"Do you want to kiss me now?"

"Of course I do."

"So do I," she says and leans toward me.

I can't resist that beautiful mouth and I meet her lips with mine. All of my sexual feelings are aroused and I put my arms around her, draw her close to me, feel her breasts against mine. I know where this is going to lead but I can't stop. Well, I've warned her. I pull away, ready to ask her to come upstairs to bed with me. But she has an odd look on her face.

"Turn around," she whispers.

"What?"

"Turn around."

I do.

Kip stands just inside the living room door, suitcase at her feet.

"Well, girls," she says tartly, "how long has this been going on?"

Oh, boy.